An Algonquin Maiden
A Romance of the Early Days of Upper Canada

G. Mercer Adam

Contents

AN ALGONQUIN MAIDEN
A ROMANCE OF THE EARLY DAYS OF

UPPER CANADA

BY

G. Mercer Adam

AN ALGONQUIN MAIDEN.

CHAPTER I.
THE YOUNG MASTER OF PINE TOWERS.

I t was a May morning in 1825--spring-time of the year, late spring-time of the century. It had rained the night before, and a warm pallor in the eastern sky was the only indication that the sun was trying to pierce the gray dome of nearly opaque watery fog, lying low upon that part of the world now known as the city of Toronto, then the town of Little York. This cluster of five or six hundred houses had taken up a determined position at the edge of a forest then gloomily forbidding in its aspect, interminable in its extent, inexorable in its resistance to the shy or to the sturdy approaches of the settler. Man *versus* nature--the successive assaults of perishing humanity upon the almost impregnable fortresses of the eternal forests--this was the struggle of Canadian civilization, and its hard-won triumphs were bodied forth in the scattered roofs of these cheap habitations. Seen now through soft gradations of vapoury gloom, they took on a poetic significance, as tenderly intangible as the romantic halo which the mist of years loves to weave about the heads of departed pioneers, who, for the most part, lived out their lives in plain, grim style, without any thought of posing as "conquering heroes" in the eyes of succeeding generations.

From the portico of one of these dwellings, under a wind-swayed sign which advertised it to be a place of rest and refreshment, stepped a man of more than middle age, whose nervous gait and anxious face betokened a mind ill at ease. He had the look and air of a highly respectable old servitor,--one who had followed the family to whom he was bound by ties of life-long service to a country of which he strongly disapproved, not because it offered a poor field for his own advancement, but because, to his mind, its crude society and narrow opportunities ill became the distinction of the Old World family to whose fortunes he was devoted. Time had softened these prejudices, but had failed to melt them; and if they had a pardonable fashion of congealing under the stress of the Canadian winter, they generally showed signs of a thaw at the approach of spring. At the present moment he had no thought, no eyes, for anything save a mist-enshrouded speck far off across the waters of Lake Ontario. All the impatience and longing of the week just past found vent through his eyes, as he watched that pale, uncertain, scarcely visible mote on the horizon. As he reached the shore the fog lifted a little, and a great sunbeam, leaping from a cloud, illumined for a moment the smooth expanse of water; but the new day was as yet chary of its gifts. It was very still. The woods and waves alike were tranced in absolute calm. The unlighted heavens brooded upon the silent limpid waters and the breathless woods, while between them, with restless step, and heart as gloomy as the morning, with secret, sore misgiving, paced the old servant, his attention still riveted upon that distant speck. The sight of land and home to the gaze of a long absent wanderer, wearied with ocean, is not more dear than the first glimpse of the approaching sail to watching eyes on shore.

Was it in truth the packet vessel for whose coming he had yearningly waited, or the dark wing of a soaring bird, or did it exist only in imagination? The tide of his impatience rose anew as the dim object slowly resolved itself into the semblance of a sail, shrouded in the pale, damp light of early morning. Unwilling to admit to his usually grave unimpressible self the fact that he was restless and disturbed, he reduced his pace to a dignified march, extended his chosen beat to a wider margin of the sandy shore, and, parting the blighted branches of a group of trees, that bore evidence of the effect of constant exposure to lake winds, he affected to examine them critically. But the hand that touched the withered leaves trembled, and his sight was dimmed with something closely resembling the morning's mist. When he again raised his eyes to that white-sailed vessel it looked to his hopeless gaze absolutely becalmed. The slow moments dragged heavily along. The mantle of fog was wholly lifted at last, and the lonely watcher was enveloped in the soft beauty of the morning. A light cloud hung motionless, as though spell-bound, above the mute and moveless trees, while before him the dead blue slopes of heaven were unbroken by a single flying bird, the wide waste of water unlighted, save by that unfluttering sail.

And now, like a visible response to his silent but seemingly resistless longing, a boat was rapidly pushed away from the larger craft, and the swift flash and fall of the oars kept time to the pulsing in the old man's breast. Again ensued that inglorious conflict between self-respecting sobriety of demeanour and long suppressed emotion, which ended only when the boat grated on the sand, and a blonde stalwart youth leaped ashore. The old man fell upon his neck with tears and murmured ejaculations of gratitude and welcome; but young impatient hands pushed him not ungently aside, and a youthful voice, high and intense from anxiety, urgently exclaimed:

"My mother! How is my mother?"

"She yet breathes, thank God. She has been longing for your coming as a suffering saint longs for heaven. She must see you before she dies!"

The young man turned a little aside with down-bent head. His positive blue eyes looked almost feverishly bright; and the lip, on which he had unconsciously bitten hard, now released from pressure, quivered perceptibly; but with the unwillingness or inability of youth to admit the inevitableness of a great grief he burst forth with:

"Is that all you have to say to me?" And then, as his keen eye noticed the tears still undried upon the cheeks of the old man, he sighed heavily. "Can nothing be done? Is there no help? It doesn't seem possible!" He ground his heel heavily into the sand. "Say something, Tredway," he entreated, "anything with a gleam of hope in it."

Tredway shook his head. "The only hope that remains is that you will reach home in time to receive her last words. This is the second time that I have come down expecting to meet you."

The young fellow with his erect military air and noticeably handsome face betrayed a remote consciousness that he was perhaps worth the trouble of coming after twice. As they together hastened up from the beach the younger of the two briefly narrated the cause of his delay--a delay occasioned by stress of weather on the Atlantic, and the state of the roads in the valley of the Mohawk, on the journey from the seaboard. He had lost not an hour, the young man said, in obeying the summons of his father, the Commodore, to quit England and return to his Canadian home ere his much-loved mother passed from the earth.

Eager to reach that home, which was on the shores of Lake Simcoe, the young Cadet bade the old servitor hasten to get their horses ready when they would instantly set forth. As they were about to mount, the younger of the two was accosted by an old friend, now an attache of Government House, who, learning of the arrival of the packet, and expecting the young master of Pine Towers, had strolled down to the landing-place to welcome the newcomer and ask him to partake of the Governor's hospitality. The young man, however, begged his friend to have him excused, and with dutiful messages of respect for the Governor and his household, and a cordial adieu to his former boon-companion, he rapidly set off for home, closely followed by his attendant.

Coming up the old military road, cut out between York and Holland Landing by His Majesty's corps of Queen's Rangers, under the *regime* of Governor Simcoe, both horsemen fell into a brief silence, broken by sorrowful inquiries from the younger man regarding the subject which lay so close to the heart of each. "Dying!" he exclaimed in deep sadness, and with the utter incapacity of young and ardent life to conceive the reality of death. "And my own mother. It seems natural enough for other mothers to die--but mine! Heaven help us! We never know the meaning of grief until it comes to our own threshold."

The old steward viewed with a desolate stare the May landscape, brightly lit with sunshine and bloom, and said wearily:

"But what can one expect in this wretched, half-civilized country? Now in England--"

His voice lingered long upon that fondly loved word, and his young master concluded the sentence with,

"There would be little hope, but in this 'brave new world,' where the odour of the woods is a tonic, and the air brings healing and balm, how can death exist? Ah, Tredway, this is a beautiful country!"

"To me there is but one beautiful country--that is England." Again there was that lingering intonation.

Edward Macleod gave vent to a short melancholy laugh. The allurements of an old civilization were over-ripe to his taste. Promise appealed to his imagination; ful-

filment was a dull fact. Along with the unmistakable evidences of birth and breeding in his person, there was in his fresh youth and buoyancy something joyously
akin to the vigorous young life about him.

"England," said Tredway, with his disapproving regard fixed upon the wilderness around, "is a garden."

"And I take no delight in gardens," declared Edward. "I was never intended for
a garden statue. This long day's journey under the giant trees of the wild, uncon-
quered woods seems to gratify some savage instinct of my nature. The old country is
well adapted to keep alive old customs, old notions, old traditions; but for me I am a
Canadian, my mind is wearied with over-much civilization. I hate the English love
of land for land's sake. That line of hills, swelling in massive curves, and crowned,
not with a tottering ruin, serving to hang some legendary romance or faded rag of
superstition upon, but with stately trees--that is my idea of the beautiful."

He struck into a sharp gallop, his bright head above the dark blue military cloak
forming a picturesque feature in the woodland, and the flying heels of his spirited
horse seeming to add a rattling chorus of applause to his patriotic sentiments. The
old retainer ambled along in his wake, but more slowly. His idea of the beautiful
was not quite so recklessly defiant. Presently, for he was still jaded from the effects
of his long journey on the previous day, he relaxed his attempt at speed, and soon
lost sight of his companion altogether. The vision of waving cloak and flying steed
vanished in the green aisles of the forest.

Along the Oak Ridges--situate some thirty miles from York--which the two
horsemen now neared, a Huguenot settlement had been formed about the close
of the eighteenth century. The settlers were French officers of the noblesse order,
who, during the French Revolution, when the royalist cause became desperate, emi-
grated to England, thence to Canada, where, by the bounty of the Crown, they were
given grants of land in this portion of the Province of Upper Canada. Here many
of these *emigres* had made clearings on the Ridges, and reared *chateaux* for themselves and their households after the manner of their ancestral homes in Languedoc
and Brittany. Into the grounds of one of these mansions had the younger horseman
disappeared to pay his hurried respects to the stately dame who was its owner, and
who, with her fair daughter, were intimate friends of the Macleod family.

Almost before the old man had time to wonder what mad freak had kept his young master so long from the beaten road, he was at his side again.

"I have been trying to get a glimpse of my little friend, Helene," he said, in explanation of his absence, "but the DeBerczy mansion is as empty as a church on Monday. They still go to Lake Simcoe in summer, I suppose. But what does this early flight portend?"

"It was caused solely by the serious nature of your mother's illness. Madame and Mademoiselle have been now five weeks at 'Bellevue.'"

The young man's face darkened, or rather lost the brightness that habitually played upon it, like gleams of sunshine on a stream, which, when disappearing, show the depth of the tide beneath.

"You would scarcely know the young lady now," continued Tredway. "The difference between fifteen and eighteen is the difference between childhood and womanhood."

"I suppose she has grown like a young forest tree, and holds her graceful head almost as high."

"She is well grown, and very beautiful, but not bewitching like your sister Rose."

"Ah! dear little Rose! But she, too, I doubt not, is a bud no longer. It's odd how much easier it is for a girl to be a woman than for a boy to become a man." There was something vaguely suggestive of regret in the gesture with which young Macleod lightly brushed his short upper lip, whose hirsute adornment was not, in its owner's estimation, all that it ought to have been. "I was twenty-one last winter. Do I look very young?" he inquired, with the natural anxiety of a man who has recently escaped the ignominy of being in his teens.

"You look altogether too young," dryly returned the ancient servitor, "to appreciate the worth of a country where old customs, old ideas, and old traditions are respected."

"Then may youth always be mine!" exclaimed Edward, looking round him with the glow in his heart, sure to be felt by the devout worshipper of Nature in the large and beautiful presence of her whom he adores. The region about him, esteemed the epitome of dreariness in winter, held now in its depths a vast luxury of vegetation. The wild vines ran knotted and twisted about the trunks and branches of multitudinous trees, and the fallen logs were draped with moss, lichens, and delicate ferns.

Passing through this boundless wilderness, they seemed to look into a succession of woodland chambers, thickly carpeted with wild flowers, gorgeously festooned with creeping and parasitical plants hanging from the branches, and secured in their leafy seclusion by walls of abundant foliage. In one of these natural parlours they paused for their mid-day repast--mid-day in the world without, but here, where only vagrant gleams of the spring sun pierced the forest solitudes, gloomy with spruce and pine, there was a sense of morning in the air. This appearance was heightened by the delicate curtains of cobweb, strung with shining pearls, which still might be seen after the fog at early dawn. There was no sound except sometimes that of an invisible bird, singing in the upper air, or when a partridge, roused by approaching steps, started from the hollow, and rapidly whirring away directly before them was again startled into flight when they overtook it.

The road they followed cut straight through the forest, and, disdaining to enclose the hills in graceful curves, attacked and surmounted them in the direct fashion common to our forefathers, when they encountered obstacles of any serious nature. The absence of human sight or voice gave a strangeness to the sound of their own utterances, and there were frequent lapses into that sad silence which fell upon them as naturally as the gloom from the overshadowing boughs above. The old attendant who viewed every member of the family whom he served and loved just as the first man regarded the world at his first glimpse of it--that is, as an extension of his own consciousness--was deeply moved at the sight of his young master's sombre face. Edward's heart, indeed, ached painfully. The perpetual repetition of this luxuriance of young fresh life in the woods of May was a constant reminder of a life that until lately had been as vigorously beautiful, and now perhaps had passed away from this world forever.

Leaving their weary horses at Holland Landing, they took boat down the river and bay, desiring to hasten their arrival at the family mansion, nearly opposite to what is now the prettily situated town of Barrie. Edward sat apart and gazed long and silently at the waving tree lines, dark against a luminous, cool, gray sky, with its scattered but serene group of clouds. All his desire for home and for her who was the sunshine of it had resolved itself into a yearning that gnawed momentarily at his heart. Instead of the fair sky and landscape and silent waterways of his New World home, he saw or rather felt, the hush of a dim chamber, whose wasted occupant had travelled far into the valley of the shadow of death. His wet eyes, looking abroad upon the outer world, were as the eyes of those who see not. The afternoon sunshine paled and thinned, but beneath the chill of the spring day there lay a warm hint of the untold tenderness of midsummer. Unconsciously to himself the prophecy brought a feeling of comfort to his heart, in its reminder of the glory of that summer to which his mother might even now be passing--"the glory that was to be revealed."

It was early twilight when Edward Macleod reached his beautiful home over-looking Kempenfeldt Bay. The broad, solid-built house, with its commanding po-sition, and spacious verandas, seemed just such a mansion as an old naval officer, who was reduced to the insipid necessity of a life on shore, would choose to dwell in. One might almost be tempted to call it a fine piece of marine architecture, in some of its fanciful reminders of an ocean vessel. Its solitariness, its pointed turrets and gables, its proud position on what might be termed the topmost wave of earth in that region, the flying flag at its summit, and the ample white curtains that flut-tered sail-like in the open windows, all heightened the resemblance. From its portal down to the bay, extended a noble avenue of hardwood trees--oak, walnut and elm--never planted by the hand of man. Their gracious lives the woodman had spared, and now, with their outstretched branches, catching the faint evening breeze, they seemed to breathe a sad benediction upon the returning youth, who walked hur-riedly and tremblingly beneath them.

As he stepped from their leafy shadow upon the sunset-gilded lawn, he was startled by an apparition which seemed suddenly to take shape from a sweet-scent-ed thicket of lilacs now in profuse bloom at the rear of the house. A dark, lissome creature, beautiful as a young princess, but a princess in the disguise of a savage, darted past him. So sudden was the appearance, and so swift the flight of this dusky Diana, speeding through the blossoming shrubs of spring, that his mind retained only a general impression of a face, perfect-featured and olive-tinted, and a form robed in a brilliant and barbarous admixture of scarlet, yellow, and very dark blue.

But the next moment every sensation and emotion gave way to overwhelming and profound grief, for his sister Rose, hurrying to meet him, threw herself into his arms with an abandon of sorrow that seemed to leave no room for hope. The fatal question burned a moment on his lips, then died away unuttered, leaving them pale as ashes, and a big tear fell upon the bright head of the girl whom he now believed to be with himself motherless. But in a moment his father took his hand in a tense, strong grasp, and drew him quickly forward. "She yet breathes," he whispered, "but is unable to recognize any of us. Heaven grant she may know you. For days past her moan has been, 'I cannot die until I see my son, until I see my first-born.'"

His voice broke as they entered the chamber of death. The young man, feeling strangely weak and blind, sat down beside the bed, for the awful hush of this darkened room weighed heavily upon him. As in a terrible dream he saw the sorrowing forms of his younger brother and sister, crouching at his feet, poor Rose drooping in the doorway, his father's trembling hands grasping a post of the high, old-fashioned bedstead, and, on the other side of the bed a youthful stranger, whose black dress and very black hair divinely framed a face and throat of milky whiteness. These objects left but a weak impression upon his dulled senses, for all his soul was going out in resistless longing towards the fast-ebbing life that seemed to be slipping away from his feeble grasp. He stroked the little bloodless hand, and kissed repeatedly the wasted cheek, uttering at the same time low murmurs of entreaty that she would look upon him once more before she died. All in vain. Utterly still and unresponsive as death itself, she lay before him. "Dear mother," he implored, "it is your son, your own Edward that calls you. Can you not hear? Will you not come back to me a single moment? Ah, I cannot let you go; I cannot, I cannot!" His voice sank in a passionate murmur of grief. "You will look at me once, will you not? Oh, mother, mother, mother!"

He had fallen to his knees, with his face on the pillow close to hers, and his last words smote upon her ear like the inarticulate wail of an infant whose life must perish along with the strong sustaining life of her who gave it birth. The head turned ever so slightly, the eyelids quivered faintly and lifted, and her eyes looked fully and tenderly upon her son. Then, with a mighty effort, she raised one transparent hand, and brought it feebly, flutteringly, higher and higher, until it lay upon his cheek. A strange faint light of unearthly sweetness played about her lips. It was a light as sweet and beautiful as her own life had been, but now it paled and faded--brightened again--flickered a moment--and then went out forever.

The sad sound of children weeping broke the silence of the death-chamber. Edward still knelt, and Rose was bowed with grief; but the old Commodore's courageous voice sounded as though wrung from the depths of his sorely-stricken heart:

"The Lord gave, and the Lord--" his tongue failed him, but after a momentary struggle he continued in shaking tones--"and the Lord taketh away. **Blessed**--"

He could say no more.

Surely the blessing that, for choking sobs, could not find utterance on earth, was heard in heaven, and abundantly returned upon the brave and desolate spirit of him who strove to pronounce it.

CHAPTER II.
AN UPPER CANADIAN HOUSEHOLD.

The breakfast-room of Pine Towers, on a bright, sunny morning, some three or four days after the death of its much-respected mistress, held a large concourse of the notables of York, and other private and official gentry of the Province. They had come to take part, on the previous day, in the funeral obsequies; and were now, after a night's rest and bountiful morning repast, about to return to the Capital. Among the number gathered to pay respect to the deceased lady's memory, as well as to show their regard and sympathy for the bereaved husband, the good old Commodore, were many whose names were "household words" in the early days of Upper Canada. Sixty years have passed over the Province since the notable gathering, and all who were then present have paid the debt of nature. Hushed now as are their voices, the Macleod breakfast-room, on the morning we have indicated, was a perfect babel of noise. The solemn pageant of the previous day, and the sacred griefs of those whom the grim Enemy had made desolate, seemed at the moment to have been forgotten by the departing throng; and for a time the young master of Pine Towers, as he bade adieu to his father's guests, witnessed a scene in sharp contrast to yesterday's orderly decorum. It was with a sigh of relief that Edward Macleod saw the last of the miscellaneous vehicles move off, and the final guest take the road to the bateaux on the lake, to convey him and those who were returning by water to Holland Landing, there to find the means of reaching the Capital.

Entering the house, empty now of all but those who were left of its usual inmates, including his sister's friend, the beautiful Helene--whom he had hardly had an opportunity to more than greet on his return from England--an overpowering sense of desolation fell upon him. Seating himself near his mother's favourite window, the young man's loneliness and bereavement found vent in tears. All the past came vividly before him--a mother's life-long devotion and tender care; her thousand winning ways and loving endearments; her pride in his future career and prospects; and the recollection of the many innocent confidences which a mother loves to pour into the ear of a handsome, grown-up son, whose filial affection and chivalrous devotion assure her that she still possesses charms to which her husband and his contemporaries of a previous generation had been wont sedulously to pay tribute. "Ah, beautiful mother, it is not to-day nor to-morrow that I shall fully realize that I am to see thee no more on earth," said the young man musingly, as he left his seat and strode nervously up and down the room, while his favourite hound from a rug by the large open fire-place eyed his agitated movements.

Presently the young man's soliloquies were interrupted by the timid entrance of his sister, Rose, followed by the more decided and stately tread of the charming Helene.

"Ah, Edward," said his sister, "you are alone. Have all our guests gone?"

"Yes," was the reply, "and I am not sorry to have the house again to ourselves."

"You, of course, include Helene among the latter," observed Rose interrogatively.

"I do, certainly," was Edward's instant and cordial response, as he offered Helene his hand to conduct her down the steps into the conservatory and out on to the lawn. "Miss DeBerczy, of course, is one of us, though you told me this morning that she, too, expressed a wish to be gone."

Helene interrupted these remarks with the explanation that her wish to take leave was owing to a mandate of her mother's which had reached her that morning.

"We shall all be sorry at your leaving us so soon," was Edward's courteous rejoinder. "But, when you go," he added, "you must permit me to accompany you to 'Bellevue,' for I wish to pay my respects to your mamma; it is a long time now since we met. Besides, I have to deliver to her the cameos I brought her from England and the family trinkets your uncle entrusted to my care."

"Mamma, I know, is eager to receive them, and will be delighted to welcome you back. In her note, by the way, she tells me that Captain John Franklin has written to her from York, asking permission to call upon her on his way north. You know that the Arctic Expedition is to go overland, by way of Penetanguishene and Rupert's Land, and is to effect a junction with Captain Beechey's party operating from Hudson's Bay."

"So I learned before I left England," replied Edward. "I hope my father," he added, "will be able to meet the members of the Expedition. It would rouse him from his grief, and I know that he takes a great interest in Captain Franklin's project."

The conversation was now monopolized by the ladies, for Helene took Rose aside to tell that young lady that her mamma had given her some news of a young and handsome land-surveyor, of Barrie, of whom she had heard Rose speak in terms of warm admiration.

The gentleman referred to was Allan Dunlop, who, Helene related, had been very useful at York to Captain Franklin, in giving him information as to the route to be followed by his Expedition on its way to the "hoarse North sea."

Rose visibly coloured as she listened to the young man's praises, in the extract Helene's mother had enclosed from Captain Franklin's communication. That young lady protested, however, that Allan Dunlop was her brother's friend, not hers. "Indeed," she added, "we have only occasionally met at the Church at Barrie, and I have not even been introduced to him."

"Ah, and how is it that his name is always on your lips after every service I hear you have attended across the bay?" queried Helene archly.

The tints deepened on Rose's sweet, bright face as she apologetically urged "that at such times there was doubtless nothing better to talk about."

Happily for Rose the embarrassing conversation was interrupted by the return of her brother, who rejoined the ladies to say that on the highway, at the end of the avenue down which he had strolled, a party of marines and English shipwrights, in command of a naval officer, had just passed on their way to the post, near Barrie, to proceed on the morrow by the Notawassaga river to the Georgian Bay, and on to the new naval station at Penetanguishene. A Mr. Galt, who accompanied the party, and was on his way to the Canada Land Company's reserve in the Huron district, had brought him letters from York, among which, he added, was one from his old friend, Allan Dunlop, condoling with him on the loss of his mother and sending his respectful compliments to his father and his family.

"How curious!" observed Helene, "why, we've just been talking of Mr. Dunlop."

"You mean to say," interposed Rose, "that *you* have just been talking of him."

"Well! that is quite a coincidence, Miss DeBerczy, but do you know my friend?" asked Edward.

"No, I've not that pleasure," replied the beautiful Huguenot. "but your sister, I believe, knows him--"

"Oh, Helene! I do *not*!" said Rose, interruptingly.

Edward turned towards his sister, and for a moment regarded her lovingly. After a pause, he said, "Well, Sis, if you *do* know him, you know one of the best and most promising of my early acquaintances, and from what I have heard of him since my return, I feel that I want to improve my own acquaintance with him, and shall not be sorry to know that he has become your friend as well as mine."

"But, Edward, you must wait till I *do* know him," said Rose with some emphasis. "I know your friend by sight only, and have never spoken to him; though, I confess, I have heard a good deal of him in the recent election, and much that is favourable, though papa has taken a great dislike to him on account of his political opinions."

"Ah, papa's Tory prejudices would be sure to do injustice to Dunlop," Edward rejoined; "but, I fear," he added, "there is need in the political arena of Upper Canada of just such a Reformer as he."

At this stage of the conversation the old Commodore was observed on the veranda, and Tredway approached the group to announce that lunch was on the table.

Commodore Macleod, as may be inferred from his son's remark about his father's Tory prejudices, was a Tory of the old school, a member of the Legislative Council of Upper Canada, and a firm ally and stiff upholder of the Provincial Executive, who had earned for themselves, by their autocratic rule, the rather sinister designation of "the Family Compact." As a trusted friend and loyal supporter of the oligarchy of the day, whom a well-known radical who figured prominently in the later history of the Province was wont to speak of as that army of placemen and pensioners, "Paymasters, Receivers, Auditors, King, Lords and Commons, who swallowed the whole revenue of Upper Canada"--the reference to a man of the type of young Dunlop, who aspired to political honours, was particularly distasteful, and sure to bring upon the object of his bitter animadversion the full vials of his wrath.

Ralph Macleod was a grand specimen of the sturdy British seamen, who contributed by their prowess to make England mistress of the seas. He entered the navy during the war with Holland, and served under Lord Howe, when that old "sea-dog," in 1782, came to the relief of Gibraltar, against the combined forces of France and Spain. He served subsequently under Lord Rodney, in the West Indies, and was a shipmate of Nelson's in Sir John Jervis' victory over the Spanish fleet off Cape St. Vincent. For his share in that action Macleod gained his captaincy, while his friend Commodore Nelson was made a Rear-Admiral. In 1797 he was wounded at Camperdown while serving under Admiral Duncan, and retired with the rank of Commodore.

Early in the century, he married an English lady and came to Canada, where for a time he held various posts on the naval stations on the Lakes, and was with Barclay, on his flagship, *The Detroit*, in the disaster on Lake Erie, in September, 1813. Narrowly escaping capture by Commander Perry's forces at Put-in-Bay, he joined General Proctor in his retreat from Amherstburg to the Thames, and was present at the battle of Moravian Town, where the Indian chief, Tecumseh, lost his life.

When the Treaty of Ghent terminated the war and left Canada in possession of her own, Commodore Macleod, with other old naval officers, retired from the service, and took grants of land in the neighbourhood of Lake Simcoe. Being possessed of considerable private means, the Commodore built a palatial residence on the borders of that lake, and varied the monotony of a life ashore by an engrossing interest in politics and the active duties of a Legislative Councillor. The illness of his wife, to whom he was devoted, had in the past two years almost entirely withdrawn him from political life, and lost to his colleagues in the Upper House the services of one who took grim pleasure in strangling bills obnoxious to the dominant faction which originated in the Lower Chamber. His temporary withdrawal from the Legislative Council, and the lengthened absence in England of Dr. Strachan, that sturdy ecclesiastic who was long the ruling spirit of the "Family Compact," emboldened the leaders of Reform to inveigh against the Hydra-headed abuses of the time, and sow broadcast the dragon-teeth of discontent and the seeds of a speedy harvest of sedition.

Already, Wm. Lyon Mackenzie had unfolded, in the lively columns of *The Colonial Advocate*, his "plentiful crop of grievances;" while the harsh operations of the Alien Act, the interdicting of immigrants from the United States, the arrogant claims of the Anglican Church to the exclusive possession of the Clergy Reserves, and the jobbery and corruption that prevailed in the Land-granting Department of the Government, all contributed to fan the flame of discontent and sap the loyalty of the colony. In the Legislative Assembly each recurring session added to the clamour of opposition, and emphasized the demand for Responsible Government and Popular Rights. But as yet such demands were looked upon as the ravings of lunacy or the impertinences of treason. Constitutional Government, even in the mother-land, was not yet fully attained; and, in a distant dependency, it was not to be expected that the prerogative of the Crown, or the rights and privileges of its nominee, an irresponsible Executive, were to be made subordinate to the will of the people. "Take care what you are about in Canada," were the irate words William IV. hurled at his ministers, some few years after the period of which we are writing. "By--!" added this constitutional monarch, "I will never consent to alienate the Crown Lands nor to make the Council elective."

With such outbursts of royal petulance and old-time kingcraft, and similar ebullitions from Downing Street, exhorting the Upper Canadian Administration to hold tight the reins of government, the reforming spirit of the period had a hard time of it in entering on its many years conflict with an arrogant and bureaucratic Executive. Of many of the members of the ruling faction of the time it may not become us now to speak harshly, for most of them were men of education and refinement, and in their day did good service to the State. If, in the exercise of their office, they lacked consideration at times for the less favoured of their fellow-colonists, they had the instincts and bearing of gentlemen, save, it may be, when, in conclave, occasion drove them to a violent and contemptuous opposition to the will of the people. But men--most of all politicians--naturally defend the privileges which, they enjoy; and the exceptional circumstances of the country seemed at the time to give to the holders of office a prescriptive right to their position and emoluments.

At the period of which we are writing, there was much need of wise moderation on the side of the governed as well as on that of the governing class. But of moderation there was little; and the nature of the evils complained of, the non-conciliatory attitude of the ruling oligarchy, and the licence which a "Free Press,"--recently introduced into the colony,--gave in formulating charges of corruption, and in loosening the tongue of invective, made it almost impossible to discuss affairs of State, save in the heated terms familiar to irritated and incensed combatants. It was at this period that the young land-surveyor, Allan Dunlop, entered the Legislative Assembly and took his seat as member for the Northern division of the Home District. Though warmly espousing the cause of the people in the ever-recurring collisions with the different branches of the Government, and as warmly asserting the rights and privileges of the popular Chamber in its struggles with the autocracy of the Upper House, the young Parliamentarian was equally jealous of the reasonable prerogative of the Crown, and temperate in the language he used when he had occasion to decry its abuse. He was one of the few in the Legislature who, while they recognized that the old system of government was becoming less and less suited to the genius and wants of the young Canadian community, at the same time wished to usher in the new *regime* with the moderation and tact which mark the work of the thoughtful politician and the aims of the true statesman. It has been said that one never knows what is inside a politician. What was inside the Reformer, Allan Dunlop, was all that became a patriot and a high-minded gentleman.

CHAPTER III.
"WHEN SUMMER DAYS WERE FAIR."

Afterwards--for close upon the coming of every grief, however great, fall the slow, dull footsteps of Afterwards--, the bereaved Macleod family took up again the occupations and interests of life in the benumbed fashion of those whose nerves are slow in recovering the effect of a great shock. Edward alone bore a brave front, though his heart at times failed him. He was something of a puzzle to the friend of his sister, who could not reconcile the tears which she saw in his eyes one moment to the jest she heard from his lips the next, and who marvelled in secret that the utter abandon of his grief at the bedside of his dying mother had not been followed by a state of settled melancholy after her death. To the cool, steadfast nature of Mademoiselle DeBerczy this alternate light and shade, gaiety and grief, in the heart of Rose, as well as of her brother, was difficult to understand; but now she began faintly to perceive that to their ardent temperament sunshine came as naturally as it did to the first day of spring, which, while it ached with the remembrance of winter, could not wholly repress on that account its natural brightness. Certainly Edward Macleod, though his unusually pale face gave evidence of the suffering which he had lately experienced--nay, which he was even now experiencing--could not say that life for him was utterly without consolation. For the sake of the stricken household, for the sake of her who had left them desolate, he would be a man; and, being that complex creature, a man, involves not only the lofty virtues of courage and self-forgetfulness, but also a tender susceptibility to the charms of these perfect spring days, and to the no less alluring charms of a maiden in the spring-time of youth.

Nearly a week had elapsed since the funeral of Mrs. Macleod, and now a second message from home had been received by Helene DeBerczy, reminding her that her invalid mother had claims which could no longer be set aside. If Madame DeBerczy's language was seldom imperative, her intention abundantly made up for the deficiency. Consequently, her daughter was now reluctantly turning her face homeward--a dull outlook, brightened only by the prospect of a boat-ride down the bay with Edward and Rose.

"And to think," said Edward to Helene, as the trio paced the long avenue together, "that I scarcely recognized you on the evening of my return!"

"That is not surprising. I am an entirely different person from the one you left three years ago."

"Let me see," mused the young man, "three years ago you were a little inclined to be haughty and cold, occasionally difficult to please, and sometimes exacting. On the whole, 'tis pleasant to reflect that you are an entirely different person now."

He turned towards her with a merry glance, but her face was invisible. She wore one of those long straw bonnets, no doubt esteemed very pretty and stylish in that day, but marred by what a disciple of Fowler might call a remarkable phrenological development of the anterior portion. This severely intellectual quality in the bonnets of that time naturally stood in the way of the merely sensuous delights of observation. Edward had barely time to be reminded of an unused well, in whose dark, shallow depths his boyish eyes had once discovered a cluster of white water-lilies, languidly opening to the light, when the liquid eyes and lily-like face in the inner vista of this well-like bonnet again confronted him.

"Is that the sort of person I used to be?" she queried, with the incredulity one naturally feels on being presented with a slightly exaggerated outline of one's own failings. "What pleasant memories you must have carried away with you!"

"I did, indeed--myriads of them. Some of the pleasantest were connected with our last dance together. Do you remember it?"

A slight warmth crept up, not into her cheeks, but into her eyes. "I have never forgiven you for that," she said.

"And you don't deserve forgiveness," declared Rose, championing the cause of her friend.

"Ah, well," said the culprit, "perhaps I had better wait till I deserve it before I plead for it."

How strange and far away, almost like part of their childhood, seemed the time of which he spoke. Like a painted picture, suddenly thrust before their view, the scene came back to them. A windy night in late Autumn, illumined without only by the broad shafts of light from the Commodore's mansion, and within by the leaping flames in the big hall fire-place. The young people had improvised a dance in the great hall, and Helene had tantalizingly bestowed most of her favours upon Fred Jarvis, a handsome youngster of twenty, who frequently improved his opportunities of becoming the special object of Edward's boyish enmity. To fall a willing victim to the pangs of jealousy formed, however, no part of this young gentleman's intention. Returning late in the evening, he caught a glimpse of Fred and Helene dancing a stately minuet together, and, lightly securing his horse at the door, he entered the hall, just as Helene was protesting that she was too tired to dance any longer. "Just once with me," he pleaded; and their winged footsteps kept time to the tumultuous throbbing of the music. The young girl suddenly grew faint. "Give me air," she cried, and at the words Edward's strong arm swept her across the broad veranda, and up on the waiting steed. Mounting behind her, like another young Lochinvar, they dashed wildly off, but just in what direction could not be told, for Helene, in mingled consternation, exhaustion, and alarm, had fainted in earnest, and Edward, in the endeavour to hold her limp, unconscious figure before him, had dropped the reins. The steed, however, with a prudent indisposition for pastures new at that hour of the night, turned into a stubble-field, and brought up at a haystack. How, in the utter darkness, and with the wind blowing a gale, the young man managed to restore his companion to consciousness and bring her back to the house, were mysteries which Rose could never attempt to penetrate with any degree of satisfaction. Helene, of course, was superbly angry, and even this bare mention of the escapade brought fire to her eyes and a loftier poise to the well-set head. Strongly set about the heart of this young Huguenot were barriers of pride, that could not be overleaped in a day--scarcely in a life-time.

"It is a bargain, then," said Edward, with a mischievous light in his smile, "you will never forgive, and I shall never forget."

"I wish, if it isn't asking too much, that you would allow me to forget. I particularly want to forget everything unpleasant on a morning as beautiful as this," rejoined Helene.

It was indeed an ideal morning. The sky was as soft and warm, as blue and white, as only the skies of early summer can be. Treading the mingled shadow and light, thrown from the interlacing boughs above, they came at last to the blue curves of Kempenfeldt Bay, whose waves lapped lightly on the beach. Here they found the two younger Macleod children, who had come to see the party off. Just as the latter arrived, the youth, Herbert, who had been amusing himself rocking a punt in a creek by the shore, managed to upset the craft and precipitate himself into deep water. The mishap had no more serious result--for the lad was a good swimmer--than to frighten Rose, and deprive her of the anticipated pleasure of a visit to "Bellevue" with Helene and her brother Edward. Bidding the former a hurried goodbye, with injunctions to her brother to take care of her friend, Rose disappeared with the children into the woods.

The young man now released a row-boat from its bondage to the shore, helped his companion into it, and pushed it far out upon its native element. A new day in the New World, and a long boat-ride before them--what could they wish for more? Edward, at least, enjoyed the prospect extremely, especially when he could get the bonnet rightly focused. This was a matter somewhat difficult of achievement, as its owner had to his mind a heedless habit of dodging, and his remarks, instead of being didactic and improving in their nature, were necessarily exclamatory and interrogative, in order to gain the attention of his fair *vis-a-vis*. Being a young gentleman of literary tastes he thought of Addison's dissertation upon the fan, and its great adaptability to the purposes of the coquette. To the mind of this impartial critic, a fan was not half so effective and terrible a weapon as the present style of bonnet.

"Bother Addison!" he suddenly exclaimed aloud.

"I beg your pardon," said a voice from the depths of the obnoxious head-gear before him.

"I was thinking of the author of *The Spectator*. You know Johnson says we ought to give our days and nights to the study of Addison. Don't you think it would be more profitable for us to devote our days and nights to the study of Nature?"

"Undoubtedly; and especially in this short-summered region, where there are only a few months of the year in which one can pursue one's studies out of doors. My days are spent on the shore, and as for my nights--well, even at night I often go to sleep to the fancy that I am drifting over the water with just such a gentle movement as this."

"I hope," said Edward gravely, "that you have an efficient oarsman. You couldn't row and sleep at the same time, you know."

He looked up to see if his companion was struck with the force of this observation, but although they were moving towards the east, the bonnet pointed due north. There was also a slight suspicion of the wintry north in the tone with which she replied:

"Oh, there is no labour connected with it; I am merely drifting--drifting to the Isle of Sleep."

"That is a pretty idea, but it is too lonely and listless to suit me. I should prefer to have a young lady in the boat--and a pair of oars."

"In that case you would have to row," and, with a slightly mocking accent, "you couldn't row and sleep at the same time, you know."

"In that case I should never want to sleep. No, please, Miss DeBerczy, don't look to the north again. Every time your gaze is riveted upon that frozen region my heart sinks within me. I feel as if I were not entertaining you as well as I should."

"Oh, don't let that illusion disturb you. I have never doubted that you were entertaining me as well as you--could."

A brief silence fell upon them, broken only by the regular plash of the oars. In the young man's conversational attacks there had been nothing but a light play of sunny humour, but in this last retort of hers there was something like the glimmer of cold steel. It wounded him, yet he was unwilling either to conceal or reveal the hurt. But Helene DeBerczy had this weakness, common to generous souls, that she could not utter an ungenerous remark without suffering more than her victim. So, scarcely more than a minute elapsed before she said appealingly,

"You are not going to leave me with the last word, are you?"

"Is not that what your sex specially like to have?"

"Perhaps so. I should prefer to have the *best* word, and--"

"And let a certain well-known gentleman take the hindmost?" supplied the young man smilingly.

"If he only would! What a shocking thing to say, but with me it is always conscience who has the very hindmost word; and my conscience is perfect mistress of the art of saying disagreeable things. At the present moment she is trying to make me believe that I have been unpardonably rude to you."

"She is mistaken then, for even if it were possible for you to be rude, I could not fail to pardon you immediately."

"There! now you have had the best word. It is useless for me to try to say anything better than that. Perhaps the most becoming thing I could do would be to relapse into ignominious silence."

"Silence! Desolation! And with a two-mile pull yet before us! If I have had the best word you have uttered the worst one. What so terrible as silence?"

"It is said to be golden."

"And, like the gold that Robinson Crusoe discovered on his island, it is of no particular use to anyone."

"It is one of the charms of Nature."

"A charm that I have never discovered. What about the ever-present hum of multitudinous insects, the song of birds, the moan of winds, the laughter of leaping water? It seems to me that Nature is all voice."

"Then, suppose," said the undaunted young lady, lifting her languorous lids, "that we listen to her voice."

There was no answering this; but, as the bonnet now veered towards the sunny south, and the boat rounding the sharp corner of the bay abruptly turned in the same direction, the young man was surprised to find himself looking his companion fully in the face, caught in the sudden sunshine of her smile.

"I was about to remark," he said, emboldened by this token of favour, "that there is nothing I delight in so much as listening to the voice of nature--that is human nature."

The smile deepened into a rippling laugh. "I am in one of my inhuman moods this morning," she said, "but I believe my forte is action rather than speech. Let me take your place, and those oars, please."

He resigned them both, and at once; not because the unusual exertion had made any appreciable inroad upon his strength, but because he foresaw new phases of picturesqueness in the young girl's dainty handling of the oars. Nor was he disappointed. The skirt of her dress was narrow and long, beginning, like an infant's robe, a few inches below the arms, and thence descending in softly curving lines to her feet, with as little hint of rigidity or compression about the tenderly rounded waist as about the full fair throat above it. She stretched out a pair of shoes, incredibly small and unmistakably French, and bent her slender gauntleted hands blithely to their task. The newborn sweetness of the spring morning was about them. On the heavily wooded shore the great evergreens towered darkly against the sun, but its beams fell with dazzling brightness upon the meadowy undulations of the lake. Above them they heard at times the wild cry of the soaring gull, or the apparently disembodied voice of some unseen bird. Behind them they left the beautiful stretch of Kempenfeldt Bay, gleaming in the sunshine, and now they slowly ascended the waters of Cook's Bay, called after the great circumnavigator, under whom many of the naval officers who had settled in the region had served, Governor Simcoe's father, after whom the old Lac des Clies--as the French called it--had received its modern name, being a shipmate.

But, now, Helene, whose slender strength had succumbed to the difficulties of propelling their little craft, resumed her old seat, and her bonnet, like a dark lantern, sometimes allowed a charming light to be reflected upon surrounding objects, and then as suddenly withdrew it. In the blue distance, near the mouth of the Holland River, they caught the first glimpse of "Bellevue"--the home of the DeBerczy's. The long sunlit run had after all been too brief. Edward began to realize that some days might elapse before this pleasure could be repeated. He drew in his oars, and let the boat rock idly on the tide. His companion gave him an inquiring glance. "I wish," said he, "that you would do me a favour."

"Isn't that rather an extraordinary request?"

"Not at all. It is a very natural remark. It has not yet advanced so far as to be a request."

"Oh! well, of course, I can't grant what isn't a request."

"Does that mean that you can grant what is one?"

"Sometimes."

"How good of you! But, as I said before, I had only expressed a wish. Aren't you in the least interested in my wishes?"

"If you were interested in mine you would take up those oars again."

"And thereby shorten the term of your imprisonment by me! Your kindness emboldens me to make known my desire. I wish you would let me examine something that appears to be hanging to your bonnet."

"Is it a grub--a caterpillar--a spider?" These horrors were mentioned in the order of their detestability, and with a rising accent.

"Really, I wouldn't like to say, unless you remove the bonnet." She gave a convulsive twitch to the strings, and pulled them into a hard knot. "Can't you brush it off?" she asked Edward breathlessly.

"Pray do not be so alarmed. No, indeed, I couldn't brush it off. It sticks too fast for that. I wish," he said, as she made a frantic lurch towards him, "that you could be mild but firm--I mean not quite so agitated." Her breath came in quick perfumed wafts into his face, as his steady fingers strove to undo the knot in her ribbons. But even after this lengthy business was concluded his trouble (if it could rightly be called a trouble) was only half over, for the careful Rose, with a prudent foreknowledge of the power of lake breezes to disarrange, if not carry away altogether, the headgear of helpless woman, had by some ingenious arrangement of hair-pins fastened the bonnet to the raven locks of her friend in such a manner that it could not be removed without endangering the structure of her elaborate hair-architecture. So it was among the dark waves of rapidly down-flowing tresses that Helene's voice was again heard beseeching him to tell her what it was.

"Your scientific curiosity seems to be almost as great as your fear of the insect creation. But, really, it is quite a harmless little fellow. See!" and he pointed to a steel beetle set with a view to ornamental effect in the centre of a little rosette of ribbons.

"Oh, shameless!" exclaimed the young girl, sinking her lily-white face again among the abundant waves of her hair.

"Yes, I daresay he is ashamed enough to think that he isn't alive when he sees that you regret it so much."

It is very annoying to be obliged to laugh when one has just made up one's mind to be very angry; but Mademoiselle DeBerczy, with all her haughtiness, was endowed with a sense of humour; so it was with only a weak show of reproachful indignation that she at last threw back her head and exclaimed:

"How could you--when I have such a horror of every sort of creeping thing-- and you knew what it was all the time!"

"Oh, excuse me, I did not know--that is, I wasn't positive. At a distance I thought it was some sort of a big fly--a blue-bottle. Now I see it is a blue beetle."

The young lady deigned no reply.

"I am sorry that you were frightened, but you don't seem to be a bit sorry on account of my sufferings."

"Your sufferings?"

"Yes, see how surprised you are even to know that they existed! But they are over now. At frequent intervals, all through this long voyage, I have been forced to look at a heavenly body through a telescope--that is, when I could get the telescope properly adjusted to my vision. The difficulties of adjustment have cost me a world of trouble."

She gazed at him a moment in wide-eyed amazement, and then without at-tempting to solve the riddle of his remarks, proceeded to reduce her wind-blown locks to something like their usual law and order. The dark heavy waves, rioting in the breeze, seemed to offer a problem to the deft white fingers that fluttered among them, but they were speedily subjugated, and the despised bonnet was added as the crowning touch. Not a moment too soon, for the boat grated on the sandy beach, and the austere windows of her home were looking coldly down upon her. A pair of austere eyes were also fixedly regarding her; but of this Helene was happily un-conscious. Perhaps it was the instinct of hospitality alone that made her smile so brightly upon the brother of her friend, as they walked up to the house together. The grounds about "Bellevue," not so ample as those surrounding the home of the old Commodore, gave equal evidence of wealth and taste, and reminded one of a little park set in the midst of the wilderness. The garden borders were bright with crocuses and snowdrops and rich in promises of future bloom, while from the or-chard slopes on the left came a fair vision of wall-like masses of foliage, frescoed with blossoms and the perfumed touch of the blithe breezes at play among them. Entering the quaint, dimly-lighted hall, they passed under long plumes of peacock feathers, o'erhanging the arched doorway leading into the drawing-room. The floors were waxed and polished, the apartments spacious and lofty with elaborate cornices and panels. Leaving her guest in mute contemplation of a tiny wood fire in a great fire-place, the young girl ran lightly up the broad, low stairway, pausing at the half-way landing to gaze dreamily from a casemated window out upon the sparkling waters of the lake. Some of its brightness was reflected in her eyes, as, with a step less discreet and deferential than that which usually characterized her approaches to her mother's bedchamber, she passed on to a half-closed door, tapped lightly upon it, and then pushed it wide open.

"Ah, my daughter, what tidings do you bring?"

"He has come!" declared the girl, proclaiming with unaffected gladness what was at that moment a great event in her life.

"He!"

The chilly palm which the elder lady had extended, without rising, for the customary greeting, was not so chilly as the tone with which she uttered this of-fending pronoun. Helene, suddenly remembering with deep self-reproach the grief that her mother must feel in the loss of her old friend, took the cold fingers in both her warm white hands, and whispered tenderly:

"She has gone!"

Madame DeBerczy was not overcome by this intelligence. She had indeed learned the sad truth from Tredway, who had been despatched to "Bellevue" by the Commodore immediately upon the death of his wife. Consequently, at this mo-ment, her heart did not suffer so much as her sense of propriety--which her enemies asserted was a more vital organ.

"I trust," she said, not unkindly, but with a sort of majestic displeasure, "that you do not mention these facts to me in what you consider the order of their importance."

The young girl was chilled. She moved away to one of the spindle-legged chairs near a window, and played absently with the knotted fringes of the old-fashioned dimity curtain. "I mention them in the order of their occurrence," she said gently. "Dear Mrs. Macleod could scarcely close her eyes on earth until they rested upon her son. He brought me over in his boat this morning, and is waiting below to see you. Do you feel able to go down?"

"I hope I shall always be able to respond to social requirements, and the son of my old friend must not be slighted. Were you about to suggest that I receive him in my bedchamber?"

Helene, who had risen with charming alertness at the first intimation of her mother's intentions, now confronted that frigid dame with the subdued radiance of her glance. "Ah, dear mother!" she murmured deprecatingly. Daughterly submissiveness, tender consideration for an invalid's querulous moods, gentle insistence upon her own right to be happy in spite of them, were all radiated from the softly spoken words. Rigid propriety may have slain its thousands, perhaps its tens of thousands, but the elder lady foresaw with terrible clearness that it would never find a victim in this blithe girl, who refrained from dancing down the stairs before her simply because her happiness was accustomed to find expression in her looks, not in her actions. However, motherly allegiance to duty might curb if it could not altogether control. "Is it possible that I heard you humming a tune as you came through the hall?" she inquired.

"No, no; it is impossible! I hummed it so low that you certainly could not have heard it!"

Dignified rebuke was out of the question, as they had reached the foot of the stairway. In another moment Edward Macleod was bending profoundly over the hand of his hostess. The aristocratic, little old lady, with her delicate faded face, always seemed to him like some rare piece of porcelain or other fragile, highly-finished object. He led her to the easiest chair, and drew his own close beside her, only interrupting the absorbed attention which he gave to her remarks by soft inquiries regarding her health, or compliments upon the way in which her not very vigorous constitution had withstood the severity of the Canadian winter.

This noble dame, though she had been accustomed to a Northern climate, had never reconciled herself to it. She still longed for *la belle France*. Those who accompanied her husband to this portion of Upper Canada, on the outbreak of the French Revolution, had either returned to France or had gone to settle in French Canada, at the capital of which Helene was born shortly after the death of her father. The old friendship of General DeBerczy for Commodore Macleod, and the fact that the latter was the executor of her husband's estate and the guardian of her daughter, had led her to return to the Huguenot colony on the Oak Ridges, and summer always found Madame and her household at her northern villa, near the Macleod residence, on Lake Simcoe. Here Edward passed the day gossiping with the old lady, and sauntering about the trim grounds with the stately Helene until the afternoon was far advanced.

After taking his leave of Madame DeBerczy, Edward cast a fugitive glance about him in search of her daughter, but that young lady, for reasons of her own, was absent. He suffered a vague disappointment, as he took his way to the shore, but at the water's edge a girlish form overtook him, and a superb bouquet of hothouse flowers was placed in his hand.

"I brought them for you to place upon--upon--"

She hesitated. It sounded like wanton cruelty to say "your mother's grave" to him, whose idea of everything lovely on earth must be signified in the word "mother," everything terrible in the word "grave." But he understood her, and thanked her, while his heart and eyes filled fast. On that lonely homeward row the burden of his bereavement lay heavily upon him, and the remembrance of his happy morning with his childhood's friend, though sweet, was almost as faint as the fragrance exhaled from the rare exotics at his feet. The pure tender curves of the white camellias reminded him of Helene. She herself was the rare product of choicest care and cultivation--the flower of an old and complex civilization. The fancy pleased him at first, and then woke in his mind a certain vague disdain. What place had hot-house plants, either human or otherwise, in this wild new land, whose illimitable forests as yet were almost strangers to axe and fire?

In a remote and solitary corner of his own domain, the Commodore had made for his dead wife a last abiding-place. Thitherward, and alone, the motherless youth bent his steps in the soft glow of sunset. The stillness of the place was broken only by the whisper of the trees overhead, the faint hum of insects, and the low murmur of the lapping waters of the lake. Walking with downbent head and step so light that his footfall made no slightest sound upon the young grass in his path, he did not see the form of a half wild, wholly beautiful girl, emerge from the deep gloom of the woods before him. Nor did she observe him, for her attention was wholly bent upon the armful of forest-flowers, which she let fall upon the grave with a passionate gesture of grief. The young man, looking up in startled amaze, recognized the strange, fantastic figure that had fled before his approach on the evening of his return home. He scarcely noticed her odd costume of mingled blue and yellow, so drawn was he to the dusky splendour of her face. The warm vitality of the mantling cheek, and the charm of the lustrous lips, were matched in hue by a blood-coloured 'kerchief, carelessly knotted about the supple, tawny throat, behind which streamed a profuse abundance of deep-black hair. Giving him one frightened glance, she turned and sped like some strange tropic bird upon the wind. Moved by wonder, curiosity, and admiration, the young man gave stealthy chase; but, after following in the wake of her flying feet by bush and brier, and through the tangled thickets of the forest, he had the poor satisfaction of losing sight of her altogether, and then gaining one last glimpse of her, as, from the dense shadowy point where she became invisible, shot out a birch-bark canoe, and the dying sunset illumined with all the hues of victory the superb form of an Algonquin maiden rapidly rowing away. Hot, irritated, and tired, Edward returned home, nor did he observe that, in this fruitless chase, one of the pure buds that Helene had given him had fallen from his breast, on which he had pinned it, and had been rudely crushed beneath his heel.

CHAPTER IV.
INDIAN ANNALS AND LEGENDS.

The last flame of sunset had gone out on a horizon of ashy paleness, as the light bark of the Indian girl swept up the beach, and its occupant, after making it secure, loitered idly home. Here, undismayed by observation, she was as gracefully at ease as a fawn in its leafy covert, and as quickly startled into flight at the tread of a stranger.

So lightly did her moccasined feet press the underbrush that no sound preceded her coming, until she reached the blanketed opening of a wigwam where sat an aged Algonquin chief, very grave, very dignified, very far from being immaculately clean. The young girl was not intimidated by this picturesque combination of dignity and dirt. Perhaps it was the absence of these qualities in the young cadet that caused her sudden flight from him. Seating herself on a bearskin, not far from her foster-father, she interchanged with him mellow syllables of greeting. The chief placed a finger upon her moist brow, and inquired the cause of her haste.

"It was the young kinsman of the Wild Rose who followed me. His head is beautiful as the sun, but he moves, alas, yes, he moves more slowly."

"Then, why this haste?" queried the Indian, who, though he could boast all the keen and subtle instincts of his race, was apparently in some matters as obtuse as a white man.

The girl bowed her face upon her slim brown hands.

"I do not like the glances of his eye," she said. "They are strong and dazzling as sunbeams on the water."

The chief smoked in meditative silence. "You go too often to the dwelling of the Wild Rose, my daughter."

"Ah, yes; but to-night her pink face is dewy wet, I know, and she is alone. The Moon-in-a-black-cloud has gone to the home of her people."

"Then let her seek consolation in the slow moving sun. The pale-faced nation are not fit associates for an Algonquin maiden. Mother Earth has no love for them; they are quick to wash away her lightest finger-touch upon them. They are pale and lifeless as a rock over which the stream washes continually. Their men are afraid of the rain; their women of the sunshine."

"It is even so. The Wild Rose covers her head, and even her hands, when she leaves the house."

At this mournful assent the chief warmed to his task of depreciation.

"They are degraded, these pale faces, they are poor-spirited, mean, contemptible; unable to cope with the wild beasts of the forest, they settle down in weak resignation to grow vegetables; nothing stirs them from their state of ignoble content except the call to battle, and that is responded to not in defence of the lives of their fathers, their wives and children, but merely to settle some petty quarrel between the chiefs of their nations.

"Ah, they are a strange, servile race! They work with their hands." The Indian paused and looked down at the wrinkled yet shapely members that lay before him. "They look upon the grand forest as their natural enemy, burning, cutting, mutilating, until they have made that odious thing 'a clearing,' when a house is built with the dead bodies of the beautiful trees that have fallen by their hand."

"But surely they are not wholly bad," pleaded the girl, her kind heart refusing to accept the belief that even the lowest of humanity could be utterly worthless.

The chief was not to be turned from the swift current of his thoughts by idle interruptions.

"Their religion is dead, buried in a book, and they put it from them as easily as they put the book on the shelf. Our religion is alive, broad as the earth, deep as the sky. They go into a ***house*** to worship; ***our*** temple is fashioned by the great Spirit, and our prayers ascend continually like the white smoke from our wigwams. Ah, but they should be pitied not blamed. They are far from the heart of nature--they have ceased to be her children."

"It is money they worship, and the soul of a man becomes like that which he adores. They mourn bitterly for their dead, because they feel how great is the distance between them and the land of spirits. I have heard that there are white men who do not believe that this land exists, but that cannot be true."

There were some depths of degradation that even his far-reaching imagination failed to compass. Wanda listened wearily, though she manifested no signs of impatience.

"The pale-faced women are sometimes very beautiful," she said.

"Yes; but they are strange, unnatural creatures. In times of anger they attack their helpless little ones, talking in a harsh voice, pinching, beating, slapping them, doing everything but bite them."

His listener did not shudder. The Indian, no matter how much his feelings may be stirred, is unaccustomed to evince emotion.

"With us," continued the old man, "an angry woman frequently pulls her husband's hair; for is he not her husband to do with what she likes? but to fall upon her own flesh and blood--that is unnatural and horrible. It is as if she should wilfully injure her own person, bruise it with stones or sear it with hot irons. Perhaps it is because the pale-faced tribes suffer so much in childhood that they are weak and cowardly in manhood. They shrink and cry like a wounded panther at the touch of pain."

The girl who had not dwelt upon it except in her thoughts was nevertheless filled with a gently uplifting sense of race superiority. Her admiration of Rose was tinged with pity. Poor garden flower, confined for life to the dull walks and prim parterres of a fixed enclosure, when she might roam the wild paths of the forest; condemned to sleep in a close room, on stifling feathers, and bathe in an elongated tub, when she might feel the elasticity of hemlock boughs beneath her, inhale the perfumed breath of myriad trees, and plunge at sunrise into the gleaming waters of the lake. It was indeed a pitiable life.

They entered the wigwam, and seated themselves on the rush mats that lay upon the ground. About them were carelessly disposed some dressed skins of the beaver and otter, a brace of wild duck, fishing tackle, and the accoutrements of the chase, a rifle, powder-horn and shot pouch. The chief himself, in his buckskin garment, tightened by a wampum belt, his deer-skin moccasins, scarlet cloth leggings and blanket, was not the least picturesque object of the interior. Usually reticent, he found great difficulty to-night in withdrawing his mind from the subject that had taken such violent possession of it.

"The influence of the white race is spreading," he said. "Like the poison vines of the forest it touches all who come near it with fatal effect. The tribe of the Hurons is infected with it, and they are becoming mere tillers of the soil--miserable earth-worms! Men were made to be free as the bounding deer or the flowing stream, but they have paled and weakened, they have become wretched grovellers on the ground."

Wanda's large eyes held a smouldering fire of repressed indignation. Her mother had been a Huron.

The story of that dark time, far back in the annals of Canada, when the Huron hunting-grounds in this region were laid waste by the destroyer, had been told her so often that her childish imagination had been filled with horror, and a passionate sense of outraged justice and impossible revenge stirred within her at the bare mention of her mother's martyred tribe. She did not vent her feelings in bitter or retaliatory speech--that is the weakness of fairer-faced women--but through her brain rushed like a swift stream a vivid recollection of the tragic tale as it fell from the lips of her Huron mother upon her young horror-stricken heart.

Less than two hundred years before, the poetry of Indian life among the peaceful shades of this virgin wilderness was turned into a tale too ghastly for human imagination, too terrible for human endurance. At that time the Huron settlements on the borders of Lakes Simcoe and Couchiching, and between Nottawasaga and Matchedash bays, numbered from twenty to thirty thousand souls. The picturesque country, thickly dotted with Indian towns, was for many years the scene of Champlain's zealous efforts to erect in these western wilds the standard of the Cross. While he won, among the Hurons, converts to his faith and a colony to his country, they found in him a leader in a fateful attack upon their ancient and most obdurate enemies, the Iroquois. The result of the expedition was failure and discomfiture, but years afterwards, when Champlain was dead, and the "great-souled and giant-statured Jean de Brebeuf" became known as the apostle of the tribe, this foray brought most disastrous consequences upon the unsuspecting Hurons.

Not far from the present site of Barrie was the frontier town of St. Joseph, where the Jesuit Fathers, in view of the perils surrounding them, had concentrated their forces in a central stronghold, with a further inland defence at Ste. Marie, near the site of the present town of Penetanguishene. Here, at St. Joseph, after years of incessant labour, of discomforts and discouragements without parallel in the annals of our country, the ardent souls whose enthusiasm for faith and duty had become the dominant principle of their life, were swept away in the red tide of blood that was opened by the Iroquois. One still fair morning in the summer of 1648, while most of the warriors were absent at the chase, and a company of devout worshippers were celebrating Mass in the Mission Chapel, their brutish enemies descended upon their peaceful domains, and by means of every torture conceivable to the savage imagination practically exterminated the tribe. Before the century had half-ended the mission post of St. Ignace was similarly invaded by the Iroquois, who, after they wearied of the pastime of hacking the flesh off their prisoners with tomahawks and hatchets, and scorching them with red-hot irons, bound them at last to the stake and mercifully allowed the swift-mounting flames to end their sufferings.

Whole families were bound in their houses before the town was set on fire, and their wild cries mingled with the wilder laughter of their inhuman captors. The few who escaped were so wounded and mutilated that before they could reach a place of safety numbers of them died frozen in the woods.

The remembrance of this dark tale never failed to stir the young girl to a sort of slow self-contained fury, but the blood of the peace-loving Hurons was in her veins, and could not long be dominated by the vengeful propensities of her haughty Algonquin father. Invariably with the mixture of blood comes the warring of diverse emotions, the dissatisfaction with the present life, the secret yearning for something better, the impulse towards something worse. She sighed furtively, and half-impatiently went outside to tend the evening camp-fire. The blazing branches illuminated the starless summer night, and cast a superb glow over the beautiful half-clothed figure crouching not far from them. Beyond, the dark blue bay ebbed and flowed languidly.

Some days elapsed before Wanda again made her appearance in the neighbourhood of the Commodore's mansion. This was caused partly by shyness, partly by fear of meeting the bold-eyed youth, whose interest in her had been so painfully apparent. At length Rose, who had noted with wonder and a little anxiety this unusual absence, suggested to her brother that they call upon one of her Indian friends. To this Edward demurred, on the ground that the work in which he happened to be engaged at the time could not possibly wait. But when he learned that the beautiful Wanda was the friend alluded to he agreed to go with her at once, saying that the work he was doing could wait as well as not. Such was the manner in which brotherly affection was manifested sixty years ago.

It was a still, almost breathless evening in June. From the meadows, thickly starred with dew, rose the thin high chorus of the crickets, while above, the commingling of gray cloud and crimson sunset had subsided into dusk and golden twilight, which were giving place to the white radiance of the moon slowly climbing the warm heights of heaven. It was so quiet that the sound of waves and insects seemed like the softest whispers of nature. Rose and Edward had rowed down the bay for Helene, who usually accompanied them on their impromptu excursions by lake and wood. Seen in the pale brilliance of sky and water her loveliness had an almost unearthly quality, perfectly akin to the night, but giving her a strange effect of soft remoteness from her friends. The light from a brazier, fitted into a stanchion in the prow of the boat, in which some pieces of birch-bark were kindled, brought the deep dark shadow of the woods into sharp relief, and gave a more vivid brilliance to the immediate surroundings; but along the dimly-lit path in the forest all the magical influences of the night held sway. Beneath the tangled underbrush they caught glimpses of the rich and fantastic vegetation with which the earth was clothed, while above them, intermingled with the shadows cast by the vaulted boughs, played the vivid brightness of the moon. Some of the trees were deeply girdled--a slow method of killing them. These lingering deaths affected the trio with melancholy. A wounded inmate of the grove, standing in mute and pathetic resignation to its fate, loses first the feeling of the sap that, blood-like, circulates through every limb, then all its leafy honours fade, and its death is slow and inevitable as the death of a forsaken woman who carries a deep hurt at the heart.

Near where a group of lofty elms lifted their beautiful heads up to the moonlight they found the old chief busily engaged in mending his seine. He greeted them with entire self-possession, rising and giving his hand to each, after which he resumed his occupation in tranquil content, as though the duties of hospitality were now over. The young ladies, however, without waiting for any further exhibition of courtesy, seated themselves on a mossy log, and bestowed upon their host and his employment the flattering attention, which, if it failed to make an impression upon him, would certainly prove him more--or less--than mortal man. Edward, meantime, finding a convenient bough a few feet above his head, amused himself in swinging by his hands, with a view to muscular development. The contrast between the sad dignity of the aged Indian, the lone survivor of a despised race, and the light-heartedness of the fair boy, upon whom all the hopes of his family centred, struck both girls forcibly. After a few sympathetic inquiries regarding the health of the chief, Rose asked after the whereabouts of Wanda.

"She is not here," he replied. "She flies from our home as a bird flies from its cage, returning only when she is weary, or when the shades of night are upon the land."

"Do you know where she is?" inquired Edward, dropping to his feet, and seating himself on a log facing the others.

"Somewhere in the forest," replied the Indian, indicating the direction by a broad sweep of the hand, which might include a thousand acres.

This was sufficiently indefinite. "It appears to be characteristic of this young lady that she is either a vanished joy, or just on the point of becoming one. Have you any idea how far away she is?" he asked.

"Something more than twice the flight of an arrow," tranquilly answered the Indian--"yes, much more. It used to be that she went short distances, but she now goes a papoose's journey of half a sun--sometimes further." He viewed his impatient guest a moment with gravity, and added, "yes, much further."

"And you trust her all alone?"

"She is an Algonquin maiden. She fears nothing."

"And why is an Algonquin superior to a Huron, for instance?" The young man, leaning idly back, and caressing the Indian dog of the chief, pursued his questions without any definite purpose, but merely to draw out his reserved-looking host.

"Why is the fleet deer that spurns the soil better than the dull ox that tills it? Or why is the eagle better than the hen that picks up corn in your doorway? But there was a time when in all the land no Indian could be found who was tame and stupid--what you call civilized."

"Tell us a legend of that time, will you not?" pleaded Rose, who had been watching in silence for a fitting opportunity to make her favourite request.

"Ah, please do," said Edward, and the three settled themselves comfortably to listen.

"It was a great many moons ago," began the chief, "long before the time of my grandfather. All the Indian races were then as one people, living in peace, and speaking one tongue. Not one of them worked with his hands. The deer, the beaver, the otter, the antelope, and the bear flourished and fattened for all, and were caught with scarcely any skill or effort. The men were never wearied in the chase, nor the women with pounding corn. None of the white races had as yet come upon the earth to molest and insult the guardian spirits of hill and stream and stately wood, and the red men, then as now, were in the habit of propitiating these deities by offerings of maize, bright coloured flowers, or belts of wampum laid upon the mountains, or dropped into caves or streams. Yes, every one lived without fear of his neighbour, and the red ochre with which our tribes paint their faces in war was used only to decorate the pipe of peace.

"One day it happened that a few chosen ones of all these tribes were met together upon a plain, about the distance of four bow-shots across. Very green and shining it looked to the eye, for it was in the Flower-moon, and the great star of day was bright in the heaven. By its clear light they saw, far in the distance, two strange, enormous things moving towards them. But whether these things were writhing wreaths of thunder clouds descended to earth, or gigantic trees denuded of their foliage and suddenly gifted with the power of motion, or whether they were wild beasts of a size never seen before, they could not tell. But presently they found them to be immense creatures in the form of rattlesnakes, poisoning the air with their vile effluvia, and destroying every green tree and living thing in their path. Every delicate plant and creeping thing was poisoned by their breath, and the larger animals were devoured in the flap of a bird's wing. With them came terrific lightnings that rent the trees and cleft the solid rock, and thunders which caused the earth to reel like a man who had drank many times of fire-water. Nearer and nearer they approached, and now the chosen residents of this fair plain were filled with alarm for their lives, and at once began to build fortifications against the terrible intruders. The snakes, who appeared to prefer the flesh of man to that of the other animals, crawled up close to the defence of their enemies, and flung their long horrible bodies against it, but in vain. It was useless to attack them with bows and arrows, on account of the scales which enveloped them like an armour. Those who ventured without the walls were instantly swallowed, while those within, who had fasted many suns, were growing weak from want of food.

"Now there was among them a chief, called the Big Bear, who was very brave and cunning. He had been a hunter of the deer and wolf ever since he had been pronounced a man. No danger was so great that he could not find a trail out of it. So when he began to speak all the people who remained gathered round him.

"'Brothers and chiefs,' he said, 'I perceive that one of our enemies is a woman, because she is less sluggish in her movements than the other, and her eyes are bright and deceitful. Besides she cares not to eat all the time, but she will sometimes go to view herself in the river, or when she thinks no one is looking will slyly turn her head to see the graceful movements of her tail. Brothers, my plan is this: Let me contrive to win the heart of this vain squaw-snake, and then with her aid I shall be able to destroy her husband; afterwards we may compass the destruction of the faithless wife. If I perish it is in a good cause, I am a willing martyr.'

"This good man proceeded that very night to carry out his noble purpose. The sky was full of shining lights as he mounted the fortification, and bent toward her, murmuring: 'Ah, beautiful creature, thy form is graceful as a winding stream, and thine eyes are two stars reflected in it. That stupid man-snake, lying in heavy sleep, how can he appreciate you? He is withered and worthless as a last year's leaf. As for me I flee to you from the dull women of my tribe, who are like so many dead trees, that stand even after life has left them. You are alive and beautiful in every movement, like the long curving wave that breaks upon the beach.'

"Oh, there is no doubt that Big Bear knew all about the best way to make love, for very soon the squaw-snake began to show great discontent with her husband, to scold him in a high voice, and to wish that he were dead; whereas she greeted Big Bear with much affection, warming her glittering head in his breast, and embracing him several times by coiling round and round him. But she was careful to turn her head away, so as not to poison him by her breath. As for Big Bear, though he was glad to win her love, he wished her not to love him too well as she had a wonderful dexterity in snapping off the heads of those whom she admired. Her consent to the death of her husband was easily gained, and she bade him dip the points of two arrows in the poison of her sting. This he did and after retiring within the fortification he levelled one arrow at the head of the husband, while he deposited the other in that of the wicked wife. The horrid monsters rolled over in agony, and rent the air with their death-shrieks, while all the people gathering about Big Bear, called him their brother, because by his wonderful knowledge of the arts of flirtation he had delivered them from great peril. But the most grievous result of the danger through which they had passed was this, that the poison ejected by the snakes in their death-agonies affected all the tribes of the earth to such an extent that each began to use a different language which could not be comprehended by the others. Since that time a young man of one race very seldom weds with the daughter of another, because she does not understand the lies he tells."

"Is it necessary for him to tell her what is not true, in order to marry her?" asked Edward.

"It is customary," replied the chief, gravely returning to his task, without the suspicion of a smile.

"Oh, strange peculiarity of the red men," softly exclaimed Helene. She begged for another legend, but the Indian had relapsed into his normal state of imperious dignity; so, after thanking him for the extravaganza, to which they had listened with admirable self-possession, they returned to the beach, the dog plunging joyfully into the green depths of the forest before them. The great woods were warm, odorous, breathless. Rose pushed back the damp blonde locks from her brow. "I wish you could have seen Wanda," she said. "The girl is quite a beauty. Half wild, of course, but with a sort of barbaric splendour about her that dazzles and bewilders one. You will understand when you see her, why the Indians speak the word 'paleface' with a contemptuous inflection."

"I suppose," mused Edward, "that paleness to them means weakness, lack of blood, vitality, courage, and all that most becomes a man. Yet as a matter of taste I prefer white to copper colour." His blue eyes were bent upon the lily-like face of Helene.

"Wait till you see her," was his sister's laughing response.

"And that will be many moons hence, to use the language of our story-teller, if she continues as elusive as the wind. I have had glimpses of her, or rather of the flutter of her vanishing raiment. A being with a wonderfully perfect face, clothed in heterogeneous and many-coloured garments, and educated on the amazing fictions with which her foster-father's memory seems to be stored, would be worth waiting to see."

But he had not long to wait. As he stood on the beach in the absence of his companions, who were carefully retracing their steps to the wigwam in search of a glove, presumably dropped by the way, he caught sight of the Indian girl, her back turned towards him, lazily rocking herself in his boat. For a moment he thrilled with the excitement of a hunter in the presence of that desirable object, "a splendid shot." Then he crept stealthily forward, sprang into the boat, and before the startled girl could recover from her amazement, he was rowing her far out on the moonlit bay. "There!" he cried, exultantly, bending an ardent yet laughing gaze upon her, "now you may run away as fast as you like."

The girl neither spoke nor moved. A great fire of resentment was burning in her heart, and its flames mounted to her cheeks. "My soul!" he murmured, "how beautiful you are!" She faced him fully and fairly, with the magnificent disdain of an empress in exile. In some way she gave him the impression that this brilliant little escapade was rather a poor joke after all. "Do me the favour of moving a muscle," he pleaded mockingly, and his request was lavishly granted. Before he could guess her intention she was in the water, knocking an oar from his hand in her rapid exit, and swimming at an incredible rate of speed for the nearest point of land, from which she sped like a hunted thing to the woods.

Left alone in this unceremonious fashion the young man paddled ruefully after his missing oar, and then struck out boldly after the escaped captive, with the intention of apologizing for what now seemed to him rather a cowardly performance; but the footsteps of the flying maiden left no trace upon the beach. His discomfited gaze rested on no living thing save the approaching figures of his sister and her friend, whose humane inquiries and frequent jests concerning the half wild, wholly dripping, vision that had crossed their path, contributed in no way to the young man's enjoyment of their homeward row.

CHAPTER V.
THE ALGONQUIN MAIDEN.

Early on one of those matchless summer mornings, for he loved to adopt the hours kept by the birds, Edward set forth alone on a voyage of discovery. The wilds of his native land had a great and enduring fascination for him. He never ceased to enjoy the charm of a forest so dense that one might stay in it for days without the danger of discovery. Wandering as he listed, hurrying or loitering as it pleased him, and resting when weary beneath the outstretched arms of the over-shadowing wood, he drank deeply of the simple joys of a free and careless savage life. His whole nature became sensitive and receptive, like that of a poet, an absorbent of the beauty and music of earth and air.

The long bright hours of this particular day were spent in exploring bayous and marshes, and in paddling among the ledges and around the lovely islands of Lake Couchiching. The dazzling blue expanse--mirror of a sky as blue--was broadly edged with reeds and rushes, flags and water-lilies, and framed by the thickly wooded shore and the green still cliffs that overhung the quiet waves. The air was laden with the sweet faint odours of early summer, and a soft breeze was lightly blowing under skies as soft. The youthful voyager went ashore, and for a long time lay stretched on the sand with his gun watching for wild-fowl.

The woods were brilliant with flowers, blue larkspur, scarlet lichens, the white and yellow and purple cyprepedium, or lady's slipper, called by the Indians 'moccasin flower,' the purple and scarlet iris, the bright pink blossom of the columbine, and all the other wind-blown and world-forgotten flowerets of the forest.

As the day grew warmer he betook himself for coolness to a quiet leaf-screened nook, beneath a rudely sculptured cliff, mantled in foliage. Here he reclined after his midday lunch, gazing out upon a sky so blue that it seemed a sea washing the invisible shores of heaven, and dreaming of as many things as usually occupy the fancy of a young man on an idle June day. But one event of which he did not dream was rapidly approaching. A wild bird more brilliant and beautiful than any he had so patiently waited for with his gun was preparing to fall at his feet. Just above his head the Algonquin maiden, Wanda, who like himself had strayed far from home, was reposing warm and wearied in utter unconsciousness of the proximity of any human being. The shining waters of the lake beneath her gave her a sudden charming inspiration. Springing up with the alertness of one upon whom fatigue lies as lightly as dew upon the sward, she swiftly disrobed, and remained a moment graceful as a young maple in autumn, standing in beautiful undress, its delicate limbs bare of leaves, and all its light raiment fallen in a many coloured heap to the ground.

In the natural ***abandon*** of the situation, Wanda neared the edge of the overhanging cliff, and sprang far out into the water. Edward, who was still lounging under the rock, was startled by the flashing outline--like a meteor from the heavens--of a human figure, which, in the twinkling of an eye, had cleaved the smooth surface of the lake, sank far into its depths, and reappeared some distance off. The glistening waters seemed to set in diamonds the beautifully shaped head and neck of the Indian maiden as she disported herself in the cool lake, and made for a point of land where a winding pathway, covered to the water's edge by a profuse growth of young trees, led up to the cliff above.

Recalling the classical story, familiar to his youth, and the judgment of the gods--"Henceforth be blind for thine eyes have seen too much!"--the young man concealed himself from view from the lake and waited for some time before venturing to regain the cliff overhead.

The fear of not being able to overtake the Indian beauty prevented Edward from remaining a prisoner quite as long as his sense of propriety dictated. But his fear was justified. She had almost reached the vanishing point of his vision when he finally emerged from his involuntary hiding-place. When at last he came up with her she confronted him with the wide innocent gaze of a child suddenly startled in its play. Then the swift instinct of the savage, the uncontrollable desire to fly, took possession of her. But the young man laid a light detaining hand upon her slim brown wrist. "Don't leave me," he entreated, "I want to ask you the way home."

It was the only pretext he could invent on the spur of the moment, and it answered his purpose admirably. She stopped to view with undisguised amazement, tempered with faint scorn, a human being who was so ignorant of the commonest affairs of life as to lose himself in the woods. She never dreamed of doubting his word. "I will be your guide," she said, with grave friendliness.

"You are very kind. I am afraid," said the youth with well-feigned discouragement, "that we are a long way from home."

"This is my home," said Wanda, as they stepped into the shadow of the limitless forest. "It is only white men who are content to live on a little patch of ground and shut the sky away from them. The Indian is at home everywhere."

"That is certainly an advantage, for when a person's home is spread all over the continent he can never be lost. What should I have done if I had not met you?"

She made no reply. Flitting before him like some gorgeous bird, he was obliged to follow her at a pace that was anything but agreeable on this hot afternoon. Presently she turned and came back. He was leaning against a tree, breathing heavily, and exhibiting every symptom of extreme fatigue.

"You are forcing me to lead a terribly fast life," he declared. "You have no idea of how tired I am."

She laid a smooth brown hand upon his heart. If it beat faster at the touch it was not sufficiently rapid to cause alarm. "You are not tired at all," she declared with the air of a wise physician who is not to be imposed upon, "besides there is need for haste. It is going to rain."

And indeed the intense heat of the summer afternoon threatened to find relief in a thunder shower. The atmosphere suddenly cooled and darkened. The strange, shrill, foreboding chirp of a bird was the only sound heard in the forest, except the rushing of a new-risen hurrying wind in the tree-tops. Then came the loud patter of rain on the leaves overhead, accompanied by a heavy crash of thunder.

"The Great Spirit is angry," murmured the young girl, her eyes dilating, and her breast heaving.

"Well, experience teaches me that the best course to pursue when people are angry is to keep perfectly still until the storm blows over. It's no use talking back. Ah! don't do that," he implored as she stooped and kissed the ground.

"But I must. It will propitiate the angry spirit and preserve us from danger."

"Oh, how can you waste your sweetness on the desert earth, in that fashion? It *may* preserve us from danger, but it is likely to have a contrary effect on me."

The temporary shelter afforded by the interlacing branches overhead was now beaten down by the strength of the storm, which descended in torrents. "Ah! you are afraid," he observed softly, drawing nearer to her.

"It is for you," she responded, "The rain is no more to me than it is to a red squirrel, but you, poor canary bird, your yellow head should be safe in its own cage."

This anxious, motherly tone brought a smile to the lips of the young man. A sudden thought struck his guide. Grasping his hand she drew him swiftly along until they reached the hollow trunk of an immense oak, into which she hastily thrust him. "There is not room for both," she declared, looking like a dripping naiad, as the rain-drops thickened about her. "Then there is not room for me," responded Edward, whose sense of chivalry rebelled at the idea of looking from a place of security upon an unprotected woman, exposed to the fury of the storm. He drew her reluctant form beside him, but she was impatient and ill at ease in her enforced shelter, as though she had been one of the untamed things of the wood, caught and prisoned against its will. Outside the rain fell fast, while within crouched this beautiful creature as remotely as possible from her human companion, and gazing longingly forth upon the wild elements of whose life her own life seemed to form a vital part. Her pulse beat fast in sympathy with the fast beating rain. Her large liquid eyes were dark as woodland pools. She did not pay her companion the compliment of being embarrassed in the slightest degree by his presence. Her only feeling was one of physical discomfort in her cramped position, and impatience with the man who could imagine that for her such protection was necessary. It crossed his mind that here was a veritable child of nature, untamed, untamable, not only in her habits and surroundings, her modes of life and thought, but in her very nature, in every fibre of her being, every emotion of her mind. Her superb unconsciousness chagrined and then irritated him. A beautiful woman might as well be a beautiful statue as to persist in behaving like one. A sudden rash desire took possession of the youth to test the quality of this superhuman indifference. The opportunity was tempting, the moment auspicious; he might never be so near her again. He laid one hand upon her arm, and bent his fair head till it reached her shoulder. Then he bestowed a lingering kiss upon the lovely curve of her cheek where it melted into her neck. She turned her proud head slowly, and looked at him through eyes that deepened and glowed.

"Wanda!" he breathed softly.

For answer he received a stinging blow on the face. Nor was he consoled by the spectacle of a wild girl darting from under the shelter of the tree, and vanishing from his sight.

CHAPTER VI.
CATECHISINGS.

A June Sunday in the country, radiant, cloudless, odorous with the breath of countless blossoms, thrilled with the melody of unnumbered voices, was just beginning. The first blush of morning lay warm upon sky and lake--the splendour above perfectly matched by the splendour below,--as Rose Macleod opened her casement window fronting the east, and looked out upon the myriad tender tints, the new yet ever familiar harmonies of light and colour with which the world was clothed. The gray walls of the Commodore's home on this side were hung with climbing plants, and as his pretty daughter leaned out of her chamber window a dewy branch of roses, loosened from its fastening, struck her softly on the cheek. The touch gave her a thrill, delicately keen--a pleasure, sharp as pain. No life was abroad yet except the birds, but the morning-glories were all awake. She could see their wealth of tender bloom outspread upon the rugged heap of rocks, warm with sunshine, that separated between a corner of the flower-smothered turf and the dark shadow of the almost impenetrable woods.

With her golden head drooped in drowsy meditation upon her folded arms she would have made a picture for a painter, a picture rose-tinted and rose-framed. But no painter was there to look upon her except the sun, and his ardent attentions becoming altogether too warm to be agreeable he was incontinently shut outside. She turned away with that slight sense of intoxication that comes from gazing too long upon the inexpressible beauty of a world that is dimmed only by the complaints and forebodings of querulous humanity. In the cool dimness of the pretty many-windowed room she stood a moment irresolutely, and then went in search of inspiration to a row of well-used books, over which she ran a pink reflective finger-tip. But nothing there responded to her need. It is a rare book that is worthy to hold the attention of maidenhood on a June morning.

So, as further slumber was impossible, she presently slipped down stairs, and stepped out upon the broad veranda. Afterwards came the younger children, Herbert and Eva, whose usually bright faces were shadowed now with the consciousness that it was Sunday, a fact that was aggravated rather than palliated by the radiant perfection of the weather. The Commodore, who was the most sympathetic soul alive, would, if he could have followed his own unperverted instincts, have had his children as happy on Sunday as on any other day, but it was necessary to make concessions to the Puritan spirit of the time, which ruled that a certain degree of discomfort and restraint should mark the first day of the week. But every dull look vanished as the father's step was heard, for his was one of those genial, warm-hearted, caressing natures, which are calculated to dispel the chill of even an old-fashioned Sunday. There was also a hearty brusqueness in the tone of his voice, something of the sea in the swing of his gait, and even in the movement of his full kindly gray eye, which could not fail to inspire confidence. His children flew to him at once, laying violent hands upon him, and clinging to his arms with decorously subdued shrieks of merriment, as he walked briskly to and fro.

"Where's Edward?" he demanded of his eldest daughter, as they approached that young lady, who was pensively reclining in a rustic chair.

"Not up yet, papa," she dreamily responded, uplifting her face for his morning salutation.

"Not **awake** yet," corrected Herbert, with a boy's unmistakable contempt for the luxurious habits of his elders.

"Lazy dog!" commented the Commodore, in a voice whose irateness was wholly assumed. "If I had come down late to breakfast when I was young I would have been sent back to bed again."

"That is what Ed. would like," declared Herbert. "He said it was no use calling Sunday a day of rest unless one could get all the rest one wanted, and it was hardly worth while for him to get up at all on a day when he couldn't fish or shoot or go out in his boat."

"The young barbarian! After all the care and pains expended on his bringing up. What shall we do about it, Rosy?"

"Call him again!" said Herbert, who, with the ever-fertile mind of tender youth, was never destitute of practical suggestions.

"Bright boy! run at once and ring the bell just outside his door." As the child departed to make the clangour, so much more delightful to his own ears than to those for whom it was intended, Eva observed:

"But he came in so late last night, papa, and looked very tired."

The Commodore patted the head of his little girl, but he continued to direct towards her elder sister a glance of half-humorous inquiry. Poor Rose knitted her pretty brows in troubled perplexity. She had been informed in the "Advice to Young Women," "Duties of Womanhood," and other ethical works of the day, that a sister's influence is illimitable, and she felt besides an added weight of responsibility towards her motherless sister and brothers. "I don't know, papa," she said at last, "unless we all take to the backwoods, live in a wigwam, and feast on the fruits of the chase. Edward chafes a good deal under the restraints of civilized life."

"Ah, here comes the prodigal son!" joyously exclaimed Eva, who ran to meet her favourite brother, oblivious of the smiles produced by her unflatteringly inapt remark.

"Don't kill any calf for me," entreated Edward, thrusting his younger sister's straight yellow locks over her face, until it was hard to say where her features ended and the back of her head began. "I deserve it, but I don't like it. Veal is my detestation."

"Upon my word," said the old gentleman, looking very hard at a discoloured spot just above the left eye of his eldest born, "it looks as though I had been trying to kill the prodigal instead of the calf. That's a bad bruise, my boy."

"'Tis, sir," responded Edward, in a tone which implied that meek assent was all that could be expected from him to a proposition so very self-evident. He felt uncomfortably conscious that the eyes of the assembled family were upon him, and glanced half enviously at Eva, as though the ability to shake a sunny mane over one's face at will was something to be thankful for. The breakfast bell roused them from a momentary silence, but the shadow of this mysterious bruise seemed to follow them even to the table. Herbert and Eva, aged respectively ten and twelve, had that superabundant love of information so characteristic of their tender years. They sat in round-eyed silence, bringing the battery of their glances to bear upon their unfortunate brother, who at last could endure it no longer.

"Upon my life!" he exclaimed, "one would think I was the governor-general, or some wild animal in a menagerie, to become the object of so much concentrated and distinguished attention."

"Which would you say he was, Eva?" asked Herbert.

"Which what?" inquired that young lady.

"Sir Peregrine Maitland, or a wild animal?"

"Oh, Sir Peregrine, of course. See what a lofty, scornful way he has of looking at us. And yet he is not really proud; he is willing to sit down with us at our humble board, just as though he was a common person."

"Children!" said Rose with soft reproach, but her voice trembled, and the imps were subjugated only outwardly.

"Anything particular going on in Barrie?" queried the Commodore, turning to his eldest son.

"Really, I can't say. I haven't been over in several days."

"Oh, I imagined you were there last night."

"I never go there at night," protested the young man, with unnecessary vehemence. It was clear to him now that his father and sister held a very low opinion of him indeed. Probably they thought he had been hurt in some vulgar tavern brawl, or drunken street fight. The idea was loathsome to him. He had not a single low taste or trait of character.

"I'm afraid," said Herbert, shaking his head with mock regret, "that you are a very wild fellow."

"He means that you are very fond of the wilds," interpreted Rose, hurriedly endeavouring to avert the threatened domestic storm. "Eva," she continued, taking up that irrepressible damsel before she could give utterance to the uncalled-for remark, which was but too evidently burning upon her lips, "do you know your catechism?"

"Yes," replied her sister, in rather an aggrieved tone, for she did not relish this change in the conversation, "I know it--to a certain extent."

"Eva looks as though she would prefer to catechise Edward," slyly interpolated her father; and under this shameless encouragement the young lady boldly observed:

"Indeed, I should. I should like to begin right at the beginning with, 'Can you tell me, dear child, who made you'--have that big black bruise on your brow?"

"I can," responded Edward, imperturbably. "It was a beautiful little beast, not much bigger than you are, but a great deal prettier."

"Was it, really?" Any offence that might have been taken at the uncomplimentary nature of the reply was swallowed up in eager curiosity. "What was it?"

"Well, that I can't tell you. I never saw anything like it before."

"That's queer," said Herbert. "What colour was it?"

"Oh, black and brown and all the loveliest shades of scarlet--with cruel, little, white teeth, sharp and strong as a squirrel's teeth."

"But it didn't bite you," said Rose, with a puzzled glance at the white brow, whose delicate fairness made the discolouration more conspicuous.

"No, but it looked fully capable of biting--enchanting little brute!"

"Why on earth didn't you shoot it?" questioned the Commodore, rousing himself to the exploration of this new mystery.

The young man laughed a little guiltily. "To tell the truth the idea never once entered my head. You have no idea what beautiful eyes it had."

"Oh--sentimentalist!"

"Yes, I was sentimental enough yesterday, but it will be long before I am troubled that way again."

"At any rate," said Herbert, as they drifted back to the shadowing veranda, whose flowery screen the sun had not yet penetrated, "you can't go to church."

"I wish I could take you all over in my sail-boat," said his elder brother, wistfully surveying the blue waters of Kempenfeldt Bay.

"Ed., you are a heathen," declared Miss Eva, whose usual adoring advocacy of her brother's opinions was paralized by this assault upon the proprieties; "it's wicked to ride in a boat on Sunday."

"But it's perfectly right to ride in a carriage," added Herbert, with a view to giving information, and not with any satirical intention.

There was no reply. If it is a crime to possess a too great susceptibility to the ever-deepening charm of woods and waters then Edward Macleod was the chief of sinners. In his father he had a secret sympathizer, for the old gentleman himself was not without strong leanings toward a free and careless, if not semi-savage, life. But no hint of this escaped him in the presence of the younger children, whose air of severe morality, born of renewed attacks and final triumph over the difficulties of the Sunday School lesson, he considered it unwise to disturb.

Church service was not a painfully long or tedious affair. The little wooden structure, erected for that purpose in Barrie, had the air of trying to be in sweet accord with the outlying wilderness, from the dark green drapery of ivy which charitably strove to hide its raw newness. The town itself (for in a new country everything in excess of a post-office is called a town) was wrapped in Sabbath stillness. The little church was well filled, for a bright Sunday in a country village draws the inhabitants from their homes as infallibly as bees from their hives. Workers and drones they were all there, bowed together under the sense of a common need, and of faith in a common Helper, which alone makes men free and equal.

Like a light in a dark place gleamed the bright head of Rose Macleod in the farthest corner of the family pew. A vagrant sunbeam, like a golden arrow, pierced the gloom about her, but to the disappointment of *one* interested observer, it failed to reach the rich coils, so nearly resembling it in colour. This observer presently reminded himself that he had come there to worship the divine, as revealed in holy writ, not in human beauty; nevertheless he could not forbear sending another stealthy glance, which, more accurately aimed than the sunbeam, rested fully and lingeringly upon the shadowy recess, where a glowing amber-golden head bloomed richly forth against the frigid back-ground of a bare wooden wall. The dainty little lady, enveloped in the antique richness of a stiff brocade, should have been made aware by some mysteriously occult means of a strange thrill at the heart, caused by the protracted gaze of a handsome fellow-worshipper, but to tell the truth her thoughts were piously intent upon the enormity of her own sins, and the necessity of reclaiming her brother from the very literal wildness of his ways.

Service was over; the still air seemed vibrant with the notes of the last hymn, and tender with the just-uttered words of the benediction, as this stately little damsel, with the peculiar air of distinction which set so charmingly upon her doll-like personality, passed down the aisle and out into the sunshine. She had looked on him--she had been conscious of his existence; but it was seemingly in the same way that she had noticed the wooden pews against which her rich little robe was trailing, and the floor which felt the pressure of her dainty feet. Allan Dunlop standing among the outcoming worshippers, whose greetings he mechanically responded to, silently anathematized the soulless edict of society, which forbids a man to stand and gaze after a vanishing vision in feminine form. The receding figure was not wholly unconscious, however, of the mute homage of which she had been the recipient.

A few hours later this lovely possessor of all the graces and virtues, according to the newly-awakened imagination of her unknown admirer, reclined in her shell-pink apartment, in which the breezes blowing through the lattice sounded like the **andante** of the sea, and sighed for the forbidden fruit of a half-finished novel. But the sigh perished with the breath that gave it birth. The next moment she sternly doubled a very diminutive fist, and demanded of herself whether that was the best use that could be made of her time and opportunities. Then she looked about for some missionary work. It was not far to seek, for the children, weary of purposeless drifting on the still monotonous tide of Sunday afternoon, came battering at her door with united hands and voices, demanding a story. In the midst of her recital she suddenly bethought herself of Edward and inquired after his whereabouts.

"Roaming up and down the strawberry patch," said Eva.

"Seeking what he may devour," added her brother, unconsciously giving a scriptural turn to his information.

"For shame, Herbert!"

"Shame enough! He never offered me one."

The subject of this discussion passed the open door shortly after and looked rather forlornly in upon the interested trio. On his way upstairs a casement window that stood ajar swung softly open as he passed it, touched by the invisible fingers of the breeze; and the young man was not comforted by the picture suddenly revealed to him--the picture of a slim shape in a light canoe darting bird-like over the water. Rose felt a vague pang of pity, but had no opportunity to go to him. Her ministrations were in active demand by the younger pair from whom she was unable to free herself until twilight fell, when they voluntarily resigned her to a need greater than their own. On many a summer night in years past they had seen their father and mother pace the winding length of the avenue together. Now, when the tender gloom of evening was beginning, and the solitary figure of the Commodore was seen going with drooped head toward his favourite walk, it was Rose who ran with eager step to take the vacant place at his side. If his heart was saddened by that shadowy presence, which walks at eventide by the side of him who is bereaved, it could not be wholly cast down so long as warm clinging hands were about his arm, a bright face looking up into his, and a clear voice, from which every note of sadness was excluded, murmuring a thousand entertaining nothings in his ear.

If Rose was a never-failing fountain of alluring fiction to Herbert and Eva, and the comfort of life to her father, she was the sympathizing *confidante* of her elder brother, who unburdened his heart to her in a private interview just before retiring.

"But what under the sun made you kiss her?" inquired this practical young lady.

"Oh, murder, Rose, what a question! What under the sun makes one taste a peach or pluck a flower?"

"But if the peach or the flower does not belong to you? Well, I'll not lecture you, Edward; you have sufficiently expiated your offence."

"I never dreamed," returned the delinquent, "that a kiss for a blow, which is the Christian's rule of morals, could be translated by the poor savage into a blow for a kiss."

"Probably you terrified her. That old chief has brought her up in the belief that the white man is a compound of all the vices."

"Well, she behaved as though I might be that. She never paused to consider the ruin she had wrought, but darted off like a flash of lightning."

Rose laughed; but after she departed the smile upon her brother's face quickly vanished. Not that the bruise on his brow was so severe, but he found it impossible to forgive the blow to his vanity.

"Beautiful little brute!" he muttered under his breath, "I haven't done with her yet. She'll live to give me something prettier than this in return for my caresses."

CHAPTER VII.
AN ACCIDENT.

Some days later, Edward, mounted on his favourite Black Bess, waiting for Rose to accompany him in a morning gallop, was amazed to see that venturesome young lady prepare to seat herself on Flip, a crazy little animal scarcely more than a colt, whose character for unsteadiness was notorious.

"I have set my heart on him," was all Rose could say in answer to her brother's protestations.

"Set your heart on him as much as you please," returned Edward, "so long as you do not set your person on him."

"In England," ventured, the respectful Tredway, "young ladies generally prefer a more trustworthy animal."

"Well, when we go to England," responded Rose, casting her arms around the neck of her slandered steed, "we'll do as the English do--won't we Flip, dear? In this country we'll have just a little of our own wild way."

From this decision there was no appeal. The words were scarcely spoken when there was a swift scamper of heels, a smothered sound, half shriek, half laughter, from Rose's lips, a cloud of dust, and that was all. Edward's alarm was changed to amusement as the pony, after its first wild flight, settled down into a sort of dancing step, ambling, pirouetting, curvetting, sidling, arching its wilful neck at one moment, and rushing off at a rate that bade fair to break its rider's at the next.

By fits and starts--a great many of them--they managed to make their way to "Bellevue," where the lovely Helene, arrayed in the alluring coolness of a white *neg-lige*, and with her braided locks drooping to her waist, came down the walk to meet them.

"Rose Macleod!" she exclaimed, for Black Bess was still far in the rear, and she imagined her friend unaccompanied, "and on that desperately dangerous little Flip!"

"The very same," responded Rose saucily, "but I don't know how long I may remain on him. We want you to join us in a glorious old gallop."

"Good morning, Mademoiselle," exclaimed Edward, reining in his black steed. "I hope Madame DeBerczy is better than usual, as I have some thoughts of leaving my wild sister with her. She's every bit as unmanageable as Flip."

"Leave me, indeed," retorted Rose, "as though I could trust you alone in the woods--with a pretty girl."

The last words were inaudible, save to Helene, between whom and Rose there passed a subtle glance which gave Edward a vague alarm. Could it be that Helene had received intelligence of his encounter with Wanda? No, it was clearly impossible. There was nothing of mocking in her look--nothing but the pretty consciousness of a girl who could not forget that her shoulders and arms were gleaming beneath the mist of a muslin altogether too thin, and a weight of loosened braids altogether too thick, to be proper subjects for a young man's contemplation.

She presently vanished within, and reappeared before they had time to be impatient. In her close-clinging habit, with her black braids securely pinned, a handful of lilies drooping at her waist, and the whole of her fair young figure invested with a sort of stately maidenliness, she formed a sufficient contrast to Rose, who, perched defiantly upon her wicked little steed, looked every inch a rogue. Mademoiselle DeBerczy's white horse was slim and graceful as became its owner, who glanced with lady-like apprehension at the dashings and plungings and other dog-like vagaries of Flip. "Dear me, Rose," she at last remarked rather nervously, "I can't bear to look at you."

"Then don't look at me!" exclaimed the wild girl, "go on with Edward; Flip and I are going to make a morning of it."

The young man nothing loth drew in Black Bess beside the milk-white palfrey, and began to comment upon the beauty of the morning, of the woods through which they were passing, and, lastly, of an Indian child, who, straying away from a settlement of wigwams, perched itself upon a stump, and surveyed the cavalcade with round-eyed interest.

"The loveliest Indian girl I ever saw," remarked Helene, "is Wanda, the Algon-quin chief's adopted daughter. But this is no news to you, as I hear that you were quite forcibly struck by her."

Oh, the ambiguities of the English language! There was not a quiver of an eye-lash, not the slightest curl of the scarlet lips, and the wide dark eyes were seemingly free from guile; but, nevertheless, Edward suffered again that vague alarm which had sprung into being at the gate of "Bellevue."

"I think her very pretty, certainly," he returned, "but I can't say that I admire her."

"I am surprised at that. Rose told me that she made quite an impression upon you."

Ought this to be taken literally? The lily-white face was no tell-tale. Could one so fair be so deceitful? This matter must be further probed.

"The impression was not altogether a pleasant one," he confessed with a rising flush.

"Not pleasant? You are very hard to please. She is not only remarkably hand-some but she has a vigorous personality--a sort of native force that is sure to make its mark."

"I fear I am not an admirer of force--that is in a woman."

"I am sure you have no reason to be. It is possible that even the beautiful Wan-da might not be above browbeating a man."

"Oh, she might do worse than that," said Edward, with the coolness born of desperation. "She might sink so low as to basely persecute him with her knowledge of a secret extracted from his sister. Don't you think that would be treating him very contemptibly."

"It would depend altogether upon what sort of treatment he deserved."

"It occurs to me that the unfortunate creature we have in mind has suffered enough."

It was evident that Helene thought so too. She said nothing, but the sweet eyes that had refrained from mocking at him could not hide a tinge of remorse. This pledge of peace was quickly noted by the much-enduring youth, whose gratitude might have found vocal expression had not his attention that moment been called off by an approaching pedestrian, who suddenly appeared at a curve in the Penetanguishene road, which, after partly retracing their steps, they had now reached.

"What, Dunlop, as I live!" he exclaimed, eagerly reining in his steed, and extending a cordial hand. "My dear fellow, how long have you been at home, and why have I been left in ignorance of your coming?"

The young man who had paid Helene the doubtful tribute of a disappointed glance, returned the greeting warmly, but in more measured terms. "I was at church on Sunday," he said, "for the first time since my return home. Why weren't you there?"

"Ugh!" said Edward, as though the recollection had been an icicle suddenly thrust down his back. "Why, to tell the truth, I performed an act of worship on the day before, and the consequence was so frightful that I was discouraged from further attempts at prayer and praise. I hadn't the heart to go."

"You hadn't the *face* to go!" softly corrected Helene.

"Exactly. Your knowledge of the facts is copious and profound. Excuse me! Miss DeBerczy, let me present to you Mr. Allan Dunlop, Provincial land-surveyor, member for the Home District, future leader in parliament, and a man after my own heart!"

The stranger looked as though a less elaborate introduction might have pleased him better. "Edward you are as extravagant as ever," he exclaimed, and then, turning to the lady, with a sort of shy sincerity, "Don't believe him, Miss DeBerczy. I am studying politics and practicing surveying, but that is all."

"And you mean to say that you are not a man after my own heart," demanded Edward, threatening him with his riding-whip; "then, perhaps, you will be good enough to tell me whose heart you *are* after."

An embarrassed laugh broke from Allan's lips, as he thought involuntarily of the queenly little creature, golden crowned and richly robed, whose reign had begun, so far as he knew, on the Sunday previous. Oddly enough, the same personage came at that moment to Helene's mind, and she hurriedly inquired, "Why, where can Rose be?"

"Here she comes," said Edward, after a backward glance, and here indeed she came. With her bright hair flying in the breeze, her riding hat rakishly askew, one glove invisible, and the other tucked for safe keeping under the saddle, her riding-habit gray with dust, and fantastically trimmed with thorns and nettles, her blue eyes at their bluest, her pink cheeks at their rosiest, she produced a very powerful effect upon the minds of her spectators. Perhaps it would not be too much to say that she produced three distinct effects upon their minds.

Helene was the first to recover the faculty of speech. "Why, you are a regular little brier rose!" she exclaimed laughingly, wheeling her horse about so as to remove what appeared to be the larger part of a blackberry bush from her friend's habit, and improving the opportunity to insert a pin in the ragged edges of a dreadful looking rent, which the premature removal of the blackberry bush had revealed.

Edward introduced his friend to Rose with a gravity which was too evidently born of the belief that she had never before presented quite so disreputable an appearance. Allan knew his goddess under this quaint disguise, and his heart beat a loud recognition. The cool graceful black and white propriety of Helene DeBerczy was barren of significance compared with the slightest strand of yellow wilful hair that blew about the pink-shamed face of his friend's sister.

With renewed expressions of good-feeling and the promise, by Allan, of an early visit to Pine Towers, the young men separated, the riding party moving off in the same order as before, Helene and Edward going first, leaving Rose and Flip to follow at their own discretion.

But the latter, who had exhausted every known device for his own amusement, now suddenly discovered and put into instant execution another way to annoy his pretty mistress. This was to stand perfectly still--inexorably, indomitably, immovably still. In vain Rose whipped, begged, prayed, and almost wept. But Flip was thereby only strengthened in his decision. Rose's companions had vanished around the bend in the road. Though lost to sight they were to memory obnoxious. How mean of Edward to go off in that cool, careless way, without a thought of her left behind! How contemptible of Helene to leave her without so much as a hair-pin to repair the ravages made by that horrible little horse. And now, worse and worse, Allan Dunlop, who might have had the gentlemanliness to make himself invisible as soon as possible, came hurrying back to be a further witness of her dishevelled embarrassment.

"I am afraid your horse is a little fractious," he suggested respectfully.

"Oh, no," replied Rose, earnestly, scarcely conscious of what she said. "Only--sometimes--he won't go."

This was a statement which Flip seemed in no wise disposed to contradict.

"Perhaps if you will allow me to pet him a little, we may induce a change in his behaviour." He drew near and laid his head upon the pony's mane, accidentally brushing with his moustache the warm little hand upon the reins. Its owner drew it away, while an expression of absolute pain crossed her face. "I don't know what you can think of me," she said contritely. "I lost one of my gloves in reaching for a branch above my head, and its no use wearing the other and trying to be half respectable." She was miserably conscious that she was not even that, as she tried to fasten up her loosely waving locks, and thought of the awful rent in her habit, through which that saving pin had slipped and been lost sight of forever, like a weary little missionary in a very large field of labour. The skirt beneath was deplorably short, and her feet, though small, were not small enough to be invisible. Her chivalrous attendant seemed quite unconscious of these glaring deficiencies in her appearance, as he looked up with a bright smile, and said: "There, I think he will go now." At the word Flip began a slow undulating movement, something akin to that produced by a rocking-horse, which while it "goes" fast enough makes no perceptible progress. Poor Rose, excited and unstrung by her morning's adventures, dropped the reins in disgust, and then with one hand clutching her skirt, and the other her hair, she resigned herself to a fit of uncontrollable laughter. The next moment the wilful horse made a wild plunge forward, and the wilful girl was flung with terrible force against a heap of stones on the roadside. Colourless, motionless, breathless, she lay at the feet of Allan Dunlop, whose heart turned sick as he discerned among the yellow locks outspread on the gray stones a slender stream of blood.

For a moment the young man stood horror-struck. Fortunately he was not far from home, and there he proceeded at once to take the almost lifeless girl. As he was about to lift her gently in his arms, a low moan escaped her lips, the significance of which he was not slow to catch. Unable to speak, almost unable to move, she made a slight writhing motion of the limbs, accompanied by a convulsive twitch at the torn gown. Allan Dunlop was not dull-witted enough to suppose that her ankle was sprained. His sensibilities and sympathies were exquisitely quick and fine. Catching up an end of the unfortunate riding-habit he twisted it closely about the helplessly exposed little feet--an act of delicacy which received a faint glance of grateful recognition before she lapsed into utter unconsciousness. Gathering her into his arms he carried her as he might have carried a child to the shelter of his own house. But here a fresh dilemma presented itself. Not a soul was in the house. His father had not yet returned from market, his mother and the servant were absent, he knew not where. Placing her on a couch he bathed with awkwardly gentle fingers the wound in her head, and dared even to wipe away a few drops of blood from the little pallid face. Still the white lids lay motionless over the blue eyes, and the girlish form was unmoved by a breath. He stood anxiously looking down at her, wondering what his mother would do in his place, and feeling in every fibre a man's natural helplessness in the presence of a suffering woman. "What can I do for you?" he asked, as she at last opened her eyes, and gazed half-frightened at her strange surroundings.

"Thank you, I believe I am quite comfortable, except--except for the dreadful pain. I feel so terribly shaken." And the poor child broke into uncontrollable sobs.

"Oh, don't cry!" begged Allan, who might with equal truth have claimed that he too felt terribly shaken. "I can't imagine where my mother has gone." He stared miserably out of the window a moment, and then returned to his patient, with the air of a man who is not going to shirk a duty, no matter how difficult it may be.

"If you could dry your eyes," he began with a sort of brotherly gentleness, "and tell"--

"I'm afraid I can't. I don't dare move my right hand from under me, the pain is so acute in my back, and there is something dreadfully wrong with my left arm."

Dreadfully wrong indeed! It hung limp and broken. The young man was spurred by the sight to instant, decisive action.

"Miss Macleod," he said, "I will have to leave you alone, and go at once for a physician and your father. Do you think you can be very brave?"

Her tears flowed afresh at the question. This time he wiped them away himself. "Oh, I'm afraid I couldn't be that," she said. "I never could. But I'll promise not to run away before you come back."

She *is* a brave little soul after all, he thought, as he waved his hand, and hurried off to the stable; but that is a woman's courage--cry one moment and make a joke the next.

Mrs. Dunlop, who was not as far distant from home as her son had supposed, entered the house a few minutes after his departure, followed by the servant, both bearing great baskets of raspberries. The two women were sufficiently astonished at sight of the unexpected and most unfortunate guest; but Allan's mother would scarcely allow Rose to pronounce a word of her penitent confession. It was enough for her to know that here was an opportunity for her to relieve suffering, and she improved it with characteristic tact and delicacy. The open-eyed and open-mouthed maid was sent on various small missions of mercy, which she attacked with zeal, in the hope that thereby in some way her abounding thirst for information might be assuaged.

Very soon after, the quiet farm-house became the rendezvous of an unusual number of strangers. Helene and Edward, who had returned to see if Allan could tell them anything concerning the whereabouts of the missing girl, came first. Helene, full of grief and contrition because she had not remained by the side of Rose through the entire length of her perilous undertaking, and Edward, whose brotherly sympathy was tinged by the magnanimous consciousness that nothing would tempt him to remind her that he had warned her of the evil which had resulted in her downfall. Afterwards came the physician who set the broken arm, and forbade the patient's removal, and then the Commodore, in whose brawny neck his daughter hid a wet, pitiful face.

"It was my fault, Papa," she whispered, "and it's a miracle I'm not broken up into more pieces than I am. I deserve to be. I'm as full of penitence as I am of pain. But don't you be troubled about me. Mrs. Dunlop is as good and kind as it is possible to be. I am sure they are very nice people."

Very nice people perhaps, but very little to the Commodore's taste. As he turned to greet the man, upon whose hospitality his daughter had been so literally and unexpectedly thrown, he was scarcely his frank, genial, outspoken self. There was a secret root of prejudice against this unpretending farmer, whose son's political views were as far from his own as the east is from the west, and whose social position was decidedly inferior. Not that the kindly Commodore was gifted with that microscopic eye which is too easily impressed by the infinitesimal gradations of society, but he retained too much of the Old World feeling for class distinctions to make him oblivious to the difference in their rank.

"Good heavens! Edward," he exclaimed, in a conversation with his son a few days after the accident, "what uncommonly low ground our little Rose has been suddenly transplanted to. That old farmer looks as stiff and straight as one of his own furrows, and his son, what's-his-name? is of the same mould."

"It's remarkably rich mould, Father. Not such low ground as one might think."

"Rich! What, in dollars and cents?"

"No; better than that. In knowledge and sense. Allan Dunlop is a very bright fellow."

"Oh! I *thought* the paternal acres could scarcely afford a sufficient yield of potatoes and parsnips to furnish material wealth. As for the sense you speak of, I hope your friend possesses enough to keep him from making love to your sister."

"He is far too proud to make love to one whom he considers his social superior, though she might do worse than permit it."

"Oh, dear yes; she might have been thrown into a settlement of savages, and wedded to the first wild Indian that ran to pick her up."

Edward's cheek reddened perceptibly.

"Or she might marry a snob," he said.

"Come, Edward," returned the Commodore, with a breezy laugh, "you must not insinuate that your old father is such a disagreeable sort of person. But, seriously, you don't consider Allan Dunlop your equal, do you?"

"No," said Edward, "I don't think him my equal."

"That's the sensible way to look at it. Not but that he is as good and necessary in his way as the earth he tills and the vegetables he sells."

"Oh, it is the father--who, by the way, is an old soldier--that tills and sells. The son, as you know, is a young rising politician--a radical."

"I am only too well aware of that, but why couldn't he stick to the plough? Its the unluckiest business imaginable, Edward, that we should have played into their hands in this way. They are the last sort of people to whom one cares to be under a personal obligation."

Edward had no balm to apply to his father's irritation. "When I say that I don't consider Allan my equal," he explained, "I mean that I fancy him my superior."

His father laughed aloud. "You seem to have a good many fancies," he said, tolerantly, and continued to smoke in meditative silence.

And still among the people of whom her father and brother held such entirely opposite opinions lay the helpless Rose, victim of a slow fever, which left her, as

Helene pityingly said, weak as a roseleaf. But Helene seldom saw her now. Edward and his father were also all but banished from her bedside. "Really," said Dr. Ardagh to the Commodore, "I must insist upon absolute quiet as the first requisite for my patient's recovery. Those daily visits are exciting and harmful. Mrs. Dunlop has a perfect genius for sick-nursing, and you can safely leave your daughter to her. She is really a remarkable woman!"

The Commodore made a wry face. "Not long ago Edward would have me believe that the Dunlops, father and son, were endowed with uncommon mental power. Now it appears that the mother is similarly gifted. My poor child hasn't brains enough to keep her from riding an unsafe colt, but it is to be hoped she knows enough to appreciate the advantages of her situation."

The doctor raised his eyebrows at this peculiar pleasantry, but managed to harrow his listener's heart by intimating that it would be a confoundedly strange thing if young Dunlop did not appreciate *his* advantages.

CHAPTER VIII.
CONVALESCENCE.

To be slowly recovering from a severe illness is almost like being again a very little child. So thought Rose Macleod, as she lay between lavender-scented sheets, in the quaint stone cottage, whose deep old-fashioned window seats, and low whitewashed ceilings, were becoming as familiar to her as the stately halls of her home. The protracted leisure of convalescence was growing burdensome to her. So many days had she watched the lights and shadows woven throughout the greenery, just outside her window, or listened to the weird measure of the rain when the wind surged like a sea through the foliage, or held her breath for joy when a flying bird pulsed vividly across the sky, or counted the milk-white flowers of the locust tree, as they strewed the ground with blossoms, or noted the exact moment when the morning-glories softly clasped their purple petals together, as though unable to contain a greater fulness of joy than was brought by the summer morning. It was now early evening, and Rose gave vent to a little uncontrollable sigh. Mrs. Dunlop came as quickly to the bedside as though the sigh had been the sound of a trumpet.

She was a very pleasant object for weary invalid eyes to rest upon. Her dark hair was satin-smooth, her voice and movements were quiet and refined. There was in her face that mingling of shyness and sincerity, irradiated by a look of the keenest intelligence, which reminded Rose of Allan, between whom and his mother there was a strong resemblance.

"I have something to tell you," she said gently. "As my prisoner you have behaved in such an exemplary manner, keeping all the rules of the institution, and making no attempt to run away, that I have decided to give you the freedom of another room."

"Oh, am I to go into another room?" Had a voyage to Europe been proposed to her it could scarcely have suggested pleasanter ideas of change. "A new wall-paper, and a new window! What more could I ask for? But how am I to get there? What means of transportation have you?"

"That is just what I am thinking of. I could dress you in my gray wrapper, and then--would you mind if Allan were to help me to lift you to the couch in my room?"

Rose shuddered a little. A faint pink stained for a moment the whiteness of her cheek. "I shouldn't mind it if I were senseless," she said, "but I don't want him to think I have lost my senses again. No, we'll have to give up that idea."

But Mrs. Dunlop was not the sort of person to give up an idea without good cause. "The mountain must then go to Mahomet," said she, and wheeling the couch close to the sick-bed, she arranged the invalid cosily among the cushions, and pushed her slowly into her own apartment. "If I were twice as large as you are," she added, "instead of being just your size, I should have carried you in half the time."

But another and more serious consequence followed that same evening upon the striking similarity in figure between Mrs. Dunlop and Miss Macleod. Golden twilight had changed to dim dusk, but Rose still lay with her fair head almost buried among the cushions. She expected a visit from her father that evening, and the temptation to show him what she could do and dare was irresistible. All her hostess's hints that bed-time had arrived were wasted upon deaf ears. At last, in a little anxiety as to the result of her experiment, if the Commodore did not arrive, Mrs. Dunlop went out to the front gate to see if there were signs of his approach. At the same moment Allan entered the house by the back door, and looked about for his mother. Impelled by a "fatalistic necessity" he went up to her room, the sound of his carefully modulated tread upon the stairway filling the heart of Rose with delight, for was not that her own father, who had probably been informed at the gate of the change in her condition and surroundings, and who was coming up so softly in order to surprise her. Allan, meanwhile, glancing in, saw nothing in the gray gloom but a small figure in a well-known wrapper, stretched wearily upon the couch. "Poor little mother," he thought. "She is quite tired out." He went up to her intending to bestow a filial caress upon her cheek, but before his design could be accomplished he was drawn close by a single arm around his neck, and repeatedly kissed. "You blessed darling!" she softly exclaimed, "here I've been waiting for you, and *waiting* for you and longing--*Oh*!" That silky moustache and that chin, that was *not* stubby, could they belong to a gentleman of sixty years? Her right arm fell limp and useless as the other. "I thought you were my father," she said in a weak voice of mingled disappointment, anger and shame.

"And I thought you were my mother," was all the guilty wretch could offer in extenuation of his conduct.

The people whose parts this unfortunate pair had been playing with such ill success were now heard at the door below. Allan felt like a criminal as he stole into the hall, and thence into his own room; but the Commodore could scarcely understand the propriety of a strange and otherwise objectionable young man holding a moonless *tete-a-tete* with his daughter. In any case his presence would involve disagreeable explanations. If her cheeks were as flushed as his own no doubt her doting parent would ascribe it to renewed health and strength.

But the young man, sitting alone in the perfumed darkness of that summer night, with his hot head fallen upon the window-sill, did not imagine that the fire that burned along his own veins was an indication of health. On the contrary, he feared it the symptom of a dreaded disease--the fever and delirium of love. What was that little yellow-haired girl to him? Nothing! nothing! Yet her kisses burned upon his lips, and every drop of blood in his body seemed to contradict his nonchalant nothing with a passionate everything! Yes, she was in truth the lamp of his life, but in that radiant light how pitiful his life appeared. How pitiful, and yet how beautiful, for in the tender illumination of her imagined love rough places became smooth, dark ways bright, and the heights of possible achievement were faintly flushed with all the delicate tints of dawn--the dawn of a diviner day than any he had yet looked upon. When he went to sleep it was to dream of walking in a wilderness of roses. Pale and drooping, broken and dying, red and roguish, blushing, wanton, wild and warm, each bore some fantastic resemblance to Rose Macleod, and each was set about with "little wilful thorns." The hand which he eagerly outstretched to pluck the loveliest rose of all was pierced and bleeding. Still he did not despair of reaching it. But as his longing eyes drew nearer and nearer the stately little beauty turned suddenly a deep blood-red, and then he saw that the crimson drops falling from his own wounds had worked this transformation. He hid her in his bosom, and held her there. But the closer she was pressed the richer and more fragrant was the breath she exhaled, intoxicating all his senses, and the farther into his heart went the cruel thorns, until in mingled pain and rapture he awoke.

This Allan Dunlop, though born and bred on a farm, had in him the spring of a higher and finer life. He was a man of delicate instincts, refined feelings, and great native sensibility, inherited from his mother, at whose history we may take a rapid backward glance.

Far away in one of the stately homes of "Merrie England," when the eighteenth century was old, a gentlewoman, young, charming, and full of an habitually repressed life and gaiety, waited for her cavalier, the youthful riding-master who had little to recommend himself to her gracious kindness save that deep but indefinable charm which a handsome man on a spirited charger is so prone to exert on the feminine imagination. The morning was fair, the lady was fairer, and the heart of her gallant attendant beat faster than the feet of his steed, as the flying skirt of her robe swept his stirrup, and the soft length of her mist-like veil blew before his eyes and caressed his brown cheek. It was not the only mist that blew before his eyes nor before her's either, poor child! for the rival contrast between this wild rush over hedge and ditch and bright green meadow and the stiffly guarded walks and ways of home had spurred her imagination also into a gallop. "We will never come back," he said jestingly, "we will ride away into a world of our own!" but there was something reckless in his laugh and a formidable note of earnestness in his jesting. He never dreamed that her pulse beat quicker after his careless speeches, and he was in truth a good deal in awe of her, for the buckram propriety which had encased her like a garment ever since she could remember was not easily thrown aside. This young pair, though as deeply in love with each other as it is possible for man and maid to be, had never acknowledged the fact by a syllable. Anna Sherwood was too shy and prim; Richard Dunlop too poor and proud. He had been a trooper in a cavalry regiment, afterwards riding-master in a garrison town in England, and since his coming to Canada, and before taking to farming, he held the position of fort-adjutant at Penetanguishene; at present he was tutor in equestrian arts to the young lady whom he passionately loved. Of her there is little to tell except that until this dashing young fellow crossed her path she had experienced about as much change and variety in her life as though she had been a plant grown in a flower-pot. On sunny days she was allowed the outside air; on stormy days she was kept within. She toiled not, neither did she spin. Nothing was required of her except colourless acquiescence in a life of torpid, unnatural, unendurable *ennui*.

The young lady's only guardian was a wealthy maiden aunt, who was as rich as she was old maidish--a statement likely to thrill the heart of any mammon-wor-shipper among her acquaintance--and whose special pride was the exemplary man-ner in which she had brought up her brother's child. The daring young fellow who had presumed to fall in love with this model niece followed her uninvited into the family sitting-room on returning from their ride, a proceeding which rather alarmed the gentle Anna, though her much dreaded relative was absent. He did not sit down, but took a decisive stand on the hearth-rug. He looked like a man who has something he must say, though the saying of it will all but cost him his life. She sat down with a strange foreboding at her heart of something terrible to come. The austere influences of her aunt's home were upon her. She sat in prim composure, pale hands clasped, and pale lids drooping upon cheeks that had lost every particle of the warmth and glow gained by exercise. "Miss Sherwood," he began, "there is something I have been longing to say to you for weeks past, and though it is a per-fectly useless, almost impertinent thing to say, still I cannot leave it burning in my heart any longer. It is that you are dearer to me than any woman on earth--and al-ways will be." His voice broke a little, but he went bravely on. "You need not think that I shall annoy you with frequent repetitions of this fact, or that I expect to gain anything by the statement of it. I know that you are proud and self-sufficing, and," a little bitterly, "that I can never be anything more to you than the dust thrown up by your horse's heels--a necessary evil. I don't know why I should tell you this, except that I cannot suffer in silence any longer. I am going to leave you now--to leave you forever. Won't you say good-bye? Is there nothing you will say to me, little Nan?"

In spite of himself his voice had sunk to a tone of caressing tenderness. The pale proud girl had listened to him without moving a fibre or lifting an eyelash. But now there came a great flow of blood to her face, a swift rush of tears to her eyes.

"Nothing," she said, "except"--

She wrung her hands: pride dies very hard.

"Except that I love you, Dick!"

His eyes blazed. "Then, by Heaven," he cried, "we shall never part." He caught her to his breast and held her there a moment without speaking. He was too dazed to speak. The scene was dramatic; and Miss Maria Sherwood, who entered the room at that moment, did not approve of the drama. She held that it was sensational in conduct, scurrilous in character, scandalous in its consequences; and it is highly probable that from this brief glimpse of it she saw no reason to change her opinions. Act second, as may be imagined, was stormy and exciting, gaining in interest as it progressed, and the last scene in these private theatricals saw the hero and heroine shipped off to Canada--that better country, where the lives and loves of those to whom fate has been cruel are graciously spared, under conditions adverse enough but still endurable.

That life and love can continue to exist beneath bleak foreign skies, when grim Poverty howls wolf-like at the door, and the winds of seemingly year-long winters are scarcely less fierce, was the proposition these courageous young people set themselves to prove. No day dawned so dark that was not illumined for him by the repetition of that shamelessly unmaidenly speech, "I love you, Dick." As for her, she never ceased to smile at the blindness of a man who could imagine that luxurious imprisonment for life without him could be more alluring than the greatest hardships endured in the perpetual sunshine of his love.

Of this pair, whose romance had outlasted the sordid cares and trials of life in the backwoods, Allan Dunlop, with his exquisite susceptibilities, and ambitious aims, was the honest fruit. He was not visible to Rose for some days after their emotional and wholly involuntary encounter in his mother's room, and then he brought her a great handful of her fragrant namesakes. She had been promoted for half-an-hour to a huge well-cushioned chair, in which she reclined rather languidly. The roses formed a pretext for a little desultory conversation, and then Allan, noticing the invalid's little ears were turning pink, presumably at the recollection of their last meeting, could not forbear saying:

"I feel that I ought to beg your pardon, Miss Macleod, for the way I treated you the other evening. It was a brutal assault, though wholly unintentional."

Poor Rose, who remembered that it was she who made the assault, expressed the belief that she would rather it were forgotten than forgiven.

"I'm afraid I can't forget it. Some things make too deep an impression. Of course," he added, in his embarrassment, "it was the last thing I should have wished to do."

"Of course!" echoed the miserable girl, wondering if he meant what he said.

"Allan," said his mother, entering the room at that moment, "what are you saying to distress my patient? I don't like the look of these feverish cheeks."

"I fear I have committed the unpardonable sin, as Miss Rose refuses to pardon it."

Mrs. Dunlop, who was in absolute ignorance of the subject of conversation, looked smilingly from one to the other.

"Promise her that the offence will never be repeated, Allan," she said, "and then it may receive forgiveness."

The young man coloured scarlet. "The conditions are too hard," he murmured. "I think, on the whole, I should prefer to go unforgiven." And he hastily rose and left the room.

But if Rose Macleod was not free from afflictions of a sentimental nature, her brother Edward was even less so. This young man sorely missed the girlish society which his sister in happier days had constantly drawn about her. One afternoon, when time hung particularly heavy on his hands, he decided to go over to "Belle-vue," ostensibly to give Madame DeBerczy the latest information concerning Rose, but really to solace his soul with a sight of the beautiful Helene. On his way over he chanced to overtake the Algonquin girl, Wanda, whom he proceeded to upbraid in no measured terms for the way in which she had treated him.

"Ah, don't!" she cried at last, covering her ears with her hands, "your words are like hailstones, sharp and cruel and cold."

"Then will you not say that you are sorry?" he pleaded, bending his fair head once more perilously near to the soft, brown neck.

"Sorry that you deserved the blow? yes; certainly!"

"Wanda," cried Edward, an irrepressible smile breaking through his assumed anger, "you are a witch, and a wicked witch, too. It is like your race to be cruel and merciless, indifferent to the pain you inflict, and--"

"No, no," retorted the girl, indignantly, "it is not true." She was irradiated by her wrath. The usual faint yet warm redness of her face had changed to a deeper hue, and her eyes were smouldering fires. Edward had never seen her look so handsome; but his attention was distracted from her at that instant by some rough, prickly shrubs, near which they were passing. He put out his hand instinctively to keep them from touching his companion, and a sharp thorn pierced his palm. He immediately affected to be in great pain.

"It is easy for the pale-face to suffer," she said tauntingly.

"It is impossible for your race to be pitiful," he replied in the same tone.

Again she flushed hotly, and, as if to disprove his assertion, she seized his hand, and pressed it closely to her angrily, heaving bosom, as she tried to extract the thorn from it. But it had penetrated too far, and with a quick impatient ah! she bent her warm red lips to his palm and strove to reach the thorn with her little white teeth. After several attempts she was at last successful, and looked up with an air of innocent triumph.

"I take back my cruel words," Edward said. "I am sure you can be a little pitiful." Then he put her gently but hastily aside, for they were close upon "Bellevue," and he was eager to meet Helene.

With a grieved, child-like wonder the beautiful, ignorant savage watched him, as he hurried across the velvet lawn, among beds of brilliant flowers, to greet a lily-like maiden, clad in what, in her uncivilized eyes, appeared to be a mingling of mist and moonbeams. It was the first time that he had shown a wish to leave her. Hitherto she had been the object of his pursuit, of his devotion, of his ardent desire. Now, like a cold blast, his neglect struck chill upon her heart, and she turned back into the forest solitudes with all the brightness suddenly and strangely gone out of her life.

But instead of being translated to the earthly paradise of a beautiful woman's favour, Edward, to his own great disappointment and chagrin, found himself in a very different atmosphere. Helene was cold, nearly silent, utterly indifferent. She was looking unusually well. The rich harmonious contrasts of face and hair--the midnight darkness of the one breaking into the radiant dawn of the other--never before impressed him so vividly. But she was terribly distant. The young man assured himself rather bitterly that if she were a thousand miles off she could not have been more oblivious of his presence. She was alluring even in her indifference, graceful, elegant, angelic--but an angel carved in ice. "I have been so unfortunate as to offend you," he said at parting, as they stood alone in the soft, moonless, summer dusk.

"I don't know; is it a matter of much importance?" There was an accent of weariness in her voice, but the tone was hard.

"Yes, to me. You are as cold as death!"

"What a very unpleasant fancy!" She shivered lightly, and extended the tips of her very chilly fingers to him in a last good-night.

Mademoiselle Helene was intensely proud. She had been an unobserved witness of the scene between Edward and Wanda in the wood, and, of course, had made her own misinterpretation. A man who could permit a low, untutored savage to fawn upon him in that way, kissing his hand repeatedly, and flushing with gratified vanity, presumably at his words of endearment, could scarcely expect to be treated otherwise than with disdain by the high-bred girl whom he had previously delighted to honour. As for Edward he was sorely hurt and bewildered. Helene's treatment of him he considered decidedly curt, and natural resentment burned within him at the thought. But before he reached home his anger had passed away, and with it all remembrance of the cold maiden and the unpleasant evening she had given him. In their place lived an intense recollection of a tawny woman, beautiful and warm-blooded; and his heart thrilled with a tumult of emotions at the memory of her lustrous velvet lips closely pressed within his wounded hand.

CHAPTER IX.
ON THE WAY TO THE CAPITAL.

From early summer to late autumn, from assurance of bloom to certainty of frost, is but a step--the step between life and death. The murmuring leaves and waters on the shores of Kempenfeldt Bay had learned a louder and harsher melody--the wild wind-prophecy of winter. For a brief season Indian summer came to re-illumine the despairing days, and the larches, set aflame by her hand, flashed like lights. Then through the softly tinted wood broke the Autumn brightness upon delicate shimmering birch trees, red sumachs, purple tinged sassafras, golden rod and asters; but now the oaks and beeches had changed their velvet green raiment to dull brown, and all the wild woods, after the pitiless and well-nigh perpetual rains of Fall, were stricken and discoloured. Madame and Mademoiselle DeBerczy had flown with the birds, and were now domiciled in their winter home at the Oak Ridges, whither Rose Macleod, in response to an urgent invitation from Helene, had accompanied them, and whence she wrote letters of entreaty to her father, urging him to take a house in York for the winter.

"Not that it is so particularly lively," she wrote, "but it is not quite so deathly as at Pine Towers. Edward will be willing to come, I know, desperate lover of nature that he is, for there is nothing in the woods now but eternal requiem over lost and buried beauty, of which, in the natural vanity of youth, he may be tempted to consider himself a part. As for the children they will build snow-houses, and sit down in them, thus ensuring permanent bad colds, and the other member of your family, if she returns home, will 'look before and after, and sigh for what is not.' Is not that a sufficiently depressing picture? Dear papa, you know that, like the bad little boys in a certain class of Sunday School literature, I can't be ruled except by kindness. Now see what an immense opportunity I have given you to govern me according to approved Sunday School ethics!"

She paused a moment, considering not what could be said, but what could be omitted from a missive which was to be convincing as well as caressing in its nature, when Helene entered the room.

"Love letter, Rose?" she inquired carelessly.

"Certainly," responded her friend, "all my letters are love letters. Would you have me write to a person I didn't love?"

"Why, I couldn't help it, that is supposing the letter you are writing is addressed to Allan Dunlop. Of course he is a person you don't love."

"There is no reason why I should."

"No reason? O ingratitude! After he dived under the heels of a fiery horse, carried you nearly lifeless into the house, and took off his boots every time he entered it for six weeks thereafter. How much further could a man's devotion go?"

"I am beginning to find out," said Rose, with a slight return of an invalid's irritation, "how far a **woman's** devotion can go."

Helene arched her delicate brows. "Are you offended?" she asked, anxiously. "Ah, don't be! I'll take back every word. He **didn't** take off his boots, nor carry you in, nor pick you up, and, let me see--what other assertion did I make? Oh, yes. Of course he is a person you **do** love. But oh, Rose, Rose, what are you blushing about? This isn't the time of year for roses to blush."

"Upon my word, Helene, you are enough to make a stone wall blush."

"Ah, you are thinking of the stone walls of a certain farm cottage. I can imagine you sitting propped up in bed, with a volume of hymns marking the line, 'Stone walls do not a prison make,' with a big exclamation-point, and a 'So true!'"

Rose leaned back in her chair and closed her eyes.

"Are you very tired, dear?" inquired her friend, with real tenderness.

"Very tired," was the languid reply, that was not without a satirical intonation. "It seems as though my rest was a good deal broken."

"Broken bone! broken heart! broken rest! dear me! Well, I suppose they follow each other in natural sequence."

"Helene," said her mother, "you are chattering like a magpie. What is it all about?"

"Broken utterances, mamma. Not worth piecing together and repeating."

Madame DeBerczy, seated alone at the other end of the apartment, turned upon her daughter a face of such majestic severity as effectually to quell that young lady's recklessly merry mood. But it was not for long. The irrepressible joyousness of her nature was not permanently subdued until two weeks later, when the family were surprised by the unlooked-for appearance of Edward Macleod. This young man was the bearer of good-tidings. His father and the rest of the family were even now domiciled at an hotel in York waiting for Rose to arrive in order to consult her preferences before selecting a house. The announcement made both girls happy, but when it was discovered that Edward was to take his sister away in a few hours their joy was changed to lamentation. To be separated, hateful thought! How could it be endured? They withdrew for a brief space to consider this weighty problem, leaving Edward in dignified conversation with Madame DeBerczy. He was strangely reminded of his first visit to her after his return from England. Alike, and yet how different. Then the prophecy of summer's golden perfection was in the air. But his hopes with it had too-quickly ripened and died. The coolness that had sprang up between Helene and himself had grown and strengthened into the permanent winter of discontent. He was recalled from the chilling reflections into which this thought had plunged him by the concluding words of a remark by Madame DeBerczy: "I approve of a certain amount of life and animation," she said, "but they are inclined to be too frisky."

"What on earth is she talking about?" queried Edward inaudibly. He could form no idea, but he was suddenly extricated from his dilemma by observing the antics of two pet kittens on the hearth-rug.

"Altogether too frisky," he acquiesced, "but charming little pets."

"It appears to me," said the lady, with a good deal of frigidity in her manner, "that they should be something better than that."

"Oh, you could scarcely expect such young things to be stately and dignified, Madame DeBerczy. They seem to me very pretty and graceful."

"In my day prettiness and grace were not considered so essential for young ladies as dignity and stateliness."

"Young ladies! Really, I beg your pardon, dear Madame, for my inattention. I imagined you were talking of kittens." He blushed so vividly over his mistake that a more circumspect old lady even than the one he was addressing would have found it hard not to forgive him.

But now the girls re-entered the room with looks of deep dejection. "We have decided that we can't part," said Helene. "United we stand, divided we fall."

"And so," said Rose boldly, addressing Madame DeBerczy, "we have come to ask if Helene cannot go back with us for a few days." She paused a moment, for in asking a favour of so lofty a personage as Madame DeBerczy, she was never certain whether she ought to prostrate herself on the floor in oriental fashion, or merely bend the knee. In this case she did neither. But her sweet pleading eyes spoke "libraries," so Helene told her afterwards. The imaginative objections already forming in the mother's mind vanished away, and she was prevailed upon to give her consent.

"Though it leaves me rather at the mercy of Sophia," she said, as she went out to lunch.

Edward lifted an inquiring pair of eyes.

"Sophia is my new maid," explained his hostess. "Her ideas on the subject of liberty and equality are extreme. Sometimes," she added mournfully, "I am in doubt as to whether I have hired Sophia, or Sophia has hired me."

The young people longed to exchange covert glances of amusement, but this relief was denied them. It was no laughing matter to the stately sufferer at the head of the table. Rose spoke in the decent accents of sympathy and condolence, but her brother and friend were not profuse of speech. The latter was thinking of possible explanations and reconciliations that might arise through the frequent opportunities of meeting with Edward, which a temporary residence under the same roof would entail, and the former was feasting his beauty-loving eyes upon a strikingly lovely picture on the other side of the table--the picture of two heads, golden-yellow and raven-black, against the rich background of a peacock-tinted tapestry screen.

They were much less picturesque in their winter wraps, as they whirled away under the leafless trees, but they made up for it in merriment. Edward and Helene were secretly glad of the presence of Rose. It was impossible to be frigidly formal with that sunny face beaming up now at one, then at the other. This deep young person had made up her mind that she would spare no pains to bring about a better state of feeling between the two. When conversation lagged or threatened to become formally precise, she gave utterance to some amazing piece of nonsense, which compelled a laugh from the others, or else indulged in prettily assumed alarm, lest their horse should prove untrustworthy.

"When you see a horse's ears move," she declared, "it is a sign that he is vicious. Flip's ears were never still."

"Why, Rose," cried her brother, "this horse is no more like Flip than an old cow is like a wild cat. Besides his ears don't move."

"Oh, yes, they do," remarked Helene, with the calmness of scientific conviction. "When a horse moves his ears have got to move too. They are not detachable. It is the same with other animals."

"Where is my note-book?" inquired Edward, after a fruitless search in his various pockets, while Rose observed "Well, you may say what you please, but I feel sure he is not safe."

"Indeed, he isn't," echoed the driver. "He's liable to turn around any moment and bite you. It's a good thing the livery stable man hitched him up head first, else we might all have been devoured by the ferocious beast."

Such pleasantries might have been indefinitely extended had not unusual sounds of mirth and minstrelsy coming from behind arrested their attention.

"Why, it is the Elmsleys," softly exclaimed Rose. "Dear me! I haven't seen Grace and Eleanor for months."

These young ladies hailed her with every expression of delight as the carriages came to a stand-still together. They had a prodigious amount to say. At last, as the horses were growing restive, Mrs. Elmsley invited Miss Macleod to join their family party, as they also were on their way to York.

"*Do*!" echoed the daughters, and Rose accepted with alacrity. "The horse we have isn't at all safe," she explained, "and I am quite nervous on the subject since my accident last summer."

"Rose," demanded Helene, in a low aside, but with a tragic countenance, "you surely are not going to leave me?"

The girl laughed as she accepted Mr. Elmsley's proffered assistance from one vehicle into the other. "Why, you are quite a grown woman," observed that gentleman, apparently much impressed by her mature proportions, "and it seems like only the other day that you were seven years old, and used to kiss me when we met."

"Well, I'll kiss you again," replied the saucy Rose, adding after a moment's pause,--"when I am seven years old."

"I warn you, Mrs. Elmsley," said Edward, shaking his head with doleful foreboding, "that girl knows how to look like the innocent flower she is named after, and be the serpent under it."

"Did you know," said his slandered sister, addressing the same lady, and indicating the pair she had basely forsaken, "those are the very two that were with me when I was so badly hurt last summer. Do you wonder that I am glad to escape from them?"

The party drove off amid jests and laughter, while the young ladies, applying their lips once more to a leaf of grass-ribbon each had in her hand, produced such

sounds as, according to their father, might, Orpheus-like, have drawn stones and
brickbats after them, but from a murderous rather than a magnetic motive.

"I wonder if Rose is really nervous," said Edward, breaking the silence that
bound them after the departure of the others.

"I think she is really nonsensical," said Rose's friend, not very blandly.

"Are you then so sorry to be left alone with me?"

The young lady evaded the question, but became extremely loquacious. She
intimated that almost any companionship, or none at all, could be endured on this
beautifully melancholy autumn day, and called his attention to the leaves under-
foot, which had grown brown and ragged, like the pages of a very old book on
which the centuries had laid their slow relentless fingers. In a burst of girlish confidence she told him that always, after the wild winds had stripped from the shuddering woodland its last leaves, and the pitiless rains had washed it clean, the spectacle of bare-branched trees, standing against the gentle gloom of a pale November
sky, reminded her of a company of worldings, from whom every vestige of earthly
ambition, pride and prosperity had fallen away. "Anything," she said to herself,
"*anything* to keep the talk from becoming personal."

"I can understand that," said Edward, "but the influences of unworldliness--I
was almost saying other-worldliness--are nowhere felt as in the woods. Sometimes
they exert a strange spell upon me. The petty pride and shallow subterfuges of fash-
ionable life are impossible in nature's solitudes. Don't you think so?"

"Yes;" assented Helene, not seeing whither her unthinking acquiescence might
lead her.

"That is why I dare to ask you why you have been so cold and formal towards
me, so unlike your old self, for the last three months?"

No petty pride could help her now, no shallow subterfuges come to her aid.
She had declared that they were impossible here. She could not turn her face away
from his truth-compelling gaze. Why had Rose left her alone to be tortured in this
dreadful way? How could she confess to him that jealousy and wounded vanity had
caused the change in her demeanour? "I cannot tell you," she said at last. She had
turned paler even than usual, but her eyes burned.

"I am sorry to have given you pain," he said almost tenderly, and then the confession broke from her in a little storm of pent-up emotion.

"It was because I ceased to respect you! How could I respect a man who would allow a wild ignorant creature to caress his hands and hang upon his words?"

He turned a face of pure bewilderment upon her. "If you mean the Algonquin girl, Wanda," he said, "she has never treated me otherwise than with indifference, anger and contempt." He explained the scene of which Helene had been an involuntary witness, and the proud girl felt humiliated and belittled. But he was too generous and perhaps too clever to allow her to suppose that he attributed her coldness to weak jealousy. That would have placed her at a disadvantage which her pride would never have forgiven.

"So you believed me to be a vain contemptible idiot," he said, "Then you did perfectly right to scorn me." He drove on furiously, with tense lips and contracted brow. She had misjudged him cruelly, but he would not descend to harsh accusation. Helene was decidedly uncomfortable. "I have never scorned you," she said. "It was because I believed you superior to the folly and weakness of ordinary men that it grieved me to think you were otherwise."

"It grieved you," he repeated in a softer tone. "Hereafter I wish you would confide all your griefs to me the moment you are aware of them."

"To tell the truth, I don't expect to have any more." She laughed her old joyous friendly laugh, and he stretched his arm across her lap to adjust the robe more closely to her form. Her attitude towards him had completely changed, concretely as well as abstractly, for now she sat cosily and contentedly by his side, instead of perching herself a yard away, and allowing the winter winds to emphasize the coldness that had existed between them. This wonderful improvement in the mental atmosphere made them oblivious to a change in the outer air until Helene remarked upon the peculiar odour of smoke about them. This increased until it became almost stifling. Evidently the blazing brush heap, lit by the hand of some thrifty settler, had extended further than he was aware of. The smoke blew past them, and they were in the midst of that vividly picturesque spectacle--a fire in the forest. The flames ran swiftly up the dry, dead limbs, turning trees into huge blazing torches, and the light underbrush beneath them took on beautiful and fantastic shapes of fire. The gray sky was illumined with fiery banners, while, like scarlet-clothed imps at a carnival, the flames leaped and danced among the twigs and smaller branches.

The hot breeze blowing on her cheek filled Helene with sudden alarm, and

Edward urged the horse to a quicker pace. But the frightened creature needed no urging. With a great shuddering leap he sprang forward as though a thousand fire-fiends from the infernal regions had been after him. Helene uttered a half-suppressed shriek, and clung strenuously to Edward's arm. Suddenly he gave a loud gasp of dismay. On the road directly before them a pile of brush had caught the blaze and stretched before their startled eyes like a burning bridge. All attempts to stop or turn around were useless. The horse was wholly beyond control. For a moment they were enveloped in smoke and flame, shut into a fiery furnace, from which an instant later they emerged from danger, but with a badly singed steed and an unpleasant odour of fire upon them. Edward had pushed Helene to the bottom of the carriage, and flung the robe over her. Now he drew her trembling, and sobbing a little, back to his side. She was shaking excessively, and in order to restore her equanimity there was clearly nothing else to be done but to hold her closely in his arms, let fall his face to hers, and breathe in her ear every word of sympathy and comfort that came to his mind. She lay weakly with closed eyes upon his breast, while the excitement in her pulses gradually died away. When she opened her eyes the short November day was nearly at its close, and York was in sight. She drew away to her own corner of the seat, not with any visible blushes, for her complexion never lost its warm whiteness, but her eyes glowed, and her lips were 'like a thread of scarlet.'

"I am glad Rose was not with us," she said, feeling a pressing need to say something, and in default of anything better to say, "as she is even more nervous than I am."

"Yes, I am **very** glad she was not with us," assented Edward, with an unusual amount of brotherly fervour, while he turned his horse in the direction of the only available hotel in the Capital, where the wearied travellers were content to rest for a few days before setting out in search of a new home.

CHAPTER X.
YORK AND THE MAITLANDS.

There are difficulties in the way of one who would describe an event after an immortal poet has given it a setting in lines that a worshipping world will not will-ingly let die. A tree, it is said, is never struck by lightning more than once, and it is safe to suppose that a subject is never illumined by the rays of heaven-descended genius without being as thoroughly exhausted. Nevertheless, with our tame domes-tic lantern, let us endeavour to throw a little prosaic light over the details of a scene that has been irradiated by the imagination of a Byron.

It was one of the events of the season to the social world of that foreign town, but to us it is one of the events of the century. On an evening in June, 1815, in the city of Brussels, the Duchess of Richmond gave a ball on so magnificent a scale that even the gray heads of society's veteran devotees were a little turned, and the chestnut and golden pates of their juniors tossed sleeplessly on their pillows for several nights preceding it. After all, humanity is perpetually and overpoweringly interested in nothing except humanity. On the evening appointed there was a vast beautiful throng, moving through halls as beautiful and more vast; there was the witchery of soft lights and softer sounds, of odours and colours that enchant the senses; there were banks of flowers, each of whose tiny blossoms yielded its dying breath to make the world sweeter for an hour, and among them, under the starry lights, in warm human veins, flowed a thousand streams; very blue, not so blue, and even common crimson. But all flowed faster than usual, perhaps the better to warm the lovely bare shoulders and arms, or to paint the sweet cheeks above them in the vivid hues of glad, intense young life. Intermingled with the costly robes and flashing gems on the ideal figures of fair women, gleamed the brilliant uniforms of brave men. "A thousand hearts beat happily"--with one exception. This was in the possession of the second daughter of a duke. She was even then remarkable for her beauty and for a certain imperious, condescending grace. The gay throng of which she was a part was no more to her than so many buttercups and daisies; and these sumptuous apartments, so far as they concerned her, might have been a series of green meadows. At last her indifferent glance, travelling over the room, encoun-tered an object that faintly flushed her cheek, and brightened the eyes, whose orbit of vision was now limited to the circle immediately about her. Cold indifference had changed to throbbing impatience. Ah, why did he not come! With whom was he lingering? She dared not look up lest her glance, like a swift, bright messenger, should tell him all her heart, and draw him magnetically to her side. No, he must come of his own choice, and quickly, else her mood would change. Soft strains of music arose, melting, aching, dying upon the air. Her heart melted, ached, and apparently died also, for it turned cold and hard as she glanced at her watch, and saw that it was more than a minute, nearly *two* minutes (two eternities they seemed to her) since she began to be glad that she had come.

The next instant her long-lashed lids were raised in spite of herself, and she confronted a singularly tall and attractive-looking gentleman, whose face, from its pensive sadness, had a certain poetic charm. He begged the honour of the next dance with her. She regretted that he was too late. He looked disappointed, but ventured to name the next one. She was sorry, but it was impossible. Had she room for him anywhere at all on her list? She shook her head prettily but inexorably. The handsomest coquette and the plainest school-ma'am have this in common, that they detest and punish tardiness. The young man was overpowered by his sense of loss. It was small comfort to stand and look at the beautiful girl. When the gates of paradise are closed against one it matters little whether they are made of gold or of iron. Inwardly he bestowed some very hard names upon himself for imagining that that peerless creature would be allowed to await a willing wall-flower his languidly deferred appearance.

Again those heavenly strains rose and throbbed upon the air. It was maddening. The keenness of his disappointment gave his face an intensity of ardent expression that certainly did not detract from its charm in the eyes of the girl who at that instant glanced up into it. The next moment he was pressed aside--very decorously, very courteously, even apologetically pushed aside, but still compelled by an insinuating patrician hand to make room for its owner, a gentleman whose extremely lofty title had already drawn the homage of a hundred admiring pairs of eyes upon him, and whose prevailing expression was a haughty consciousness of accustomed and assumed success. The young lady whom he now honoured with a request to dance did not think of his title, nor of his condescension, nor of him. She declined with characteristic indifference on the plea that she was already engaged, and turning placed her hand on the arm of Sir Peregrine Maitland, whose suddenly bewildered and enraptured heart, if it had never before given its assent to the time-worn proposition that all is fair in love as well as in war, certainly could not hesitate now. Perhaps the triumphs of the ball-room are not less thrilling than those of the battle-field. "Why were you so cruel to me a moment ago?" he murmured, looking down into eyes that but too clearly reflected the happiness of his own.

"For the same reason that I am kind to you now," she responded like a flash.

He did not ask her the reason. Perhaps he was intuitively and blissfully aware of it. Did ever maiden discover a more demurely daring way of telling her lover that she loved him?

But now, caressed by little wafts of perfume, and half-dazed by the blaze of lights and colours around and above them, they were drifting as on a tide upon soft swelling waves of music. In liquid undulations of sweet sound they floated insensibly down the windings of the waltz, nor dreamed of danger till the note of warning came. It was a prodigious note--nothing less than the boom of a cannon--and the signal for instant, perhaps life-long, separation.

"Who could guess,   If ever more should meet those mutual eyes?   Since upon night so sweet such awful morn could rise."

But, as we know, two pairs at least of those mutual eyes were destined to meet again, and meet as gladly and warmly as when their owners danced together on the evening before the battle of Waterloo. But the chill atmosphere of a father's disapproval lay between them. It is reasonable to suppose that the fourth Duke of Richmond and Lennox was not so susceptible to the charms of pensive and picturesque young gentlemen as was his wilful daughter. Among the names on a list of invitations to a party given by the latter appeared that of Sir Peregrine Maitland, which, coming under the cold parental eye, was promptly erased. At the same time he inquired of his daughter why she permitted that undesirable gentleman to hang about her skirts--why she did not let him go. The response was that after this decided slight he probably *would* go; she added with a little sigh that she did not know where. The duke profanely and contemptuously mentioned a locality which shall be nameless. The young lady made no reply. She believed in division of labour, and in former domestic affairs of this sort her stern parent had invariably said what he pleased, while she contented herself with merely doing what she pleased.

Proverbially, actions speak louder than words, and the present case was no exception, for while the echo of her father's speech did not go beyond the walls of the apartment they were in, her own rash performance, which was a direct consequence of it, was a few days later noised abroad through all Paris. This was an evening call at the lodgings of Sir Peregrine Maitland. She came in unannounced, flushed, eager, defiant, lovely, letting fall the rich train of her robe, which she had caught up in a swift flight through the streets, and throwing off her enveloping cloak, which scattered a shower of sparkling drops on brow and bosom, and beautiful bare arms, for a light shower had fallen. "They would not let you come to me, so I have come to you," she declared with a daring little laugh. "I have run away from my guests. There is a houseful of them and they tire me to death. Everyone tires me to-night except you." The gentleman stood before her speechless with bewilderment. "I believe," she said with a little pout, like a spoiled child, "that you are not glad to see me."

"Glad to see you," he repeated, "dearest, yes! But not in this way, at this time."

She turned aside, but the drops that glittered on her cheek now were not caused by the rain. Her shimmering silken robes seemed to utter continuous soft whispers of applause to her nervous yet graceful movements. Altogether she was an incongruous object in the unhome-like bareness of a bachelor's apartments. "You are not very cordial, monsieur," she remarked in a cold tone, as she stood with her back to him, staring hard at an uninteresting picture above the mantel-shelf; "it seems to be a pleasure to you to receive an evening caller, but not exactly a rapture." She smiled her old imperious smile as she threw herself into a tired-looking chair, while her host, with very obvious reluctance, sank into one just opposite. For an instant her beauty smote upon his brain. He leaned forward until his face touched the lapful of rare old laces that flowed wave-like from waist to knee on the dress of the girl he loved.

"Darling," he murmured, "it is a rapture"--then he suddenly drew himself very far back in his chair--"but not exactly a pleasure!"

She rose again and moved restlessly about the room. He stood pale, speechless, waiting for her to go--a waiting that was almost a supplication. "How could you have the courage to come to me," he breathed as she drew near him.

"Because I hadn't the courage to stay away from you. I am brave enough to do, but not to endure."

"My poor love! if this escapade becomes public you will have enough to endure."

"I do not care for the world." She stood facing him with the absolute sincerity and trust of irresistible love. "I care for you," she said.

He took the little jewelled hand and reverently kissed it. "Ah, don't do that!" she cried, drawing it away with a quick impatient frown. He drew away, supposing that he had offended her, while she, giving him the puzzled incredulous look that a woman must give a man when she discovers, not that his intuitions are duller than her own, but that he has no intuitions at all, continued her tour about the room.

"Sweetheart," he said, following her, but not venturing to lay a finger upon her, "you *must* go." His voice was earnest and very tender.

"The same idea has occurred to me," she said, "but I dislike to hurry. There is nothing so vulgar as haste." Her old mocking tone had returned, and in despair he threw himself back into his seat.

Something in the pathetic grace of his attitude and the beauty of his sensitive poetic face smote upon the heart that, with all its perversity, belonged alone to him. She ran to him and knelt at his side, with her white arms outstretched across his knees, and her lovely head bowed upon them. The young man realized with sharp distinctness that the fear of society is not the strongest feeling that can animate the human frame. He uttered a few passionate words of endearment, and would have gathered her closely into his breast, but she, without looking up, sprang suddenly from him and, seizing her cloak, sped wind-like to her home.

But there were consequences. Madame Grundy, who is chief among those for whom Satan finds some mischief still, openly declared that there were some forms of imprudence that could be tolerated and some that could not, and that this particular indiscretion must, with reluctance, be relegated to the latter class. The irate father of the erring one coincided with this view of things, and a speedy marriage was the result. "Not guilty--but she mustn't do so again!" had evidently been the verdict of society.

A few months later, in 1818, Sir Peregrine Maitland, his affairs of love happily settled, was appointed ruler of Upper Canada, where his attention was turned to affairs of State. But there was one subject in connection with his courtship-days which had never been satisfactorily settled, and upon which he did not venture to question his wife until several years had elapsed. Then, late one afternoon, it recurred to him in that unaccountable way in which bygone events are accustomed to rise at odd times and lay claim to the attention.

"Dear," he said, "why did you object to my kissing your hand the evening you called on me in Paris?"

"You may lay out the corn-coloured silk, Emma," said Lady Sarah to her maid, who came that moment with an inquiry upon toilette matters. Then as the girl disappeared she resumed her novel, peeping over the top of it at her husband.

"As though I wanted you to kiss my **hand**!" she said.

"*Oh*!" A sudden light seemed to dawn upon the dense masculine understanding. Sir Peregrine was very proud of his beautiful wife. At the private reception which she gave that evening the corn-coloured silk gown was the centre of a group of government officials and the social dignitaries of the time, between herself and whom the ball of conversation kept lightly moving.

She turned from them to greet an old friend. "Ah, Commodore, so you are really settled here for the winter. Rose told me that you had some thoughts of remaining out in the bush through the cold season, in the cosy but rather too exclusive manner of a family of chipmunks. What have you been doing all summer?"

"Keeping myself unspotted from the world," replied the gentleman, with a stately bow to the lady, and a sportive glance at the worthy representatives of the social world surrounding her.

"How very scriptural! Do Bibles grow on bushes in the backwoods that quotation of them comes so easily?"

"I don't know, I'm sure. Such searching theological questions are, I suppose, what a man must expect to confront when he forsakes the simple and sequestered life of the chipmunks."

"Well, I am disappointed. I supposed from the expression of your eyes that you were going to say something complimentary."

"My dear Lady Sarah, do compliments grow on street corners in the metropolis that the expectation of them comes so easily?"

"No, indeed--nor in drawing-rooms either, apparently. It is a novelty to meet a man who persists in making his conversation impersonal; but it is really cold-hearted of you to think of remaining so long away from us."

"How can you say so! Absence, you know, makes the heart grow fonder."

"Does it?" The lady made a feint of moving away. "Now if it were only possible for me to absent myself," she said, laughingly.

"Impossible! That is for me to do." And the gentleman withdrew with flattering haste.

In his place appeared a blonde young man, with deep sea-blue eyes and a bright buoyant expression, on whose arm his hostess laid a soft detaining hand. "Were you on the point of asking me to walk about a little?" she inquired. "I am going to accept with alacrity."

The young fellow, who would scarcely have made the suggestion in the face and eyes of several among the most distinguished of his fellow citizens immediately surrounding her, was not slow to respond, though he assumed an expression of alarm.

"I fear this is a deep-laid plot," he remarked. "I saw my father leaving you in haste a moment ago. Probably he has offended you, and you are about to visit the iniquities of the parents upon the children. Pray are you taking me apart in order to spare my sensitive feelings? So kind of you!"

"Well, it was not my benevolent intention to lecture you at all, either in public or private, but since you speak of it so feelingly no doubt the need exists. First tell me what you have been doing all summer."

"Living out in the wild woods among the wild flowers, wild animals, wild Indians, and--"

"What a wild young man! I am positively afraid of you."

"Delightful! Please oblige me by remaining so. It is difficult for me to be appalling for any length of time, yet the emotion of fear must be cultivated in your mind at all hazards."

"And why?"

"Because you will never dare to lecture the awe-inspiring being of whom you are in mortal terror."

"Oh! are you sure of that? I met a famous lecturer the other day, and he assured me that he never stepped before an audience without suffering from fright; yet he did not spare his hearers on that account."

"Such is the hardheartedness of man. We expect more from a woman."

"More of a lecture, or more hardheartedness?"

"More of the latter--from you."

"Well I am under the impression that you will receive, before long, a good deal of the former from a young lady present. Are you aware that we are observed?"

"I am sure that one of us is the observed of all observers."

"It is kind of you not to add that politeness forbids you to say which. But what I mean is that since we began to talk I have twice encountered a glance from the darkest eyes I ever saw."

"They must belong to Mademoiselle DeBerczy."

"They do. That girl's eyes and hair are black enough to cast a gloom over the liveliest conversation."

"But her smiles are bright enough to illumine the gloom."

"Then it is a shame that she should waste them upon that rather slow-looking young man in front of her. Will you take me back to my seat and then go and see if you can release her from bondage?"

The request was immediately acceded to, and not long afterwards Helene De-Berczy and Edward Macleod were exchanging the light talk, not worth reporting, that springs so easily from those whose hearts are light.

Meantime where was Rose? To all outward appearance she was demurely listening to the remarks of a distinguished statesman, whose opinions were held to be of great weight, and whose form, at any rate, fully merited this description. He was so delighted to think that one so young and fair could be so deep. Alas! she *was* deep in a sense the gifted gentleman never knew. For, while the sweet head bowed assent, and the rose-bud lips unclosed to utter such remarks as "Ah, indeed! You surprise me!" and "Very true!" to statements of profound national import, her maiden meditations were as free as fancy. Before her mental vision the brilliant rooms with their gay well-dressed assemblage melted away, and in their place was a fair green meadow, wide and waving and deliciously cool under the declining sun of a summer evening. The last load of the second crop of hay was on its way to the barn, when a great longing desire took possession of her to ride on it. She walked out to the field, very slowly and feebly, but still she actually walked--and the whole cavalcade came to a dead stop at sight of her, for she had never been able to go any farther than the gate since her accident. Mr. Dunlop, and Allan, and the hired man, and even the oxen all stopped, and looked at her as though they expected to hear that the house was afire, or that the servant girl had run away with the butcher's boy. But when they found that nothing was wanted except a ride on a load of hay

Mr. Dunlop said, "bless the child!" and held her up as high as he could reach. Then Allan lifted her the rest of the way, blushing as he did so. She remembered how beautifully clean he looked in his white shirt sleeves, and what clear warm shades of brown there were in the eyes and on the cheeks under the broad straw hat. She remembered, too, with a little warmth of feeling--not a *very* uncomfortable warmth of feeling--how, when the waggon made a great lurch going over a ditch, she had uttered a little scream, and laid strenuous hands of appeal upon the white sleeved arm, and how, when they came to another ditch, a brown palm had held fast to her trembling hand until the danger was over. Halfway in the barn door he made the oxen stop, until she had stood on tip toe, and put her hand among the little swallows in a nest under the eaves. Ah, what was there in the memory of new-mown hay to fill her with this sharp sweet pain? She awoke from her dream to a consciousness that the gentleman beside her was saying that it was sufficiently clear to every enlightened understanding that unless tum tum tum tum measures were instantly adopted mum mum mum mum would be the inevitable result.

"Oh, no doubt of it," said Rose, and then there was a readjustment of the group in her immediate vicinity. Lady Sarah Maitland appeared with a bewitching smile and begged to introduce the honourable gentleman, who had been discoursing with so much eloquence to a friend of hers. The 'friend' hovered in the distance, but even in perspective it was clear to be seen that he was a man of great powers of endurance.

The honourable gentleman concealed under a flattered smile his distaste for the proposition, and in a few moments his place was occupied by Lady Sarah, who took one of the little hands, soft and pink as a handful of rose-leaves, between her own.

"I wonder if I might venture to ask a favour," she said.

"I'm sure I should never venture to refuse it," returned the young girl, with all a young girl's appreciation of kindness coming from a thoroughbred woman of the world.

"Then I wish very much that you would sing one of your favourite songs. It would be a great pleasure to very many of us."

"I'll not wait to be coaxed," was the reply, after a moment's hesitation. "It is only really good singers who can afford to do that."

In spite of her dimpled figure and child-face, Rose Macleod had a very stately little way with her, and it served to repel one pair of eyes that for the first time that evening caught sight of her as she moved towards the instrument. A little queen! That was what he had always called her in his heart. *His* little queen! Oh, how had he dared to enthrone her there? Presumptuous idiot! she was as far from him as the stars are from the weeds. But the girl at the piano thought of nothing but the sharp, sweet odour of new-mown hay. Sharp as a sword and sweet as love, it pierced and thrilled her being. Then, like a fragrant blossom, a melody sprang from the hidden sources of her pain. The sympathetic musical expressiveness of her voice, and its pure penetrating quality filled the room, and riveted the attention of every one in it. Others came in from adjoining rooms, until, in the press of the throng, a young man was forced, in spite of himself, nearer and nearer to the instrument, and found himself close beside the fair girl-goddess of song, just as the last words left her lips. Like one awaking from sleep she looked at him, and then the glad light of recognition swept up to her eyes. Her dream had come true. "Oh," she exclaimed, "it is Allan!"

CHAPTER XI
AFTER "THE BALL."

She was conscious of what she had said an instant afterwards and blushed to the brow. If any one at that moment had asked her what's in a name, and she had been compelled to reveal her inmost convictions, the fair Rose, who by any other name would be as sweet, would have answered "impropriety, embarrassment, a host of unpleasant emotions." It was impossible to explain to him that she had been helping him to make hay that evening in Lady Sarah Maitland's parlours, and that that was why the name that she had heard so frequently in the meadow had left her lips so easily and naturally that night. Better try and seem unconscious. But unconsciousness, like happiness, comes unsought or not at all. As for Allan, his own name had never made such music in his ears and surely to no lone watcher waiting for the dawn could the first blush of morn be more welcome than was to him this lovely mantling bloom on the face of the girl he loved.

"Charming!" "Exquisite!" "Do sing something else!" were the exclamations rained upon her as she ceased to sing, but she looked only to him.

"How is it I have never heard you sing before?" he inquired, with the applause that the others had uttered shining unspoken in his eyes.

"You have too many professional singers about your home. I am afraid to sing before them. Did you ever hear birds called 'the angels of earth?'"

"Never."

"Well, if nobody else originated the phrase I am willing to do so--rather than that it shouldn't be originated at all."

"It may be a pretty idea," said Allan, "and yet it fails to suit my critical taste." They withdrew a little from the crowd, and found a quiet place in which to sit and chat, for now a pianist of note had been led a willing sacrifice to the place Rose vacated.

"You must be hard to please," said Rose. "What can be more like an angel than a bird? It has wings, and it sings, and it is rejoicingly happy. It seems to be particularly blest every moment of its blessed little life."

"Very likely. Nevertheless I think a flower much more closely resembles an angel."

"A flower? Why, there is scarcely a point of resemblance."

The young man laughed, but the slight whimsical frown between his brows deepened.

"Now that isn't at all what I expected you to say. I thought you might be kind enough to inquire, 'What flower?' and then I could reply, 'The queen of flowers.'"

Rose looked down a moment at the warm pink hands restlessly twining and intertwining in her lap. "I am glad I did not make the inquiry," she said.

"You don't like clumsy compliments?"

"I believe I don't like any kind from you."

"Why, please?"

"I don't know exactly, unless because it seems natural to expect something better."

Allan Dunlop was dimly aware that a compliment of a very high order had been paid to himself. "Our best friends are those who compel us to do our best," he said. "I hope you will always expect something better of me than anything I have done."

It was the speech of an ambitious young man. They both recognized the note of earnestness that seemed to place them for a moment above the frivolous crowd about them. Only for a moment; then they lapsed easily into the light talk so natural to the occasion.

"Have you had a pleasant evening?" he asked.

"Very pleasant." Her mind reverted once more to her delightful reverie, and the scent of new-mown hay was again about her. Then, as though he could read her thoughts, she brought them back to the present with a quick little blush, and mentioned the name of the gentleman who had absorbed so large a part of her time, if not of her attention, through the evening.

"Now, why should she blush when she mentions his name?" thought poor Allan, with a sharp jealous pang at his heart, for the man she alluded to was an eligible bachelor, who had successfully resisted the charms of one generation of maidens. "If you find Mr. Gallon's conversation so interesting," he said, rather forlornly, "mine will seem dull by contrast. What was he expatiating upon?"

"Politics, mostly."

"Are you interested in that subject? I think of going into politics more deeply myself some time."

"Do you, indeed? More than you have?" If he had spoken of going into a decline Rose could not have looked more foreboding. Allan glanced across half-enviously at the personage who had the power to invest that topic with interest. "He seems to be more than usually roused to-night."

Rose suppressed a yawn. "Does he talk better when he is roused than he does when he's asleep?" she asked.

"Surely he displayed no signs of sleepiness when talking with you."

"No; but I cannot answer for myself."

That senseless pang of jealousy died a very easy death after all, and the only sufferer from it would have been entirely happy were it not for the advancing form of Commodore Macleod, who came in search of his daughter, and bore her off with a speed that left her lover a little chilled and daunted.

The Canadian winter with its bright, fierce days and sparkling nights was upon them, but it held no terrors for the young hearts who met it in a mood as defiantly merry as its own. Only a suffering or morbid nature sees in winter the synonym of death and decay; fancies that mourning and desolation is the burden of the gaily whistling winds; and regards the bare trees, rid of their dusty garments, and quietly resting, as shivering skeletons, and the dancing snow-flakes as the colourless pall that hides from sight all there is of life and loveliness. Nature, when the labours of the year are over, sinks to rest beneath her fleecy coverings, lulled to sleep in the kindly, yet frosty, arms of the Northern tempest. What wild weird lullabies are sung to her unheeding ears, dulled by the lethargy of sleep. How early falls the darkness, and how late the long night lingers, the better to ensure repose to the sweet mistress of the earth! How bright the starry eyes of heaven keeping watch above her rest!

The Macleods had settled in a furnished house, through which Rose had already diffused the charm of her dainty personality. She was kneeling before the hearth, like a young fire-worshipper, one snowy afternoon, and thinking a little drearily that the close environment of a snow-storm in town rendered it almost as lonely as the country, when a visitor was announced, the sound of whose name seemed to make the solitude populous. It was Allan Dunlop, whom she instantly forgave for so soon availing himself of her permission to call, when she realized how welcome a break his coming made in the cheerless monotony of the day. He caught a glimpse of bright hair against a background of blazing logs, and then she came forward to meet him, not eagerly, not shyly, but with a charming manner in which both eagerness and shyness were suggested. At that moment all the warmth and brightness of the bleak colourless world shone for him in the eyes and hair of this sweet girl, and in the glowing fire-place before which she drew his chair.

"It is exactly the sort of day on which one expects to be free from the annoyance of callers," he said. "Ought I to apologize?"

"By all means--instantly--and in the most profuse and elaborate terms." She assumed her grand air, mounted a footstool, and stood looking over his head with her saucy chin elevated, waiting for the abject petition that did not come. The young man's heart rendered the tribute of an unmistakable throb to its "little queen;" but emotional declarations are out of place after a short acquaintance, especially when there exists a decided belief that they will be listened to in an unfriendly spirit, or, what is infinitely worse, in a friendly spirit. It was the fear of making Rose his friend that steeled Allan's determination to bide his time, and that rendered his present reply rather more stiff than sensational.

"I beg a thousand pardons," he began, when she interrupted him with--

"Oh, that is too many. Do try and be a little more moderate in your demands. Would it please you to have me spend the whole afternoon in forgiving you?"

Allan laughed--a blithe contented little laugh. "Any way that you like to spend the afternoon will please me," he said, "so long as I am not deprived of your presence. Oh, not *that* way," he added, as a little frown crept between her golden-brown eyebrows, "that way excepted."

"Very well. I'll not frown at you, but you must promise not to come so near again to the verge of a compliment."

"I promise. Anything to keep a frown from marring the--I mean from your face. But the difficulty is to think of anything that is as easy to say."

"You might better remind me of my faults."

"Oh, you could scarcely expect me to be eloquent on that subject. I didn't know that they exist--that is to say, I am incapable of speaking upon a subject so wide reaching and profound. Are they like unto the snow-flakes for multitude?"

"No, not quite so numerous, but far worse in quality. For instance, the other day I never smiled at papa the least bit when I said, good morning!"

"Horrible! what an unnatural daughter!"

"It was because he wouldn't let me dance as often as I wanted to the night before. He said he must draw the line somewhere. It is strange that the word *somewhere* in that sentence invariably means the precise point where it is most painful to have it drawn."

Allan Dunlop, who had already had some experience of the Commodore's ability to draw the line at the sensitive point designated by his daughter, murmured only, "very strange."

"Not that he was in the least unkind about it," continued Rose. "Papa is always lovely to me, no matter how I behave."

"Very lovely?"

"*Very* lovely."

"I never before was so struck with the truths of heredity," mused the young man. "You are exactly like him."

"*Oh!*" the girl dropped her face in her hands a moment, and then thrust them out with the palms toward her guest. "You have need to beg a thousand pardons and a thousand more to cover the offences you have committed. And you have broken your promise!"

"What a harsh accusation! I promised not to come to the verge of a compliment. Do you think that was on the verge?"

"No! It was too blunt--too dreadfully--"

"It is a pleasure to hear you so emphatically contradict an assertion made by yourself."

"That is a mere quibble--a legal quibble. Well, there is no doubt that you would make a very successful lawyer."

"Is that a compliment, or does it approach the verge of one?"

Before this problem could be solved Herbert, who was deeply engaged in a game of checkers with his younger sister, at the other end of the apartment, suddenly announced: "Rose, here is Mr. Galton coming across the street, making directly for our house."

"Oh, dear!" was the very inhospitable exclamation of its pretty mistress. Then as she caught an amused glance from Allan's eyes, she added demurely, "I am so glad."

"Perhaps it would be better for me to go." The words escaped with obvious reluctance.

"Better for which of us?"

"For both, I think."

"Your charities are conducted on too large a scale. Now, if you could only content yourself with benefiting *one* of us you would remain. I have a dread of that man."

"So have I, but from a different motive. As your dread increases, mine grows less."

Close analysis and consideration of this fact gave a very becoming tint to her cheeks as she welcomed the entering guest. "Ah, Miss Rose," he exclaimed, "blooming as ever, in spite of wintry days. Do you know I came very near going past your door?" He allowed the announcement of this providentially averted calamity to sink deep into her heart, while he bowed to Allan.

"This is an unexpected pleasure," murmured the young lady, with sufficient formality to prevent her words from being dangerously insincere.

"Unexpected to you and a pleasure to me?" queried the gentleman, with a keen glance at the pair, whose **tete-a-tete** he had evidently disturbed, "or do your words bear reference to the idea of seeing me going past your door?"

The amount of truth in these very good guesses startled the girl to whom they were addressed into an uncomfortable sense of guilt. "How can you accuse me of anything so horrid?" she said, drawing her chair not far from him, and looking into his face with the appreciative air and attitude that are not to be resisted.

"Mr. Galton," said Herbert, who, having completed the game, and vanquished his sister, could afford to turn his attention to the frivolous conversation of his elders, "do you know what Rose said when she saw you coming? She said, 'Oh, dear, I am so glad!'"

"Herbert," implored Rose, crimsoning under these carefully reported words, and fearing that Mr. Galton, not being aware of the motive which prompted them, would not know whether to be ecstatic or sarcastic, "you are a terrible boy!"

"Herbert has done me a great kindness," exclaimed the flattered gentleman, who considered Rose's embarrassment quite natural, and very pleasing under the circumstances. "All my doubts of a welcome he has happily removed."

In the fear that these doubts might unhappily return if he were allowed to continue conversation with a too-confiding younger brother, Rose devoted herself with nervous intentness to his entertainment, and succeeded brilliantly. Fragments of laughter and chat drifted across to where Eva was trying to persuade Allan into playing checkers.

"Just one game, please, Mr. Dunlop," pleaded the little damsel, in resistless accents.

"If you but knew what a wretched player I am," said the young man gloomily.

"Oh, *are* you a wretched player?" she exclaimed brightly, "I am so glad. Then there is some chance for me." She added confidentially, "I am even more wretched."

"I hope you may never have the same reason to be," said Allan, with a half-suppressed glance at the lively pair near the window.

A lover, from his very nature, must be decidedly unhappy or supremely blest, and it is scarcely to be expected that perfect felicity can reign in a heart whose pretty mistress is spending her smiles on another man. Allan did not believe that Rose really cared for Mr. Galton--he had seen too many proofs to the contrary--but he did believe that she was giving that objectionable gentleman every reason to think that she did care. With how many men did she pursue this course of action, and was he to believe her guilty of careless coquetry? Upon how many admirers may a rose breathe perfume and still keep its innocent heart sweet for its lover? These were the questions that rankled in his mind, while Eva set the checkers in place.

"Perhaps I can keep you from getting a king," she said exultantly.

"If I can only keep my queen," observed the young man absently.

"Why, Mr. Dunlop, there are no queens in this game; it isn't like chess."

"There! you see how little I know about it," was the regretful reply.

Despite this painful manifestation of ignorance the two combatants appeared for a while to be very equally matched. Then the advantage was clearly on Allan's side. His king committed frightful havoc among the scattered ranks of the enemy, till suddenly, as he observed the painful stress of attention and warm colour in the face of his fair little foe, a strange and unaccountable languor fell upon his troops. They seemed to care not whether they lived or died, while their shameless commander, surveying them with anxious countenance, gave vent to his emotion in such ejaculations as, "Dear me!" "Why didn't I see that move?" or, "The idea of your taking two men at one jump!" At last the announcement that he was completely vanquished was joyfully made by Eva, and incredulously listened to by Herbert, who viewed his sister's opponent with amazement, not unmingled with pity.

"The battle is indeed lost!" Herbert said, quoting the historic words in a consolatory way; "but there is time to win another."

"I'm afraid not," said Allan, rising and preparing to depart.

"I wish that you could have won the game, too," said Eva, suddenly stricken with remorse in the midst of her good-fortune.

"You are a very kind little girl. I can depend on you to consider my feelings."

The accent, ever so slight, upon the "you" aroused Rose's attention. "Why, you are not going?" she exclaimed, coming towards him.

"Such is my charitable intention," he replied, smiling with sad eyes.

"I was only waiting for you to finish your game before bringing Mr. Galton to the fire to talk politics with you."

"That is a warm topic, and a warm place."

"Perhaps Mr. Dunlop fears that we shall quarrel on the subject. You know we are on different sides, Miss Macleod."

"We shall hardly come to blows, I think," returned Allan, with the look of bright good-fellowship which made him a favourite with both political parties.

"The idea of your quarrelling with anybody!" said Rose, as she accompanied him to the door.

"I may have a very serious disagreement with him some time," replied her jealous though unacknowledged lover, "but it will not be about politics."

He ran hastily down the steps, unconsciously brushing against Commodore Macleod, who favoured him with a bow of about the same temperature as the weather. Muttering a hurried excuse, he went on into the cold gloom of the early winter twilight, shivering slightly, not from the chill without, but from the deadlier chill within. 'What a pompous unbearable old fellow the elder Macleod was. How could he endure to have him for a father-in-law? Ah! how could he endure not to have him?' The fear that he might never stand in a closer relationship to a man for whom he had so little liking lay heavily upon him.

That same evening the object of these mingled emotions laid a detaining hand upon the shoulder of his pretty daughter as she bent to bestow a bed-time kiss upon his grizzled moustache. "I wish to have a little conversation with you, my dear, on a serious subject"

"Oh, but Papa," replied the spoiled girl, "I am not at all in a serious frame of mind."

"It is highly probable that you will find yourself so at the end of our talk."

"Charming prospect! After such an inducement as that I can't resist any longer." She sank back into a low chair near a great case of books, for they were sitting in the cosy library.

"I met young Dunlop coming out of the house as I was coming in," began the Commodore. "I was sorry to see that."

"I was sorry to see it, too, Papa, but he couldn't be persuaded to stay longer."

"That is not a very respectful answer to give to your old father; nevertheless, I am glad to hear it, as it assures me that you have not reached the point when his absence will leave you sad."

"Oh, no! But I am willing to admit that over Mr. Galton's departure I did come very near shedding tears--of joy."

"I hope my little girl will have no cause to shed any other kind."

"His little girl" endeavoured to look oracular as she replied: "That will largely depend upon the nature of the information you are about to communicate to me."

"It is only a request, my dear! I wish for your own sake that you would have as little as possible to do with that young Dunlop."

There was an appreciable interval of silence. Rose stared hard at the fire. Her father added, "Of course, I do not wish you to do anything unreasonable."

"I am sure of that," said the girl softly, "nor anything unkind."

The gentleman stirred a little uneasily in his chair. "You must remember," he said, "that the greatest unkindness one can do another is to encourage false hopes in him."

"How would you like me to treat him?"

"Oh, my dear child, I can't tell. You know perfectly well yourself. Be pre-occupied, absent-minded, indifferent, when he comes. Make him repeat what he says, and then answer him at random. Look as though you had a thousand things to distract your attention, and treat him as though he were the chair on which he is sitting."

"And you think that would be an ample and delicate return for the countless kindnesses shown me by himself, and his people last summer?"

"Oh, hang himself and his people!" was the Commodore's mental comment. Aloud he said, "Well, the young fellow could hardly leave you to perish under the horse's heels. What he did was only common decency."

"Then, perhaps, it would be as well to treat him with common decency. Don't you think that desirable quality is omitted from your course of treatment?" Her tones were those of caressing gentleness, but the flame of the firelight was not more red than the cheek on which it gleamed.

"Why, bless me, Rose, I don't want you to give him the cut direct. There is no need to put him either in paradise or the inferno. Better adopt a happy medium."

"Yes; but purgatory is rather an unhappy medium."

"Well, my dear, I have nothing more to say. I suppose it is natural that you should set aside the counsel of a man who has loved you for nineteen years in favour of the attention of one who has known you about the same number of weeks."

"Papa, you are unjust!" The repressed tears came at last, but they were dried as quickly as they dropped.

"Can't you understand," he continued in a softened tone, "that I would willingly give him anything in return for his kindness--except my eldest daughter?"

"That is a gift he would never value. A society man might do so, but the idea of a young fellow of talent and energy and ambition and brains looking at a little goose like me!"

The Commodore laughed. "No doubt it would be a great hardship for him to look at you; but young men of talent, ambition and that sort of thing are not afraid of hardship. In fact they grow to love it. So you think he would not value the gift?" He laughed again very heartily.

"I am perfectly certain," declared the young girl, with impressive earnestness, "that he will never stoop to ask you for it."

"Then there is nothing more to be said," replied the Commodore, with an air of great relief. "The whole question could not be more satisfactorily settled. You are my own loyal little girl and--and you don't think me a dreadfully cross old bear, do you?"

She went straight to his arms. "How can I help it," she asked, with her customary bright smile, "when you give me such a bearish hug?"

But alone in her room, the smile vanished in a tempest of fast-coming tears. There was a reason for them, but she was unconscious of it then. Later she discovered it to lie in the fact that in her heart of hearts she was not a "loyal little girl" at all, but an "out and out little traitor and rebel."

CHAPTER XII.
A KISS AND ITS CONSEQUENCES.

It was late afternoon in a Canadian midwinter day. Cold and still, with a coldness so intense that the blinding brightness of the sun made no discernable impression on the densely packed snow, and with a stillness absolutely undisturbed by any slightest breath of blustering wind. Before the early twilight came, Rose Macleod, wrapped in furs from dainty head to well-booted feet, ran lightly down stairs, tapping softly at the library door on the way.

"I am all ready, Papa," she said, illumining the room for a moment with a pair of dark blue eyes and crimson cheeks. "Don't you think it will be a beautiful night?"

"Very beautiful, and cold enough to kill an Esquimaux. I confess it would be a pleasure to know that in a few hours you would be safe under the blankets instead of junketing over at Madame DeBerczy's."

"I shall be just as safe under the buffalo robes, just as warm, and a great deal happier."

"Very well; be off then. By the way, how many are in your party?"

"Oh, nearly a dozen at least."

"Then there is a possibility that you will not all perish. Tell the survivors to report themselves here as early tomorrow morning as possible."

There was a sound of bells and a mingling of merry voices as a sleigh-load of young people drove up to the door, and waited for Rose to join them. "Delays are dangerous," observed Edward, as his sister, after opening the door, was suddenly stung by the reflection that she had not taken a last comprehensive view of herself in the glass, and turned to the hall mirror to rectify the omission.

"Particularly, when it is below zero," said another.

"What is she doing now?" patiently inquired a third.

"Airing the hall," responded a girlish voice. "Oh, no, she is really coming! Rose," she called, "come and sit by me."

"No, there is more room here," said another voice; while still another exclaimed, "I have been keeping such a cosy little corner here for you."

She stood in smiling hesitancy a moment, when her hand, from which she had removed the glove in order to adjust an unruly hair-pin, was taken by another hand, firm and warm and gloveless, and she was drawn almost unconsciously to the side of its owner. It was Allan Dunlop who had thus taken summary possession of her, and incurred a little of her dignified displeasure.

"You left me no room for choice," she said in a slightly offended tone.

"I beg your pardon, I was thinking only of leaving you room for a seat."

She was silent. It was very difficult to keep this young man at a distance, when there was such a very little distance between them, and yet she must be true to the promise tacitly given to her father. She must be cool, indifferent, uninterested. "It isn't a matter of any importance," she said absently.

"I'm afraid it is to me," he continued in a lower tone, "I know scarcely a soul here, and declined Edward's invitation to join you on that account."

"Oh, it is very easy to become acquainted with a sleighing-party." She greeted the two young ladies on the other side of him, and introduced him to them. They were refined, attractive-looking girls, but they had a fatal defect. They absorbed social heat and light instead of radiating them. It seemed as though they might be saying: "There, now, you got us into an unpleasant situation by inviting us here, and it's your duty to make us happy; but we're not having a good time at all, and we'd like to know what you're going to do about it." Allan did the best he could, not half-heartedly, for he was accustomed to do thoroughly whatever he attempted, and his success was marked. Those grave girls, who, heretofore, had always seemed to be haunted by some real or fancied neglect, were in a gale of semi-repressed merriment. The mirth was infectious, and as the horses flew over the frozen road, the gay jingle of bells mingled happily with the joyous laughter of young voices. Poor Rose, whose natural love for society and capacity for fun-making had induced her to set very pleasant hopes upon this sleigh-ride, found herself, much to her surprise, the only silent one of the company. With Allan's gracefully unconcerned personality on one side, a middle-aged lady of rather severe aspect--the matron of the party--on the other, and just opposite a pair who were very agreeably and entirely engaged *with* as well as *to* each other, all means of communication seemed to be hopelessly cut off. It was really very unreasonable for Allan to act in this way. He was saving her the trouble of treating him badly and keeping him at a distance; but, strange to say, there are some disagreeable duties of which one does not wish to be relieved. If it were possible to be overwhelmingly dignified when one is buried shoulder deep in bear and buffalo skins--but that was out of the question.

The clear crystalline day began to be softly shadowed by twilight. Behind them lay the town, its roofs and spires robed in swan's-down, while on all sides the fallen logs and deep underbrush, the level stubbles and broad irregular hollows, and all the vast sweep of dark evergreen forest, melting away in immeasurable distance, was a dazzling white waste of snow. In the bright moonshine it sparkled as though studded with innumerable stars. Above them was a marvellously brilliant sky.

Suddenly, under a group of trees that stretched their ghostly arms across the roadway, the cavalcade came to a full stop; and Edward, who was driving, looked round with a face of gloomy foreboding at the merrymakers.

"What is the matter?" demanded half-a-dozen voices.

"We shall have to go back," announced the young man, with a look of forced resignation.

"Go back!" echoed the same voices an octave higher, "why, what has happened?"

"Nothing, except that Rose ought to take another look at herself in the hall mirror. There is something fatally wrong with her appearance."

"About which part of my appearance?" demanded the young lady, who was too well acquainted with her brother to be at all surprised or disturbed by anything he could say.

"I don't know, I'm sure. Perhaps its the ***tout ensemble***. Yes, that's just what it is."

"Do drive on, Edward, and don't be ridiculous. It's too cold to discuss even so important a subject as that."

"I am sure you must be suffering from the cold." It was Allan who spoke, turning round to her in a tone of quick, low tenderness.

"Not in the least!" Every small emphatic word was keen and hard as a piece of ice. Then, in the white moonlight, she confronted something that made her heart sink, it was the unmistakable look of mental suffering, a look that showed her that he at any rate was suffering from the cold--the sharp stinging cold of a winter whose beginning was pressing bitterly upon them, whose end, so far as they could see, was death.

The mansion of Madame DeBerczy sent out broad shafts of light through its many windows to welcome the latest addition to the brilliant throng already assembled in its ample interior. Madame herself was superb in a regal-looking gown that became her aristocratic old countenance as a rich setting becomes an antique cameo. Her stately rooms were aglow with immense fire-places, each holding a small cart-load of hissing and crackling wood, the reflected light gleaming brightly from the shining fire-irons, while a number of brass sconces--the picturesque chandeliers of the past--polished to the similitude of gold, were softly shimmering overhead. The beautiful English furniture of the last century, artistic yet home-like; the old world cabinets, covered with surface carving, solid yet graceful in appearance; tiles, grave and cheerful in design, set into oaken mantel-pieces; peacock coloured screens, and ample crimson curtains, edged with heavy silken borders of gold, all lent their aid to brighten and enrich the rooms that to-night were graced by some of the best society from Upper Canada's; most ambitious little town of York. Mademoiselle Helene, beautiful in a blush rose gown, with a few star-shaped flowers of the same shade in her silky hair, was the magical living synthesis of this small world of warmth and colour in the eyes of her lover. These eyes were more than usually brilliant from his long ride in the keen air, and the yellow locks upon the smooth white brow were several noticeable inches above the heads of those around him. As he walked down the crowded rooms, in enviable proximity to the blushing dress, his handsome face and half careless, half military air drew the attention of more than one bright pair of eyes.

"Rather a pretty boy," commented a pompous-looking gentleman, patronizingly.

"But entirely too fair," was the disapproving response of the critical young lady beside him, whose own complexion and opinion were certainly free from the undesirable quality she referred to. "Of course, a pink face is attractive--in a doll."

"Then the daughter of our hostess escapes the imputation of being doll-like."

"Oh, she is quite too overgrown for that. It's a pity she has that peculiar complexion through which the blood never shows."

In another group, an enthusiastic young creature whispered to her mother: "Mamma, do notice Miss DeBerczy's face; white as a cherry blossom, and her lips the cherries themselves. Isn't she just like a picture?"

"Yes, dear," drawled mamma, adjusting her eye-glass with an air of rendering impartial justice, "like a very ill-painted picture. Why don't she lay on her colours a little more artistically?"

"Oh, she doesn't lay them on, they're natural."

"Well, Lena, you should not be so quick to notice and comment upon natural defects. Not one of us is free from them, and it is uncharitable and unkind to make them the subject of remark."

Thus silenced and put in the wrong the young lady ventured nothing further.

"Edward," said Helene, later in the evening, "really you ought to dance with somebody else. There are dozens of charming girls here."

"Which dozen did you wish me to dance with?"

"Don't be nonsensical, please. Haven't you any preference?"

"Oh, decidedly, yes." He glanced at a *petite* maiden, whose figure and movements were light and fairy-like. "But I'm afraid she would refuse me."

"I don't think she would."

"That isn't sufficient. My vanity is painfully sensitive to the smallest danger of slight."

The fairy-like person had unconsciously assumed an appreciative, not to say sympathetic, expression. Helene smiled. "Your fears are very becoming to your youth and modesty, but I think I may go so far as to say I am sure she will not refuse."

"That is joyful news." Another set was forming, and he rose with hand extended to Helene. "You said you were sure she would not refuse," he responded to her look of blank amaze; and then, as she yielded to the irresistible entreaty in his eyes, he murmured softly, "How could you imagine I had any other preference but you?"

"One imagines a great many strange things," she replied. "Once I fancied that you preferred an Indian girl."

"*How could you!*" he repeated with intense emphasis. All that part of his life seemed vague and far away as though he had dreamed it in some prehistoric period of his existence. It refused to take the hues and proportion of reality. Yes, that was nothing but a wild fantastic dream--the sort of dream from which one wakes with a wretchedly bad taste in the mouth. This rare girl, with the flower-like curves and colours, was the only reality. And yet, was she reality? Her dress, wreathed flame-like from warm white shoulders to satin shod feet, lay in rich glowing lengths upon the waxed and polished floor. Her beautiful head, too heavily weighted with braids and coils of raven blackness, swayed slumberously upon the dainty white neck, and he could not tell whether he better liked to see the dark lashes lying upon her cheeks or uplifted to reveal the magical eyes beneath. He was very much in love. The soft intoxicating strains of music went to his head like wine. He was powerless to struggle against the thrilling illusion of the hour. When the others returned to their seats or promenaded the brilliant rooms they escaped alone and unobserved into the conservatory. Here they beheld the greatest possible contrast to the desolate wintry waste without. The air was heavy and languorous with the odour of tropic flowers. The music, almost oppressive in the crowded parlours, melted deliciously upon the ear as they wandered away. Helene, when she noticed that they were quite alone, suffered a vague alarm. She told herself in one moment that it was not possible that Edward would choose this opportunity for a formal declaration of his love, and the next moment she reminded herself that impossible things are the ones that frequently come to pass. The idea, like an ill-shaped burden, pressed uncomfortably upon her.

A maiden's heart, like a summer night, knows and loves its own secret. All through the mysterious deep hours of sleep it holds the secret closely wrapped in darkness, pure as the dew on the grass, innocent as the little leaves in the forest, glorious as the countless stars of heaven. Some time, and soon enough, the dawn will come. Then the stars will pale before a glory more intense, the countless little leaves, like delicate human emotions, will wake and stir, and the white mists of maidenliness will be warmed with heavenly radiance. But after sunrise comes the day--the long prosaic day of duty and denial, of work and its rewards, of sober, plain realities. Why should the night of mystery and beauty hasten towards the common light? Her being thrilled under the first faint approaches of the dawn, and yet--yet a little longer, oh, ardent, impetuous, all-conquering Sun! It seemed as though the girl's very soul were pleading. The rich-hued, fragrance-laden flowers in the sweet dim place bent their heads to listen, but her impassioned lover paid no heed to the unspoken prayer. The sense of her beauty--of her unsurpassable charm, mingled with the voluptuous music--pierced his heart with insupportable pain. Could she not feel his unuttered love? Her lily-like face was cool and pale, but in that warm-coloured robe it seemed as though her very body blushed. In leaning over to reach a peculiar flower that attracted her attention, a little wave of her gown rested upon his knee, and it seemed to his infatuated vision that the insensate fabric throbbed as well as glowed from the momentary contact. Helene kept up a continual flow of small talk, of which he heard not a syllable. Rising hurriedly, her long train caught in a low branch that stretched across the walk, and he bent to extricate it.

"How is it that you dare to touch the hem of my garment?" she demanded laughingly.

"Oh, I can dare more than that," he cried. The conviction that she loved him, as indeed she did, gave him a sort of desperate courage. He took her in his arms and held her close, kissing her passionately on lips and eyes and soft white shoulders. She neither moved nor spoke, but stood, when he released her, confronting him with a sort of frigid, fascinated stare. "Oh, what have I done? Helene," he exclaimed tremblingly. "I thought you loved me."

"*I*?" she questioned with haughty disdain, "*love*?" she demanded with incredulous contempt, "*you*?"

The concentrated fires of her wrath and scorn were heaped upon this final monosyllable. Every word was a fierce insulting interrogation. Surely the traditional "three sweet words" had never before been uttered with such tragic effect. She stood before him a living statue of outraged pride, clothed in a fiery robe of righteous indignation; then she turned and passed out of his sight, leaving the young man to his reflections.

They were bitter enough in all truth. He still cared for Helene, he loved her as he loved himself. But it is only fair to add that he held himself in the very smallest estimation. He had acted like a drunken fool. How would he like any man alive to treat his little Rose in that style? But then she might have behaved reasonably about it. She had trampled on his heart, and left it sore and bruised and bleeding. Very well, he was not a child to cry out when he was hurt. He went back to the gay throng, and saw, as in a cruel dream, the girl who despised him scattering profuse smiles upon others. No matter! Nothing could possibly be of any importance now. Rose was making her way with some difficulty towards him. How wan and tired she looked. Was it possible that any one besides himself was suffering? The idea was absurd.

"Isn't it time for us to go, Edward?" she said. "Madame DeBerczy has invited our party to remain over to-morrow, but I promised papa not to desert him any longer than was strictly necessary." Edward found the proposition a most welcome one. They could not leave Oak Ridges too soon, nor remain away from it too long.

His sister's drooping little figure attracted the attention of Helene. "Do you talk of going?" Helene asked. "Well, so you shall go--to bed; and the very first bed we come to." She bent caressingly over the little golden head of her friend. Their beautiful arms were interlinked. Rose glanced irresolutely at her brother.

"You will need to put on the extra wraps you brought," he said, "as it is particularly cold at this hour of the morning." Helene was ignored utterly. He did not seem to know that she was present. The proud girl was wounded to the quick. She was not visible at their leave-takings. When every one was gone she went away upstairs, telling herself at every step that she hated, hated, Edward Macleod; that he was in all things and in every way detestable. She did not weep nor bewail. The tears showed as seldom in her eyes as the blood in her cheeks, and her pride was of the inflexible sort that scorns to relax when its possessor is alone. She dropped into a heavy troubled sleep, and dreamed that she was solitary in a frozen land, whose only sunshine was the golden head of her lover. In the strange fantastic manner of dreams he seemed to be a very little child, whose light warm weight lay along her arms, close to the heart above which he had pressed those burning kisses. It was bitter cold; but the whole scene was like a picture of winter. She could not feel it--she could feel nothing but the aching of her own heart, the warm breath growing ever warmer, and the clinging hands, clinging ever closer, of the child she loved. The sense of delicious languor changed to a feeling of heaviness--almost suffocation. Every golden hair of the head upon her breast pierced her like a ray of brightest sunshine. Hastily putting him from her she fled away with the wintry winds, herself as wild and swift and soulless as they. But presently coming to look for the child, and unable to find him, she realized that he was lost, and then she woke, trembling with deep, tearless sobs.

"What is it, my dearest?" called Madame DeBerczy from the next room.

"Nothing, mother, dear, but a troubled dream."

"Ah, it is the excitement of these late hours. Try to sleep again."

But Helene could sleep no more. A few days later she heard that Edward Macleod, with a party of friends, had gone on a shooting expedition to the Muskoka country.

CHAPTER XIII.
RIVAL ATTRACTIONS.

The current of a strong human affection, when it is thrown back upon itself, must find vent in another direction. The weakest stream of passion, when its chosen course is impeded by an immovable obstacle, does not sink by gentle degrees into the earth, and thus, lost to sight, become merely a thing of memory. There is disturbance and disorder; banks are overflowed; and fields, once made fruitful and beautiful by the softly-flowing river, lie sodden and unwholesome, flooded by the dangerous waves. For days and nights Edward's brain was surging with the sound of rushing waters. The tumultuous feelings so strongly excited, so completely overthrown that evening in the conservatory with Helene, would not subside. They beat upon his desolate heart in great waves of rage, remorse, despair, and love, like the beating of lonely waters upon a shipwrecked shore.

Hence it was that he welcomed the idea conveyed in a letter from a friend in Barrie that they, with another boon companion, should go hunting in Muskoka. Edward wrote an immediate agreement to the proposition, mentioning Pine Towers as the place most convenient for them to meet and lay plans for future action. He at once made preparations to depart, for the idea of delay was intolerable to him. The very atmosphere of the town was poisonous--the demands of society not to be tolerated. He told his family that his old longing for the wilds had come upon him, the sort of **ennui** that nothing but the odour of the woods could cure. The close of the day following found him on the frozen shores of Kempenfeldt Bay, now clasped in the icy arms of winter. The wind was wild among the leafless trees along the avenue, but the desolation of his home was a visible response to the sorer desolation of his heart.

The two or three old servants remaining in the lonely house were delighted to see the young master home again. Olympia, the coloured cook, whose high-sounding cognomen was usually reduced to Olly, gave him a welcome equal to what might be expected from a whole plantation of darkies. Her eyes and teeth shone in perpetual smiles, her gaily turbaned head and dusky hands gesticulated in perfect time to the exclamations poured out upon him.

"Well, my soul!" she cried; "well, my soul! Marse Ed., its good to see you home again. Come in, chile, come right in! How mis'able you do look to be sure. Just like a ghost, so cold and white. Shan't I mix you a little something warm?"

"Oh, no, Olly, I'm all right; just a little tired after my long journey, that's all."

She recognized the lifelessness in his tone, the jaded look and air of one who is fighting a hard battle in the face of sure defeat. "You's sick, honey," she exclaimed, with the ready sympathy of her race, "and you's come back to old Olly to take care ob you. Dat's right, chile, I'll just mix you a little warm--"

"Oh, dear, no, Olly, thank you; its comfort enough just to be quiet and to be at home."

She left him in the parlour, but he pushed on after her into the great fire-lit kitchen, partly because he detested the society of his own thoughts, partly because it suited his present mood to be made much of by the kindly old woman, to whom his mother all her life had been a "chile." It was almost like being a boy again to sit in the chimney corner and tell old Olly the story of his journey in all its details. But before the recital was half-finished, something stirred in the semi-darkness, on the other side of the fire-place.

"Why, bress my heart," said Olly, "I t'ought you was a dog, Wanda, you sat dat quiet. What's de matter wid you, gal? Whar's your manners?"

The graceful shrinking figure would gladly have escaped out of sight, but at the sound of her name Edward came forward to greet the Indian girl. Olly, with many muttered protestations against the rudeness shown to her young mahs'r, lifted the trap-door, and vanished down cellar. The pale life-weary young man was alone with the sweet womanly savage.

He held the little hand she offered him very closely and kindly.

"Are you glad to see me, Wanda?" he asked.

That was the keynote of his mental state. He was not glad to see anyone or anything, but he was still interested to know that someone cared for him. In his present mood it was certainly more pleasant to feel that others were kindly disposed towards him than that they were indifferent. The Algonquin maiden, on her side, was filled with a soft delicious emotion. In the summer, when this daring young man pursued her, she repulsed him; but in the winter, when he left her, she thought of him. The natural result of her meditations upon so fascinating a subject it is not difficult to conjecture. She began to believe in the reality of his regard for her, and to fancy that he had left her because of her harshness, of which he had frequently complained. Now, could it be possible that his coming had anything to do with the thought of her? Yes, she replied, she was glad to see him; her blushing beautiful face gave eloquent testimony to the fact. He released her then, and followed Olly into the dining-room, where a small but sumptuous repast was laid, for nothing in the house above nor in the cellar beneath was considered too good for young mahs'r. "You'd be sprised, Marse Ed.," confided the old woman, "de improvement made by dat chile since I took her in han'. It jus' went agin my stomach to see her runnin' wild, widout a frien' in de worl', cept dose heathen Injuns. She t'ought a heap ob yer mudder, an' I could'nt tell her 'nough about her. Dat gave me a holt on her, you see, and dars no denyin' she's changed a lot since las' summer."

"Tell her to come in here," said Edward, "and I'll judge for myself."

So in a few moments she came in, though with obvious reluctance, and took the chair that Edward placed for her at the table. It was a novel experience to the young man to find his wishes so implicitly obeyed by this hitherto almost unapproachable girl. He felt disposed to exercise this wonderful newly-acquired authority. "You must eat something, Wanda," he observed; "I dislike to eat alone."

This was the sharpest test that could have been applied to the improvement he wished to discover, but the girl's incomparable native grace never failed her. It was impossible that she should either lounge in her chair or sit stiffly erect in it. Her use of knife and fork was marked, not by awkwardness but by extreme deliberation, and careful observation of the manner in which Edward wielded his own. She wore a dark grey dress, which he dimly remembered to have seen on his sister Rose, and which that young lady had altered to fit the Algonquin girl. The entire absence of colour in the dress intensified by contrast the rich hues of cheek and lip, and the deep blackness of eyes and hair. The only detail of her appearance which displeased his taste was the strings of cheap glass beads wound about neck and waist. Was there a vein of cheapness and vulgarity in her character to correspond with this outward manifestation? He believed not. It was so easy to believe everything that was good of this shy sweet personage. He examined her narrowly and critically in the new and remarkable *role* she was compelled to play as the guest and equal of himself. There was a surprising almost ludicrous similarity between the native unconsciousness and dignity of the Indian and that of certain high-bred dames whereof he knew, and yet there was about her the unmistakable something that proved her wholly unversed in the ways of society. Her dainty hands were very brown; her manner without being constrained was certainly not easy; and her expression was that of a bird, one moment resigned to imprisonment, the next panting for liberty. In one word she was untamed. But was she untamable? His heart beat faster at the thought. When the tea things were removed he threw himself upon the couch; while the girl, sitting before the blazing hearth, took between her hands and drew upon her knees the slender head of his favourite hound. They made a striking picture, and the blue, beauty-loving eyes of the spectator looked longingly upon it. The dark lovely face bent forward seemed more childish in its soft curves since the capacity to love and suffer had wakened in her breast. Her sweet lips trembled with repressed feeling.

"Wanda," said Edward, "don't waste caresses on that unthankful brute. He doesn't need them."

She looked at him with wide startled eyes. "Come to *me*," he breathed in resistless accents. "Ah, Wanda, you pitied me once when I had a scratch on my hand. Can not you pity me now when I have a sword in my heart?"

It was not love that called her; it was the despairing cry of one who was perishing to be loved. She rose after a moment, steadying herself by a hand on the chairback, for her beautiful frame was swayed by irresolution, love, shame and pride. Slowly, very slowly, with the sweet uncertain footsteps of a baby that fears to tread the little distance between itself and the waiting irresistible arms of love, she came towards him. It seemed at every moment that she must break away and fly, as she had flown from him in the woods of summer. When she reached his side her proud head fell, then the drooping shoulders bent lower and lower till the uncertain knees at last failed her, and she sank trembling on the cushion at his side with her arms about his face. It was the attitude of protection, not that of a weak craving for it. The fierce pain for which he asked her pity could arise from nothing else but his love for her. This was the reasoning of the simple savage--a reasoning that reached the hitherto unsounded depths of passion and pathos in her nature. The young man, who bore in his heart a bitter recollection of the scornful repulse offered by one beautiful girl, could not resist the matchless tenderness so freely given by another. He laid his face wearily against her arm, and she bent over him murmuring words of uncontrollable love and pity.

Afterwards he asked himself what in the name of all the powers of evil he meant by it; but this was some days afterwards. A long tramp through the frozen woods in search of game had brought him a single wild animal and a great many sober thoughts. In the rough log house in which he and his companions were camping for a week, there was neither room nor opportunity for private meditation; but the conviction came to him with the luminous abruptness of lightning that he had used this ignorant girl merely as a salve for his wounded vanity, and cruelly deceived her by so doing. Not that his early passion for the Indian girl had died a natural death. On the contrary it had been fanned into fresh flame by the novel charm of her sweet approachableness. None the less, but rather all the more clearly, he saw the detestable selfishness of his own course. But, unfortunately, his tenderness for her kept pace with his self-contempt. His feelings toward Helene and Wanda at the present moment were just such as a man might entertain toward the enemy who had conquered him, and the woman who, in his greatest need, had succoured and saved him. For the one a bitterness that could not rise to the crowning revenge of forgiveness, for the other a passion of gratitude that would last a life-time.

"It appears to me," said Ridout, who was the most outspoken of the party, "that we have a precious dull time of it in the evenings. Macleod, here, is about as talkative as the deer he has slain."

The trio had been smoking in silence before a huge fire, but this reference to Edward's great exploit of the day roused them to conversation.

"It is no unusual thing for Macleod to distinguish himself in that direction," said Boulton, the elder of the two. "He has long been known as the champion *dear*-killer."

This wretched attempt at a pun was loftily ignored by the subject of it.

"Alas, 'tis too true!" mourned the other. "Come, Ned, try to be entertaining for once; tell us about the pretty Indian girl you were mooning with."

"What did you say?" demanded Edward, freezingly.

"You heard perfectly well what I said."

"What do you mean by it?"

"Oh, I *mean* the pretty squaw you were *spooning* with, if that suits you better."

"Gently, Tom," interposed Boulton parenthetically, "don't mention *all* the meanness you mean."

"I would like to inquire what right you have to mention any of it," exclaimed Edward wrathfully.

"Oh, none--none, whatever. Only it was town talk in Barrie last Fall that you had become infatuated with the sweet little squaw to such an extent that your charming sister, with commendable prudence and foresight, had you put out of harm's way as speedily as possible. There's no accounting for such reports."

"I don't understand it at all," said Edward, with mingled anger and humiliation. "How can people be so silly?"

"Exactly what your slanderers inquired of each other. Impossible to tell what they meant." The young man laughed rather disagreeably as he went off to bed.

"Look here, Ned," said Boulton, bringing a sympathetic hand down upon his friend's shoulder, "don't you take any notice of what Tom Ridout or any of his set may say. Of course every young fellow makes a fool of himself *some time*, in *some* direction; it's natural and proper, and just what is expected of him. All is he shouldn't make a complete fool of himself, and nobody believes that of you."

"Ugh!" said Edward, and relapsed into gloomy silence, from which he awoke to find himself alone, with the candle sputtering in its socket. He took off his boots, and threw one of them viciously, but with unerring aim, at the expiring light, and so went despondently to bed.

"Our fair friend appears to be quite as susceptible to the remarks made upon his wild-wood acquaintance as to the wild-wood acquaintance herself." This was the observation of Ridout, as he and Boulton went the following morning to investigate the trap they had set.

"Don't be a fool, Tom," said Boulton, with a perfectly unruffled face and tone, "that is, any more of one than you can help. Of course every young cub like you is expected to be one to a certain extent, but what I mean is don't be a *big* one."

It was impossible to be angry with words so placidly spoken. "I don't know what can make you so wondrous kind to Macleod," said Ridout, "unless it is a fellow-feeling, and I wouldn't have thought that of you, Boulton. But look here," surveying the empty trap with boyish disgust, "nothing taken in but ourselves! Well, we'll have to make it unpleasant for Tommy. That's the only comfort left us."

Tommy was the coloured boy, who was cook, housekeeper and general factotum for the three. When ill-luck overtook them it was felt to be some slight compensation to be at liberty to make it unpleasant for Tommy. But one day, towards the end of their self-imposed exile, it stormed so heavily and incessantly that they were compelled to remain within doors, and here Tommy's unfailing good-nature deprived the abuse with which he was heaped of all its power to charm and console. On the principle which governs the selection of a victim by the shipwrecked and storm-beaten remnant of a crew at sea, there was nothing more natural than that Edward Macleod should fall a prey to the general famishing desire for amusement. Boulton had been idly humming the air of an Indian love-song, in which Ridout joined aloud, substituting the name of Wanda for that of the ideal heroine. As the sentiment of the song was of the most languorous and 'die-away' sort it was impossible that the two men should abstain from mingling their smiles. The conclusion of the singing was followed by a few remarks from Ridout, one of which provoked a shout of uproarious laughter. For a moment Edward's face was alive with intense suffering; the next it had paled and hardened into marble-like rigidity.

"I wonder if either of you are aware," he said, with cold distinctness of utterance, "that the subject of your conversation is to be my wife."

Tom Ridout stared a moment in unbelieving amazement, and then blushed to the eyes. "I beg your pardon," he stammered, "I never thought--I didn't dream--" He broke down completely, unable to grasp the statement that shed such a different light upon their idle talk. Boulton was not subject to fluctuation of emotion, and there was no visible manifestation of a change in his feelings. The match he struck while Edward was speaking went out. He reached for another; it also went out.

"It seems to me," he said mildly, taking his unlighted pipe from his lips, "that these are the worst matches I ever saw."

Ridout had recovered some of his usual self-assurance. "It seems to *me*," he declared boldly, "that it's the worst match I ever heard of."

"Worst or best," said Edward, with dogged resolution, "it will be necessary for you to speak of it with respect--in my presence."

This seemed to be the end of the matter; but Boulton, who had at last got his pipe agoing, could not forbear offering a few final words on the subject.

"It's all right, Ned," he remarked, in his gentlest and kindest tones, "perfectly right and natural that a young fellow should make a fool of himself. That's exactly what's expected of him. But it isn't necessary that he should make an *everlasting* fool of himself. Not--strictly--necessary."

Edward rose and left the room.

To leave the room in a region upon which unpicturesque prosperity has not yet descended is equivalent to leaving the house, and that is exactly what the young man did. Of course there was a loft above that was reached by a perilously steep pair of stairs; but he was not a cur to creep away into a kennel. He went out and battled with the pitiless storm, a fiercer storm beating within his breast than that which raged without. The crazy words he had just uttered were not spoken simply to stop the idle talk of his companions; they were the ultimate expression of the thoughts over which he had brooded for days past. Helene was dead to him, and her mocking ghost haunted the desolate chambers of his heart, filling them with scornful laughter. But now upon the door of this wretched habitation had timidly knocked another guest--a guest of blooming and throbbing flesh and blood. Should he deny her admittance? Unlearned was she as one of the shy birds of the forest, but then she was eminently teachable. If his love for her could not be called a liberal education was it not something better? Was it not a liberal and lasting joy? After all, what did women know, any way? A few miserable half-learned accomplishments, the aggregate of which did not amount to so much as the eagle's feather on the proud little head of his darling. Yes, he dared to say it--his darling! He pictured her in winter as sitting by his side, before the fire, the delicate head of his pet dog encircled by her arm; in summer they would roam in blest content together through the endless forests of this beautiful new world.

And so with all his doubts triumphantly set aside he returned to the house, and during the remainder of their stay his continued flow of exuberant good spirits seemed to confirm the rightfulness of his conclusions. On his way back to York he stopped a few hours at his old home, for the sake of a brief stolen interview with Wanda. She met him with little low murmurs of tenderness and joy, and parted from him as a girl parts from the man in whose love she has absolute confidence, for whose sake she would willingly die.

When he reached home, his appearance of high health and persistent overflow of liveliness were ascribed by his family to continuous out-door exercise, nor did they dream that the sweet fever and delirium of love was upon him. Rose gave him an anxious glance or two, but poor Rose had trouble enough of her own. That cold night at the Oak Ridges, which had completely killed Edward's hopes with regard to Helene, had cast a light but lasting frost over her own. It had been painful enough to avoid Allan, but it was no less painful to be deprived of that privilege. The truth was he had given her very few opportunities to put into practice the course of treatment recommended by her father. Had she been the heroine of a novel there would inevitably have been misunderstandings of the most serious and complicated character. But she was mortal, and withal a very tender-hearted little maiden, and the secret of her cold tones and wistful glances, though for a while it sorely puzzled Allan, was at last divined by the sure intuition of love. They met frequently at various social gatherings, but it was as though a solid sheet of glass intervened between them. Through this apparently impalpable medium they could see, and smile, and speak, but no tender touch of palm, or breath of love, or thrill of quickened heart-beat could be felt between. How many times had Allan Dunlop been tempted to outstretch his hand and shatter this glassy surface! It were easily done but at the price of possible sharp pain and aching wounds, and the greater horror of seeing the sweet grieving face on the other side shrink away from him, startled by the shock. No, he would bide his time. And so, while his eyes grew hollow, his close shut lips remained very resolute. Love **can** wait (though waiting is the hardest task ever assigned it), but only on condition that it is given the food it needs.

Allan kept his love alive on glimpses of sunny hair, and sad little smiles, and fragments of talk, that, light and conventional as they might seem to chance listeners, were to him clothed with lovely hidden meanings. Sometimes when the eyes met by chance the small warm hands plucked nervously at the flowers she carried, or there was a restless consciousness in step and glance, or a scarcely perceptible quiver of the curved lip, or a piteous droop of the regal little head. Very slight things were these, yet out of them Memory and Imagination made a sumptuous feast, at which Love, like a starveling prince in exile, sat down with never sated appetite.

CHAPTER XIV.
MUDDY LITTLE YORK.

If the course of true love could be persuaded to forsake its ancient uncomfortable method in favour of a single harrassed lover, surely the trials of Allan Dunlop might soften its harsh turbulence, and move it to a gentler flow. Rose was devoted to her father, and the tie between them, made stronger by her mother's death, was not of a nature to be affected by the sighing breath of a mere lover. Then she was as lovable as she was lovely, and there was nothing in the cordial liking of a host of friends to encourage the growth of any morbid desire for the affection of a poor and insignificant outsider. There were other insurmountable points on the mountain chain of circumstance that lay between him and his heart's dearest wish. The Commodore's inherent reverence for birth and breeding, and his comparative indifference to brain, was one of them. The obstinate pride of Allan's undistinguished and ambitious self was another.

Of all sorts of pride the sort that goes with inferiority, not of person, or behaviour, or talents, but of mere social position, is the most inveterate. This unreasonable feeling was the mightiest of all the obstructions that, mountain-like, lay between them; but on its rough sides--flowers on an arid rock--grew the yearning affections, seemingly rootless, yet continuing to bloom in secret, scarce discovered beauty. Of what use was it, he asked himself in bitterness, to brood over these impassable barriers, to cultivate a faith in the power of his own affection strong enough to remove them, to cherish the vain imagination that this incomparably sweet girl and his own plain self were made for each other, and that no earthly obstacle could suffice to separate them? Upon his soul had fallen the edict of society, "What man hath put asunder let no higher power join together!"

And so he hardened his heart and closed his eyes to the heavenly vision of girlish beauty and purity that shone forever in the upper skies of his consciousness, as clear as the star of evening, and almost as far away. But tears flow as easily beneath closed lids as when the eyes are wide open, and to the hardest heart come moments of reverie, of sudden waking from sleep, or involuntary lapsing into day dream, when, like a sword in the heart, comes the thought of one too dearly loved. Do his best he could not escape these moments of exquisite torture. The poem he was reading fell fantastically into the tune of the last waltz down which he and Rose had drifted together. The prose--and very prosy--work he impatiently seized in the hope of banishing that witching melody from his brain, simply followed the perverted feet of the poem. Down the dull page danced the meaningless syllables, keeping time to the delicious strain in a way that was simply appalling to a mind whose intellectual processes were, as a rule, thoroughly well regulated. If he walked the street there was small chance but that some half-turned head or fluttering robe among the women he met would remind him of the sweetest head and prettiest drapery in the world.

Always along the misty aisles of his consciousness sped this little lovely vision, now hasting, now delaying, now bending with melting tenderness toward him, now mockingly eluding his grasp, never out of sight, never within reach. No wonder he grew pale and heavy-eyed and *distrait*. But no one of those who noticed that he ate little and spoke little, and walked with weary footsteps, knew that he was a haunted man--haunted not by any pale spectre, but by veritable flesh and blood, gold crowned, pink tinted, and illumined by the bluest eyes this side of the blue heavens. It is useless for those who are troubled in this way to say they *will not* be haunted. Celestial visits are planned with reference to anything but the convenience of their recipient.

Allan Dunlop was spoken of as 'a pushing young man,' but in affairs of the heart he did not push--he simply waited. Not that he had any faith in the so-called beneficent influences of time--for what young lover is willing to believe that the slow drag of months and years over his passion will crush all life from it at last?--but he had the delicacy of nature which forbids the gross intrusion of personal wishes and desires upon unwilling ears. He had, besides, a spark of that old-world loyalty which is prone to uphold the claim of the father in the face of despairing aspirants for the daughter's hand.

This unwillingness to take an advantage, or to push it when it was thrust upon him, was not without a certain allurement for Rose. She was accustomed to be sought after; but the man who unconsciously occupied a higher place in her estimation than any by whom she was surrounded, held himself aloof. Probably he despised her and the frivolous society in which she moved. It was a depressing reflection, for the regard of those whom we believe to be our superiors is infinitely more precious than the adoration of those who are not.

To the lover, as to the good general, the knowledge of when not to approach is of inestimable importance. Scarce are the girls upon whose hearts a tender impression can be made in the middle of an ordinary work-a-day forenoon, or who can give sigh for sigh immediately after a hearty dinner. Very few are those who, at all times, are equally approachable and appreciative. Allan's stern, self-denying course of action, to which he considered himself forced, could not have been better chosen had he had nothing at heart but the aim of furthering his own interests. In Rose's imagination he had always formed an admirable contrast to the purposeless, objectless young men of her acquaintance, and his wise withdrawal after he had roused her interest, she interpreted as indifference. So let it be, thought the young lady, assuming a feeling of entire content. But assumed feelings are not lasting. She who had been the life of society now grew very weary of it. She yawned secretly in rooms of entertainment, or invented lame excuses for her non-appearance there. "I can't think what is the matter with me," she said to herself. "I never cared for solitude, and I don't now; but I care less for common people and commonplace talk."

It was perfectly consistent with this state of feeling that, on one of the most disagreeable of all disagreeable March days, she should go out alone for a long walk which had no definite direction nor object. There was a certain satisfaction in matching her restless mood with the restless weather, in feeling herself now gently buoyed along, now almost lifted up and borne away on the strong wings of the rushing wind. Great soft flakes of snow were falling, and yielding up their heavenly purity at the first touch of earth, and the dull sunless day, weary of its own existence, was with seeming relief dying into night. Rose walked very fast without being aware of the fact. It is a peculiarity of windy weather that it begets a mental exaltation, in which even the clumsiest body seems to partake of the immortal energy of the soul. Rose's trim figure moved as softly and swiftly as a sail-boat before the wind. Nevertheless it was with a feeling of dismay that she found herself at the edge of night and far from home. She had been dreaming as she walked, and now--the usual fate of dreamers--she found herself abruptly brought face to face with reality. The big flakes were still falling, the wind still urging her forward, as she turned to retrace her steps. But now progress became difficult. The wind was in her face, and the snow blinded her eyes. She had turned so suddenly that the broad-shouldered, heavily-coated young pedestrian, who had been following in her wake, was astounded to see her, with down-bent head, swiftly advance and abruptly fling herself upon him with an impetuosity born of sightless but determined resistance to the rampant breezes. The next instant, with a movement equally impetuous, and a deeply drawn "oh!" she swept aside and looked straight into the eyes of Allan Dunlop. "I didn't know it was you," she murmured, her cheeks turning to flame beneath his gaze.

"No, you usually treat me with more *hauteur*. I never expected you to make all the advances in this way."

"Oh, shameless!" exclaimed Rose, clasping both daintily gloved hands first to her ears, then to her eyes. Then, mockingly, she responded, "I never expected to find you so approachable."

They were very glad to meet again. They did not say so, but what necessity existed for the verbal expression of a fact so apparent in the face looking down and in the face that for more than a moment at a time was unable to look up. She laid her hand within his arm, and they faced the storm together. "What were you doing at this end of the town?" she asked, fearing he would make the same inquiry of her.

"Following in your footsteps," he replied. "I was not sure who it was, but your gait reminded me so much of yourself."

What light words to make a little heart beat faster! The wind would have blown them away if she had not caught them.

"Ah, yes, no doubt a moving spectacle, but," glancing at the rough pavement which had grown worse and worse, until in pure self pity it came to an end, "I'm afraid that for the last half-hour I have led you a hard life of it."

"It was hard--very. This side-walk is a disgrace to the town, and it usually has a depressing effect on me to be out in windy, uncertain kind of weather, but I think"--the wind blew an end of her long silken scarf caressingly about his neck--"I think it was worth while."

In his heart he added, "Little darling, what rough road would I not travel in pursuit of you, if only you would turn at last to throw yourself in my arms."

They walked on for a little in silence. When love looks out of the eyes, and hesitates on the lips, and trembles in the arm that feels the confiding pressure of a tiny hand, it seems as though words were a crude, primitive method of communicating ideas. Nevertheless, so strong is the power of habit, that there are few who can resist the imagined necessity to talk if one feels like it, and make talk if one does not. So presently Rose remarked upon the beauty of the town. Even in his love wrapt state the idea struck Allan as slightly absurd.

"Where do you find it?" he asked in amused perplexity, looking at the little wooden houses and shops, the meagre beginnings of a city that as yet had no time to be beautiful, and noted the vile mud with which the streets were thickly overlaid. "Though, of course," he added, "there is scarcely anything to be seen save darkness, and that element is strictly necessary to an appreciation of the beauties of 'Muddy Little York.'"

"Oh," exclaimed Rose, "don't you see the lights flashing in the windows, and in every little muddy pool on the street? Think of the concentrated life in these little human nests set against the vast wilderness. Look at those faint yellow rays mingling with the slanting lines of snow, with the deep woods and dark sky in the distance. If it isn't beauty it is poetry."

Her foot slipped a little on an unexpected piece of ice, and his arm felt the momentary pressure of both hands. "It is everything heavenly you can mention," said Allan devoutly.

He noticed the slight instantaneous withdrawal, and was impelled to be practical, if possible; so he began to dilate at length upon the future glories of York. "This will be a great city, some day," he said.

"Possibly, but who loves greatness? People may say what they please against muddy little York. To me it is dear because it is so little."

"Yes, there is an unexplainable charm in littleness." He glanced thoughtfully down at the dainty figure beside him, while Rose wondered if it would be possible for her to make a remark to which he could not give a personal application. It was impossible for them to walk on in silence, as though this were a lover's idle stroll. Her face warmed at the mere fancy. No, she must e'en try again.

"Particularly when it is a little breeze," she said. "Now, a huge, awkward, overgrown affair like this changes what ought to be a caress into an assault."

"Yes; but you brave little creature, how blithely you face it. I wish I could shelter you from the storm. I wish I could defend you from all the storms of life."

His voice broke, and the girl felt as though her heart would burst. No bold, imperious, master spirit was this, demanding her love and life as if they were his by natural right. It was as though she had been newly roused by a faint knock at the door; and now, before her foot was set upon the stair that led down to the entering guest, he had turned away again.

"I like your way of meeting the tempest," he continued. "You face it for a moment with mocking defiance, then you step aside to escape a fierce gust, or turn your head to avoid at least half its violence. You seem to be coquetting with old Boreas. For me, I can't play with the foe; I simply have to meet him and fight him till my strength is exhausted--then rest till I can get breath--then up and at it again. Do you remember those old lines:

"'A little I'me hurt but not yett slaine,   I'le but lye down and bleed awhile, And then I'le rise and fight againe!'"

"Oh, heaven help me," thought poor Rose, "what **can** I say now? There is nothing in the world to say." She fell to crying bitterly, as she safely could under cover of the snow and the darkness; but after a minute she controlled herself, and was, to outward appearance, tranquil and buoyant as before.

They had reached the house. He stepped inside the warmly-lighted hall just for a moment, as Rose, with a gesture of dismay, threw off her wraps, and disclosed an inappropriately elaborate little gown, partially soaked by the storm. "I suppose I need not have put on anything so fine as this to go out in on a wet day, but I am fond of dressing, not for others, but for myself. I prefer feeling effects to producing them. Do you think me very selfish?"

"Oh, yes; everything that is hard, unfeeling, and unlike your sweet little self."

She had already mounted a few steps of the stairway, as he had said he could not stay. His outstretched hand held hers in a last good-by, but instead of going he touched a fold of the damp edge of her gown. "It is very wet," he said. "You are shockingly careless." And then, without daring to meet the divine eyes bent upon him, he lifted her hand reverently to his lips, and so went forth into the night and the storm.

"Rose," said the Commodore, interrupting her at the head of the stairs, "who is it that has just gone?"

"Mr. Dunlop," said his daughter hesitatingly; "he overtook--he met--I met him on my way home, and he came with me." The young girl's face was a flame, and her heart was a song. She felt that she was aggressively, barbarously happy, and tried to modify the unruly emotion out of deference to her father's anticipated anger. He looked extremely annoyed.

"I am sorry to seem arbitrary," he said, "but in future, my dear, it will greatly oblige me if you will so conduct yourself towards that young man as to discourage him from meeting or overtaking you, or accompanying you home."

"Very well, Papa." Not a ray of light faded from her eyes, not a particle of warmth from her smile. She had heard him make similar remarks before, and they affected her the same as if he had said: "It is yet winter; don't be deceived into supposing that spring-time is coming." Ah! but under the snows of winter, what power can hinder the countless delicate roots of spring flowers from thrilling into life?

CHAPTER XV.
POLITICS AT THE CAPITAL.

But more was destined to burgeon into blossom than the flowers of spring. Allan Dunlop's fame as a politician had grown concurrently with the growth of his love. In the Legislature he had won for himself a prominent position, and was known as a sagacious counsellor, a persuasive speaker, a ready and effective debater, and a good steady worker on Committees. No name carried more weight in Parliament than his, and his influence in the country was as marked as was his influence in the House. This was as readily conceded by his political opponents as it was claimed by his friends. He had, moreover, a prepossessing manner, a comely presence, and a countenance which, when animated, was not wanting in expression or fire. He was, withal, the most modest and lovable of men; and had he not sat on the Opposition benches he would have been courted by the Tory supporters of the Government and been fawned upon by the leading members of "The Family Compact."

Allan Dunlop had, however, entered the House as a radical, but of a moderate type; and though he dealt the Executive many trenchant blows, and did yeoman service in advancing the cause of Reform, he was too loyal a man to rank with the "heated enthusiasts" who were threatening to overturn the Constitution and make a republic out of the colony, and too judicious and right-minded to affirm that the Administration of the Province was wholly evil and corrupt. On the contrary, while he insisted that the Executive should pay more deference to the voice of the Parliamentary majority, and so avoid the ever-cropping-up conflicts between the Administration and the popular Chamber, he recognized the fact that the evils complained of had their origin in defects in the Act which gave the Province its Constitution; and being engrained in the paternal system of government that had long been in vogue could not possibly be at once and satisfactorily remedied.

It was true that in none of the other Provinces was power so firmly centralized in the hands of a dominant and exclusive class, as was the case in Upper Canada. But this state of things, Allan Dunlop conceded, was a legacy from the period of military rule which followed the Conquest, and the natural consequence of appointing members to seats in the Executive and Legislative Councils *for life*. Dunlop was also well aware that the social condition of the Province, at that early period, tended to centre power and authority of necessity in the hands of a few leading men. All the public offices were in their gift; and the entire public domain, including the Crown and Clergy Land reserves, was also in their hands. Hence it was that through the patronage at their disposal the "Family Compact" were enabled to fill the Lower House with their supporters and adherents, and, in large measure, to shape the Provincial Legislation, so as to maintain their hold of office and perpetuate a monopoly of power. That the ruling oligarchy used their positions autocratically, and kept a heavy hand upon the turbulent and disaffected, was true; but their respect for British institutions, and their staunch loyalty to the Crown, at a time when republican sentiments were dangerously prevalent, were virtues which might well offset innumerable misdeeds, and square the account in any unprejudiced arraignment.

But though Allan Dunlop possessed a mind eminently fair and judicial, and, Reformer as he was, could dispassionately discuss the "burning questions" of the time, there were abuses connected with the mode of governing which he stoutly strove to remedy, and injustice done to loyal settlers in the iniquitous land system that prevailed which roused his indignation and called forth many a bitter phillipic in the House. These trenchant attacks of the young land-surveyor were greatly feared by the Executive, and were the cause of much trepidation and uneasiness in the Legislative Council.

For a time Commodore Macleod, who had now returned to his accustomed duties in the Upper House, took pleasure in replying to Dunlop's attacks in the Lower Chamber; but the young Parliamentarian, though he treated his opponent with courtly deference, had so effective a way of demolishing the Commodore's arguments and of genially turning the shafts of his invective upon his adversary, that he soon abandoned the attempt to break a lance with his young and able antagonist. Dunlop's temper was habitually sweet and always under command, and this gave him a great advantage over his sometimes irascible opponents. His manner, however, was at times fiery--especially when exposing cases of hardship and injustice, when his arraignment of the Executive was vehement and uncompromising. But the "Family Compact" was at the period too firmly entrenched and buttressed about by patronage for Allan Dunlop to effect much reform in the system of government, though his assaults were keenly felt in the Upper House, and they made a powerful impression in the country, which heartily endorsed the young land-surveyor's strenuous appeals for the redress of long-existing abuses, and the concession of Responsible Government.

"What a noble fellow that young Dunlop is!" said Lady Sarah Maitland to her escort in the House, as the youthful tribune closed an impassioned appeal on behalf of settlers from the United States, who had been subjected to great hardships and outrage by the tools of the Government.

"A pestilent rascal!" was the testy rejoinder of the old Commodore, who, with his daughter Rose, had accompanied her Ladyship on the day in question to the House of Assembly.

"Nay! you shall not say that of him, Commodore, for I mean to invite him to accompany us to Stamford Cottage at the close of the Session, if he will give me that pleasure," said Lady Sarah, warmly.

"Sir Peregrine will have something to say to that, Madame," was the Commodore's blunt reply, "and Mr. Attorney-General, here," he added, "ought to arrest you for wishing to consort with seditious agitators and evil-disposed persons."

"I think I ought to take you both into custody," interposed Attorney-General Robinson, "for spoiling with your quarrel the effect of young Dunlop's speech. It was admirable, both in tone and matter, and I shall at once look into the grievances he complained of. Don't you think, Miss Macleod, that your father is unreasonably prejudiced against the member for your section of the Home District?"

"I think him everything harsh and unpaternal when politics is the subject of conversation," replied that young lady guardedly.

"Ah! politics is an unclean game," observed the courtly leader of the House; "but it would be vastly sweeter and cleaner were all our politicians of the type of Dunlop. I think him a grand fellow--but, I agree with you, Commodore, that he should be on the other side."

"Or we should be on *his* side, Mr. Attorney-General," said Lady Sarah, with a meaning glance at Rose Macleod.

At this juncture, the Attorney-General, having to address the House, took leave of the ladies, and the Government House party rose and left the Chamber.

Later in the day, the Attorney-General took occasion to refer to Dunlop's speech, and to commend its temperate and courteous tone, though the matter his young friend brought to the notice of the Government, said the Attorney-General, if true, severely reflected on the management of one of the Departments, which, the speaker added, he would take care at once to inquire into.

Other matters occupied the attention of the House for the remainder of the afternoon, and when the Speaker rose to retire a buzz of conversation ensued on the stirring topics to be brought up at the evening's sitting. Two of these topics related to matters which, at the period, convulsed the community, and threatened to overthrow the fabric of society in the colony, if not the Constitution itself. One was the case of Captain Matthews, a member of the Assembly, who was charged with disturbing the tranquillity of the Province by requesting the orchestra, at the theatre of York, to play sundry seditious tunes at the close of an entertainment, and thus inferentially to pay disrespect to His Majesty's crown and person. The other was the escapade of a number of young people in York, of respectable standing, who had committed a gross breach of the peace in breaking into and ransacking the printing-office of Wm. Lyon Mackenzie, smashing the presses of that martyr to Reform, and throwing into the lake the type which had been used in setting up some pungent articles against the Government.

"Behold how great a matter a little fire kindleth!" the moralizing bystander of the period might have observed, as he took note of the electrical condition of the political atmosphere of York, and, indeed, of the whole Province--the result of the indiscretion of one man, and the partisan frolic of half a dozen lads, who had inherited, with the bluest of Tory blood, the prejudices of their fathers. The wrecking of the Mackenzie printing-office was, of course, a serious conspiracy against the peace of a youthful and law-abiding community. But it will occur to the modern reader of the transaction, that the act was scarcely so heinous as to bring it before the country's legislature, and become the subject of a grave Parliamentary inquiry.

The act has to be viewed, however, in the light of preceding events, and with a knowledge of facts in the thrilling drama of Reform, at the time being enacted on the political stage of Upper Canada. Society in the Province was long wont to poise itself between two opinions, as to the degree of justification for the course which Reform took at the time of the Gourlay agitation, and which, in Mackenzie's day, culminated in rebellion. The issues of the conflict have, however, settled that point; and though Tory bias loves still to stand by the "Family Compact," the popular sympathies are with the actors who were whilom outlawed, and on whose heads the Crown did them the honour, for a time, to set a high value.

Chief among these actors, at the time of which we are writing, was he whose printing-presses had just been ruthlessly demolished, and whose fonts of type youthful Torydom had gleefully consigned to the deep. The provocation had been a long series of intemperate newspaper criticism of the Government, numerous inflammatory appeals to the people to rise against constituted authority, and much scurrilous abuse of leading members of the "Family Compact," who wished, as a safeguard against revolution and chaos, to crush the "patriot" Mackenzie, and drive him from the Province. But though thorny as was then the path of Reform, and galling the insult and injury done to its martyrs, Mackenzie did not shrink from pursuing the course he had cut out for himself; and his intense hatred of injustice, and sturdy defiance of those whom he held responsible for the maladministration of affairs, gained him many adherents and sympathizers. The outrage that had just been committed on his property vastly increased the number of the latter, while popular indignation compelled the Government to disown the act, and to make it, as we have seen, the subject of Parliamentary inquiry. From the Parliament the matter went to the Courts, and there the scapegraces, who had been concerned in the outrage, were mulcted in a large amount, which their parents, high government officials, had ruefully to pay over to the aggrieved printer and incipient rebel. Thus ended one act in the drama of these distraught times. How shall we keep our countenance and deal with the other?

Let us first tell the story, as we gather it, in the main, from the Journals of the House. For some time previous to the meeting of the Legislature, in 1826, partisans of the Administration had got in the habit of noting defections from the loyal side among men of substance and position in the colony, and particularly among members of the representative Chamber, where the cry for Responsible Government was waxing loud, and where sullen protests were almost daily heard against the system of official patronage and favouritism that prevailed in the government of the Province. The Administration being now in the minority in the popular Chamber, and "the long shadows of Canadian Radicalism" having begun to settle upon the troubled "Family Compact," it became important to note the increasing defections, real or fancied, in the Legislative Assembly, so that, if possible, the "bolters" might be coaxed or bribed back, or, failing that, that they might, in some way, be jockeyed out of the House and made to suffer for their defection. Among those who had recently taken the bit in their teeth was a Captain Matthews, a retired officer, in receipt of a pension, who represented the county of Middlesex, and had of late gone over to Democracy. For this act he was "put upon the list," and became a marked man on the mental tablets of the myrmidons of the Executive.

About this time there came to York a company of strolling actors from the neighbouring Republic, whose fortunes were at a low ebb, and whose dignity had very much run down at the heels. To revive their fortunes, they gave an entertainment in the extemporized theatre of the town, under the kindly proffered patronage of the members of the Legislature. It was New Year's Eve, and the fun--the age was still a bibulous one--waxed fast and furious. At last the curtain dropped, and the modest orchestra struck up "God save the king!" Hats were at once doffed, and from among the standing audience came a loud but unsteady voice, calling upon the orchestra to "play up" Hail Columbia! or Yankee Doodle.

The sober section of the play-house was stunned. Was it possible that Democracy could go to such lengths--within sight of the "royal arms," over the Lieutenant-Governor's box, and with the decaying notes of the national anthem in Tory ears?

It was but too true. Again and again rose the shout for the seditious tunes. Abashed loyalty sought to escape from the house, but the crowd jostled and intervened. The scene now became uproarious. Affrighted Conservatives were seen to jam their hats on their heads--the only mark of disapproval possible--and glare defiance at those who impeded the exit. The Tory member for Stormont--it was afterwards admitted in evidence--stripped his coat and threatened to knock any two of the opposing Radicals down. Meanwhile the orchestra, unable to accomplish the higher flight of "Hail Columbia!" struck up the commoner and more objectionable tune; and three grave legislators, it is said, danced while "Yankee Doodle" was played. The Democratic orgie at last spent itself with the music, and after a while all breathed the outer, communistic air of heaven.

After the racket comes the reckoning; and Captain Matthews, whose share in inducing the play-house fiddlers to discourse republican music to monarchical ears was reported with due exaggerations and aspersions on his loyalty, to the military authorities, speedily found himself the victim of an infamous plot. Distorted accounts of the scene at the theatre had been sent to the Commander of the Forces, at Quebec; and the member for Middlesex was specially singled out as the seditious rioter on the occasion, and the leader in what was termed "a disloyal and disgraceful affair." Presently there came an order for Capt. Matthews to report himself to the military authorities at Quebec, and at that port to take ship for England, where he was to be tried by court-martial. To enable him to obey the summons it was first necessary to obtain leave of absence from the Legislature; and the motion that was to come up in the Assembly that evening, was, whether the House, on the evidence before it, would agree to release the incriminated officer from his Parliamentary duties so as to face the frivolous charge at the "Horse-Guards" in London.

The discussion opened by the presentation to the House of the report of the Committee of Inquiry that had sat upon the matter--a report which exonerated Captain Matthews from the charge preferred against him, and relieved him from the scandalous accusation of disloyalty. The report closed with a protest against the tendency, on the part of the Government, to resort to espionage and inquisitorial measures, in endeavouring to rid the Province of those obnoxious to the ruling faction, and in attempting to undermine the independence of the Legislature by scandalizing its members and awing them into political subserviency. The conviction was reiterated that there was no ground for the charge against Captain Matthews, the malignity and falsity of which was due to political hostility to that gentleman.

A lively debate ensued on the motion to receive the report, members of the Government fiercely objecting to its reception by the House, and the Opposition as warmly insisting on its acceptance. The temper of the Government was not improved when young Dunlop rose, and, in a few quiet and well-chosen words, asserted the right of Parliament to protect its members from officious military arraignment on frivolous and vexatious pretexts. It was the duty of the Government, remarked the young tribune, to calm, not to augment, the fever of popular excitement by acts of an arbitrary and autocratic character,--such as instigating ridiculous prosecutions, and casting doubt on the loyalty of men who had long and faithfully served the Crown, and whose only fault was to set their country above their party.

That the existence of Upper Canada as a colony of the Crown--Dunlop continued--was imperiled by paying some exigent actors from the other side of the line the compliment of calling for a national air dear to republican hearts and ears, he did not for a moment believe. He was, at the same time, he affirmed, keenly sensitive to the beguiling effects of enlivening music, and--falling into a lighter vein--he confessed that he did not know what might be the consequence if the members of the Government organized themselves into a well-trained minstrel troupe and entered the neighbouring Republic singing the pathetic airs of the Old Dominion, artfully interspersed with the soul-stirring strains of the "British Grenadiers" and "Rule Britannia." He thought, moreover, that if the grave and reverend seigniors of the "Family Compact" would blacken their faces as they had blackened their hearts, and "star" it through the lowly hamlets of the Province, singing, say, the Jacobite airs of a previous generation, it would do more to cement the attachment of Canada to the Crown than all the efforts of the combined army of officials, placemen, and henchmen of the Government *plus* the Judges, the Sheriffs, the Recorder, the Incumbents of fat Clergy Reserves, the Gauge's, Tollmen, Hangmen, Customs Officers, Turnkeys, and Landing-Waiters.

Seriously, Allan Dunlop added,--and he had no apology to make for indulging in levity in discussing this frivolous matter--it was beneath the dignity of the House to occupy itself with the further consideration of the charges against the honourable member for Middlesex. These charges were so trivial and ill-founded, and they originated in such a trumpery fear lest the Crown should suffer indignity where indignity was in no wise offered to it, that he begged the House to dismiss the matter forthwith and refuse Captain Matthews leave to absent himself from his Parliamentary duties. After a scattering fusilade of small talk from both sides of the House, the report of the Committee was received, leave was refused, and the disturbing question was laid at rest.

Those who have followed, it may be with interest, this veracious piece of history, and are curious to learn the fate of the honourable member for Middlesex, will find the story graphically told in Mr. Dent's "Canadian Rebellion," Vol. I., chap.

6. The authors take the liberty of appending Mr. Dent's closing paragraph: "But though Captain Matthews," says the historian, "had been cleared by the Legislature, he had still to run the gauntlet of the military inquisition. They could not compel his attendance during the existence of the Parliament then in being, but they possessed an effectual means of reducing him to ultimate submission. This power they exercised; his pension was stopped--a very serious matter to a man with a large family and many responsibilities. He continued to fight the battles of Reform with dogged courage and pertinacity as long as his means admitted of his doing so, but he was soon reduced to a condition of great pecuniary distress, and was compelled to succumb. Broken-hearted and worn out, he resigned his seat in the Assembly, and returned to England, where, after grievous delay, he succeeded in getting his pension restored. He never returned to Canada, and survived the restoration of his pension but a short time. Thus, through the malignity of a selfish and secret cabal, was Upper Canada deprived of the services of a zealous and useful citizen and legislator, whose residence among us, had it been continued, could not have failed to advance the cause of freedom and justice."

CHAPTER XVI.
LOVE'S PROTESTATIONS.

During the rest of the dreary winter the memory of that enchanted walk through mire and darkness and driving snow, kept two hearts--Rose's and Allan's--fully awake. A pity, too; for sleep covers a multitude of sufferings, and when the most impressible part of our being is wrapped in unconsciousness, we can make shift to go through the world with only an endurable number of the usual aches and ailments. If these young hearts had ever really slumbered since their owners met for the first time, less than a year before, it had been rather an uneasy repose; and now that they were fully awake, it was to find not the glory of the dawn, but a dark bleak day, whose beginning could scarcely be distinguished from the night out of which it emerged, whose end was so far--so drearily far away. Things went on as before in their old monotonous manner. Winter relented into spring, and the intimacy that had warmed almost into acknowledged love that wild March evening had apparently died of its own intensity. Rose and Allan met occasionally, but with mutual avoidance; she from innate loyalty to her father--he from a pride that was too strong to plead. So the endless conflict went on, but not alone in the minds of the lovers.

The doughty Commodore was daily suffering in his own person the just punishment, which is but too apt to overtake the man, who in a point of difference with a woman ends by having his own way. This stern parent liked to think of himself as generous, compassionate, and tender-hearted; and he had been grievously cheated out of this agreeable sensation. His daughter's absolute and sweet-natured loyalty to his will sharpened his sense of deprivation. Was it possible that he was unnatural and tyrannical? The answer to this question was what Rose's pale cheeks seemed to require of him, and he chafed under the mute, unconscious, persistent repetition of the query. He recommended her to take long walks, but she came back from them paler and more lifeless than before. He began to see that it was possible to gain one's own point and lose something infinitely more precious. It hurt him to see her suffer, and he despised himself as the suspected cause of her sufferings. He asked himself how he could have endured it if, in his courting days, he had been shut out from the woman he loved. She was infinitely his superior, he thought with a swelling heart, and then his arm fell on the back of the chair beside him, and his hand clenched, as he grimly wondered what bolts or bars would suffice to have kept them apart. If she was alive now would she have taken this cruelly peremptory course with their daughter? He revolved the question with a sore heart. It admitted of but one answer. In all her sweet and gentle life his wife had never been either peremptory or cruel.

Unknown to Rose her father's stout heart showed signs of thawing with the weather. He began to inform himself warily, and by indirect means, with regard to the character, circumstances, and prospects of Allan Dunlop, in much the same way as we make a study of the drug, hitherto supposed to be a poison, but now believed capable of saving the life of a loved one. In his present mood of despondency and anxiety it seemed that every fresh fact that he learned served to raise Allan and lower himself in his own estimation. It is difficult to atone for a wrong so delicate that one shrinks from expressing it in words, and yet the need of making at least one attempt at reparation was pressing sorely upon him.

So it was with almost a girlish bound of the heart that the Commodore read aloud, one morning, in all the polysyllabic glory of newspaper English, an account of the heroic way in which a young child was saved from drowning by the prompt and daring action of Allan Dunlop. It was an opportunity for praising his enemy, and the worthy gentleman was almost as relieved and happy as the rescued child. "Upon my word, Rose," he said, turning to the silent girl at the other end of the breakfast table, "that young Dunlop is a much finer fellow than I supposed him to be."

"Yes, Papa," she assented meagrely. She had no idea of undoing the work of weeks--the work of steeling herself against the sweetness of recollection--by too warm an interest in the subject.

"The idea of a child paddling about alone in a boat during that horrible storm," continued the Commodore, more impatient, if the truth were known, with his daughter's lukewarmness than with the waifs recklessness. "Not one man in a thousand," he continued abruptly, "would have ventured out on Lake Ontario in that raging tempest."

"People of plebeian origin usually have a well-developed muscular system," remarked Rose.

"But they are not fond of risking their life in the interest of their muscles," returned the gentleman, annoyed at the girl's obstinacy, nor dreaming how sweet from his lips sounded his praise of her lover.

"It depends upon what their life is worth. Common folks, who suffer under the well-merited contempt of their social superiors, must grow at last to despise what better educated people know to be despicable."

"No doubt, it is as you say," replied her father. He was thoroughly irritated, and all his benevolent notions took flight, as they are apt to do when the object of our philanthropy proves perverse. "I was about to suggest that you invite him to your party to-morrow night; but in the present state of feeling perhaps it would be better not."

"I haven't the least idea that he would come," returned the girl. "He isn't the sort of person to allow himself to be taken up and dropped at random."

"Well, settle it to suit yourself," he concluded. She reflected bitterly that this privilege came when it was too late. Nevertheless, she was grateful for it, and scolded herself soundly for giving her father undutiful replies. She also remarked in the solitude of her own room that she did not care a particle whether Allan came or not, and then with a fluttering heart she wrote him a note of invitation. When Tredway was requested to deliver it that ancient servitor manifested so much interest in his errand that the blue eyes of his young mistress lingered on him a moment in surprise.

"I am under very great obligations to Mr. Dunlop," he said. "I may say that I owe my life to him?"

"You, too!" laughed the girl. "Why it was only the other day that he rescued a strange child from the wild waves."

"He rescued me from the wild woods," said the man, with the impressiveness of one who wishes to celebrate the most remarkable escape on record. Tredway had a profound objection to the woods. In the previous summer he had, with great reluctance, served as commissary general to a party of young men, who went in pursuit of a week's sport to Burlington Bay. Edward and Allan were of the number, and when Tredway was lost on a little expedition of his own, to the nearest shanty in quest of provisions, it was Allan who went in search of him, and after some difficulty brought him back to camp. The event had been a source of some amusement to the rest; but to the mind of its hero it had lost nothing of its tragic aspect. "The woods are very confusing to a person of my life and habits," he observed deprecatingly.

"Oh, yes, indeed," returned Rose, "and so very different from England."

The gratitude with which Tredway listened to this remark was not unmixed with regret that the tone in which it was uttered was sportive rather than serious. He was consoled, however, by the reflection that national differences could not be expected to oppress the heart of unthinking youth as it did that of sad maturity.

The unreasoning joy that flamed in Allan Dunlop's face, as he glanced over the dainty note, faded into ashen paleness as he remembered what its response must be. "Sit down, Tredway," he said mechanically, "I will have an answer ready in a moment." Grateful to be relieved of the pains of indecision by the necessity for prompt action he took up a pen and wrote rapidly:

"DEAR MISS MACLEOD:

It is very hard for me to refuse your kind invitation to be with you to-morrow night, but it is impossible to accept it. If I were invited to Paradise, 'for one night only,' with the knowledge that I must forego my share of its delights thenceforth, I should wish to return the same answer. Have I no right to hint that your presence is my Paradise? Forgive me for it, and for my rudeness and perverseness, which all arises out of my consuming and indestructible love for you. The only thing I can say that can condone this offence is that I never cease trying to destroy your image in my heart. So far the results are extremely discouraging; but I cannot resign the hope that Time, the great healer, may also prove, like other notable physicians, the great destroyer. Ah! what am I saying? I can never say enough to you, and yet already I have said too much. God bless the sweet ruler of my life and heart forever, and grant that every ill that threatens her may fall instead upon the head of her unworthy lover.

Will you not write me a word of forgiveness for resisting the temptation to go to you?

Ever your worshipper,

ALLAN DUNLOP."

He ended with a strange feeling of the incongruity of this declaration of passion with his surroundings, the stuffy unhomelike chambers on King Street, and the rather severe presence of a man, whose existence emphasized all the hated social distinction that never weighed so heavily on him as at present. This rigorous representative of his class took the message delivered to him, and stood for a moment hesitatingly in the doorway.

"Your people are quite well, I hope, Tredway," said Allan.

"Yes, sir, thank you. Quite well, with the exception of Miss Rose. She is looking badly."

"I am very sorry. I made no inquiries about her, because, since her accident last summer, she has never been otherwise than well. I wish," and his tones were sad and sincere as his meaning, "that I could do something for her."

"Thank you, sir. It is taking a great liberty to say so, but your visits are so infrequent that I believe Miss Rose is under the impression that you did not greatly care."

"Oh, I *care* enough, quite enough," he added mentally. "The fact is there is danger of my caring too much, and nobody knows better than you, Tredway, that

that would be the greatest piece of folly I could perpetrate. Miss Rose is vastly my social superior."

The old man bowed his head as though this were too obvious a truth to need comment. Then he said encouragingly:

"Ah, there is nothing but the remains of their former greatness left to the Macleods. They are growing more and more **bourgeois** since coming to this degenerate country.

"Yes, I imagine that their family dignity, in such times as these, may be a little out of repair; but I can hardly venture to build vain hopes on the ruins. You are a good fellow, Tredway; good-bye!"

A few days later the coveted answer to his missive came.

"DEAR MR. DUNLOP:

Since I am to see you no more it seems unnecessary if not unkind of me to write and prolong the pain of parting. But if you were dying, and should tell me with nearly your latest breath what you wrote in your letter, I should want you to know that the confession was dear and sacred to me--something I should remember all the rest of my life.

I am not willing to believe that your future will be wholly bereft of consolation. One who is capable of imperiling his life to save that of an unknown child ought to know that he can never find any better company than his own. But you need never be lonely; I hear your name and career frequently spoken of with warm appreciation by your friends, among whom I hope you will always number

Yours very sincerely,

ROSE MACLEOD."

"Ah!" ejaculated Allan, as he read and re-read this brief epistle, "she does not despise my love, but she recognizes its hopelessness." With the usual bluntness of masculine perception he failed to see that it was impossible for her to ignore what he himself was accustomed to dwell upon at such dreary length. If he was profoundly convinced that there was no hope, she could scarcely condescend to suggest that there might be a glimmer. So the young man continued to be wrapped in the darkness which was largely born of his own imagination.

"What rank," he wrote, in immediate response, "shall I assign you among my friends? One's friend may be simply an acquaintance of long standing, who cherishes no special animosity toward one, or it may be the stranger of a year ago, who now is knit into the very fibre of one's being. Just so closely woven with my inmost self have you grown, dear, and to put the thought of you away from me is like putting my own eyes from me. Do you think I can be trusted as a friend? I foresee that I shall be the most faithless one ever known, for I have never been your friend, and I don't know how to begin to be one, whereas I have had nearly a year's experience in loving you. But I am jesting with a sore heart. It is strange that I can jest at all; and yet I know that I am richer and happier in owning the smallest corner of your heart, than if I possessed the whole of any other woman's."

He wrote a great deal more of the same sort, by turns light, fanciful, woful or desperate. But all this Rose ignored. "I am very glad," she wrote demurely, "that you are rich and happy on such insufficient grounds. I could scarcely deny a corner of my heart to any of my friends, but the rest of them are well enough acquainted with me to know that the possession is not a source of unmixed joy. This illusion of yours must be destroyed, and, as you will see, my share of this correspondence is going to tend gently but inexorably towards that end. I still cherish hopes of retaining your friendship. It is so much more difficult for a man to be a woman's friend than it is for him to be by turns her worshipper and oppressor--and you are made to conquer difficult things, and be made stronger by them. You have admirable qualities--self-forgetfulness, lofty purpose, a will that never falters, a heart that never faints. I discovered all these before I received your letters. Otherwise, do you think I would have discovered them at all?"

Thus preached this adorable little high-priest of heroic self-denial, and when she had made an end she burst into tears, and wished that Allan were there to wipe them away.

CHAPTER XVII.
A PICNIC IV THE WOODS.

Winter had passed, and in hot haste--literal hot haste--the time of the singing of birds had come. It was early in the season when the Macleods returned to their summer home, but "lily-footed spring" was there before them. Earth, air, and sky were bathed in a glory of sunlight, which strove to penetrate the dark labyrinth of the pines through which the wind sang. The bay was embowered in gleaming foliage. In its clear waters the Indians plunged or paddled, or lay in attitudes picturesquely inert upon its shores. Above it in graceful curves the unwearying gulls were sinking, rising, and wheeling aloft.

On one of these halcyon days of early summer Rose Macleod was re-reading a letter from her friend Helene; which, though a mere elegant scrawl in the first place, and now yellow and worn with age, has been with some difficulty deciphered by the writers of this veracious history.

"We shall return to Bellevue next week," she wrote, "though what possible benefit can accrue from our returning I cannot pretend to say. Either home is distasteful to me; so is the rest of the world; so are the people in it. Enviable condition, is it not? I seem to be afflicted with a sort of dreadful mental indigestion. Everything I see and hear and read disagrees with me, so I suppose it is only a natural consequence that I should be disagreeable. Oh, dear, dear! What is the good of living, Rose? What is the use or beauty of anything? The Rev. the Archdeacon of York half-playfully says I need to be regenerated. Dr. Widmer says my circulation is weak. Poor mamma says nothing; but she looks a world of reproach. I wish she would take the scriptural rod to me. That would improve the circulation, I fancy; and if it didn't produce a state of regeneration it might at least be a practical step towards it. But I don't know why I should make a jest of my own misery, when I want nothing on earth except to be a little child again, so I could creep off into the long grass somewhere, and cry all my sick heart away. I used to be able to cry when I was five or six years old, but now it is a lost art.

"By the way, speaking of tears reminds me that your friend, Mr. Dunlop, was here last evening, and, while shewing him some views of foreign scenes, we suddenly came across that old, little painting of yourself, in which the artist represented you as a stiff-jointed child, with a row of curls the colour and shape of shavings neatly glued to a little wooden head. You remember how we used to make fun of it. I always said that picture was bad enough to bring tears, and there was actually quite a perceptible moisture in his eyes as he looked at it. Who would have supposed that he possessed so much aesthetic sensibility?

"Well, I am only wearying you, so I will close. Don't be troubled about me, dear. Sometimes I am violently interested in my own unreasonable sufferings, and at other times I am wholly indifferent to them; but nothing can befall my perverse nature that shall alter the tenderness always existing for you in the heart of your loving

        HELENE."

Rose read all but the concluding paragraphs aloud to her brother, who, standing at the open door, was looking idly out upon the leaf and blossom of a lovely garden. "What a stream of unalloyed egotism!" he said. "In a woman it's a detestable quality."

"Oh, you should say a rare quality," amended Rose, with a smile that ended in a sigh.

"Well, it's something that can't be too rare." A fading spring lily dropped on the doorstep by one of the children received an impatient kick, as though he would dismiss the present conversation in a similar manner. "Rose," he said, "I wish you would ask Wanda to our sailing-party to-morrow."

"Why, Edward, I might as well ask a blue-bird. She will come if it happens to suit her inclination at the moment, otherwise not."

"Don't you think a regular invitation would please her?"

"Oh, dear, no; it isn't as though she were a civilized creature. You don't seem to grasp the fact that she's only a wild thing of the woods."

A pause ensued. "There are other facts," resumed Edward a little unsteadily, "that I **have** grasped. One is that she is the most beautiful woman I ever saw; another--that I love her."

Rose put up her hands as though to save her eyes from some hideous sight, "It can't be true!" she exclaimed.

"My dear little sister, it is true; and your inability to accept it is not a very flattering tribute to my good taste."

"It **can't** be true," repeated Rose. "You must mean that you have merely taken a fancy to her."

"Well, it is a fancy that has grown to enormous proportions. I cannot live without her. If that is fancy it has all the strength of conviction."

"Oh, Edward, you can't really love her. It is only her beauty that you care for."

"You might as well say that the sunflower doesn't really love the sun; it is only the sunshine that it cares for. Wanda's beauty is part of herself."

"And it will remain so a dozen, or perhaps a score, of years. After that you will have for your wife a coarse ignorant woman, forever chafing at the restrictions of civilized life; angering, annoying and humiliating you in a thousand ways, a woman whom you cannot admire, whom it will be impossible for you to respect."

Edward's eyes blazed. Not until that moment did his sister realize how complete was his infatuation for Wanda.

"It is you who are ignorant and coarse," he cried, "in your remarks upon the girl who is my promised wife. No matter what befalls her, she will always be clothed in the unfading beauty of my love."

Rose was deeply grieved. She stood with clasped hands looking despairingly at her brother. "You poor boy," she breathed, "you poor motherless boy! What can I say to you?"

"Well, there are a good many things that you can say; but what I should prefer you to say would be to the effect that you will break it as gently as possible to Papa."

"I shall not break it at all," declared the girl warmly. "It would nearly kill poor father. Haven't you any consideration for him?"

"Yes; sufficient to make me wish that the truth should be clothed in your own sweet persuasive accents, when it is conveyed to him. I don't wish to jar him any more than is necessary."

"Edward, you are perfectly heartless!"

"That is the natural consequence of losing one's heart, isn't it?"

"Oh, then, you are only jesting. It's a very good joke, but in questionable taste."

"Dear Rose, believe me, I was never more in earnest than at present."

"Except when you are out hunting. I have seen you go without food and sleep simply because you were on the track of some beautiful wild creature that was forced to yield its liberty and life merely to gratify your whim. It is in that despicable way that you would treat Wanda."

The young man smiled. He perceived that his sister was changing her tactics.

"You are very considerate and tender of Wanda," he said, "but not so much as

I expect to be."

The conversation, which was growing more and more unsatisfactory, was abruptly terminated by the entrance of one of the other members of the family.

As a natural result of this interview Wanda was invited to go with them in the sail-boat next day. Rose was clear-witted enough to see that persistent opposition would only intensify the halo of romance which her infatuated brother had discovered upon the brow of the Algonquin Maiden, and that outward acquiescence would give the attachment an air of prosaic tameness, if anything could. Besides, a scandal is made more scandalous when the offender's family are known to be in a state of hopelessly outraged enmity.

Thus bravely reasoned Rose, while her heart sank within her. She was not prepared for the worst, but it was necessary that she should behave in all points as if she were; otherwise the worst might be hastened. It was impossible to view Wanda in the light of a possible sister-in-law; nevertheless, she gave her the pink cambric dress for which the Indian girl had so often expressed admiration, and supplemented the kindness with a pair of gloves, destined never to be worn, and a straw hat, whose trimming was speedily torn off and its place supplied by wampum, gorgeous feathers, the stained quills of the porcupine, with tufts of moose hair, dyed blue and red.

Certainly she looked very pretty as she stood on the shore next day, all ready for departure. Even Rose, who for the first time in her kind little life would willingly have noticed personal defects, was forced to admit that Wanda was looking and acting particularly well; the only apparent fault being a lack of harmony between herself and her dress. They were two separate entities, not only in fact but in appearance, and they were seemingly in a state of subdued but constant warfare. The truth was, that this wild girl of the woods was secretly chafing against the stiffly starched prison in which she found herself helplessly immured.

It was very pleasant out on the water. The fresh vigour of the breeze filling the sail with life, the waves swirling up about the sides of the boat, the dancing motion of their little craft upon the water, the changing tints, the shadows and ripples of the bay gave them a quiet yet keen delight. Their destination was a point of land on Lake Simcoe, where a party of picnicers was already assembled. A group of girls came down to the shore as they landed, and bore Rose and Eva away with them. In the leafy distance Edward caught a glimpse of Helene DeBerczy, and in his heart the young man thanked heaven that he was not as other men are, or even as the callow youths who were hanging upon her utterances.

After a while, Edward observed Wanda standing apart, and looking at the marauders in her loved woods as a man might look upon the enemies who, with fire and sword, were desolating the home of his fathers. Between her and these gay girls there was a difference, not of degree but of kind. They loved the forest as a background for themselves; she loved it as herself. The curious eyes fixed upon her were more respectful in their gaze when Edward quietly took his place beside her. Presently, Rose with her devoted adherents joined them, and every effort was put forth to make the Indian girl feel at home in her home. But for the most part they were futile. Wanda was thoroughly ill at ease, though she concealed the fact with the native stolidity of her race. But love's intuitions are keen, and Edward realized that his little sweetheart was very uncomfortable. What could be the reason? Her dress seemed incongruous, and yet it was perfectly in accord with the linen and lawns and flower-dotted muslins about her.

"Laura," observed a young lady behind him, in a muffled whisper which he could not choose but hear, "do look at Helene DeBerczy's costume. Could anything be more out of place at a picnic?" Edward's gaze, involuntarily straying to the garb which was so singularly inappropriate, rested upon the filmiest of black stuffs, exquisite as cobweb, through which were revealed the long perfect arms, and the tender curves of neck and shoulder. From this gracious figure was exhaled invisible radiations--the luxurious sense of refined womanliness. How gross and earthly, how fatally commonplace and prosaic seemed everyone about her. The violently high spirits of the other girls, their scramblings for flowers and shriekings at snakes, their too obvious blushes and iron-clad flirtations, seemed not to come a-nigh her. "Her soul was like a star and dwelt apart." The young man assured himself that he was not falling in love with her again; he was merely laying at her feet an involuntary tribute of admiration, the sort of admiration which he might feel for a rare poem.

Meanwhile the girl with whom he was in love had made what Edward called "an object" of herself. By this uncertain phrase he did not mean an object of admiration, poetic or otherwise. Left for a brief season to her own devices Wanda had torn and muddied her gown, lost her hat, and in other respects behaved, as a maiden lady present remarked, precisely like an overgrown child of five years, who has "never had any bringing up." All the children had taken an immense fancy to her, and she was delighting them with her dexterity in climbing trees when Edward cast a hot, shamed, imploring look at his sister, to which she responded by saying:

"Wanda, you must be very tired. Come and sit down a while and rest."

The girl, seeing Edward a little apart from the others, took a seat beside him, at which distinct mark of preference the rest smiled. Her lover alone wore a heavy frown. He glanced at the frouzy hair, to which not even the beauty of the face beneath could reconcile him; then at the scratched and sun-burned hands, and lastly at the stained and battered gown. "Wanda," he said with stern brevity, "how did you get your dress so wet?"

"Wading the brook," she replied, surveying the dripping and discoloured skirt with entire indifference.

"That is very improper. You shouldn't do such things. Why are you not quiet?"

"Only the dead are quiet; but perhaps you wish to kill me."

The remark was startling, but it was unaccompanied by a ray of emotion in face or voice. Only in the large soft eyes lay a depth of suffering such as he had seen in the look of a dying fawn, wounded by his hand. "Your words pierce like arrows," she said.

"Dear Wanda, forgive me; I am expecting too much of you. It is exceedingly cruel of me to make you suffer so."

"Wanda!" called one of a group of children, "come and swing us, please."

"Don't go," whispered Edward decisively. He himself strode over to them, lifted one chubby youngster after another into the huge swing, and sent them flying into the tree-tops. It was a form of pastime that he detested; but he was not going to have Wanda at the beck and call of "those little ruffians." At last, with the sympathetic assurance that if they wanted any more swinging they were at liberty to get it from each other, he left them, and rejoined the Indian girl.

"Wanda!" said Helene, as she spread a shawl on the ground, "just step across to our carriage, will you, and bring me a cushion you will find there."

"You must not!" declared Edward, in a low savage whisper, preparing to go himself; but the girl was off like a swallow before the wind. He met her on the way back, took the cushion from her, and presented it to its owner with a bow of exaggerated deference. Helene's black brows expressed the utmost astonishment; but as she confronted Edward's wrathful gaze her own eyes caught fire, and the two who once had been so nearly lovers now manifested no other emotion toward each other save repressed and concentrated hate.

"I wish you to understand," said the exasperated young man to Wanda, as he accompanied her to dinner, "that you are not a servant, and you mustn't obey anyone's commands."

"No," was the slow reply, "I shall obey no one's commands, not even yours;" and with these words she turned and fled into the woods. The ever-present desire to escape had conquered at last.

"How kind you are to that unfortunate girl!" observed the lady next him at dinner. "She must try your patience so much."

Edward admitted that his patience had been tried; but he was in no mood to expatiate upon the subject. He had a very slight idea of what he was eating and drinking, or of what all the talking was about. The sunshine flecking the open clearing gave him a feeling that he would soon have a dreadful headache. After it was over he lay down, and tried to forget his troubles in a noontide nap. Gradually the voices about him softened and died away. For a moment he was floating upon the still waters of sleep, and then he drifted back to shore. Opening his eyes he found himself alone with Helene, who was asleep among her wrappings at a little distance. The rest had strayed away in pairs and groups, out of hearing if not out of sight. The unconscious figure seemed clothed in an atmosphere of ethereal sweetness, and Edward caught himself wondering whether the root of an affection, whose life is years long, is ever removed from the heart, unless the heart is removed with it. He began seriously to doubt, not his constancy to Wanda, but his inconstancy to Helene. Suddenly she opened her eyes and caught his glance. He withdrew it at once, and in the embarrassment of the moment made some inane remark upon the beauty of the day. Helene rose with deliberation, put one white hand to the well-brushed head, trim and shining as a raven's wing, and with the utmost tranquillity answered "yes." Certainly she had the most irritating way in the world of pronouncing the words which usually sound sweetest from a woman's lips. He did not wait to continue a conversation so unpropitiously begun, but went off on a lonely exploring tramp along the shore.

Late in the afternoon as he was returning, he noticed a nondescript figure sitting solitary on the bank, which, as he approached resolved itself into the superb outline of his Indian love. Unconscious of observation she threw herself backward, in an attitude as remarkable for its beauty as for its unconventionality. She seemed to be luxuriating with a sort of animal content in the brightness of the sunshine, the softness of the odorous breeze, and the warmth of the water in which her slim bare feet were dabbling; she dug her brown fingers in the earth, as though the very touch of the soil was intense delight. The hated dress was reduced to ruinous pink rags, which became her untamed beauty as the habiliments of civilization never could have done. Her slowly approaching lover viewed her with mingled amusement and horror, while deep in his heart flowed the dark; current of a great despair. Hearing his footsteps she nerved herself for the expected reproaches, which he knew were worse than useless; but seeing in his face nothing but undisguised admiration, she sprang lightly to her feet and threw herself upon his neck. Edward kissed her, but it was with a thrill of ineffable self-contempt, and a sharp consciousness that the only charm this girl possessed for him was that she allowed him to kiss her. Then he drew away and brushed with fastidious glove the dust his coat retained from contact with her shoulder.

"See what I have found!" she exclaimed, holding up a small trinket that glittered in the sunlight. "It belongs to the Moon-in-a-black-cloud."

It was a little gold locket, which he had often noticed on the neck of Helene. Shortly before Wanda's abrupt flight, she had pointed with childish curiosity to the slender bright chain clearly visible beneath the transparent folds of the black gown, and the young lady had obligingly drawn the locket from its secret place upon her heart, for the gratification of its admirer. Left for a time on the outside of her dress, one of the tiny links must have severed, and the pretty trinket slipped to the ground unnoticed by its owner. The young man in whose hand it now lay was tempted to a dishonourable action. He had often begged Helene to show him the contents of this locket--a favour which had uniformly been denied. Now the opportunity was his without the asking. Nothing rewarded his curiosity save a lock of yellow hair, probably cut from the head of Rose. Queer fancy, he thought, for one girl to cherish the tresses of another. Suddenly he was struck by an idea that sent the blood throbbing to his temples. He examined the tress a second time. The bright hair growing upon his sister's head he knew had a reddish tinge, and its silky length terminated in ring-like curls. This was short and straight, of a pale colour, and showed by its unevenness that it had been "shingled." His heart beat as though it would burst. "You must take this back to its owner," he said imperatively.

Wanda slipped her hand in his. "We will go together," she said.

He glanced at her bare feet and ruined raiment, and realized with a burning flush that he was thoroughly ashamed of her. No, he could not take the hand of his future wife and face that crowd of curious worldlings. The mere touch of her soiled fingers was repugnant to him. She seemed like some coarse weed, whose vivid hues he might admire in passing, but which he would shrink from wearing on his person.

"It will be better for you to go alone," he replied. "Don't tell the lady that anyone beside yourself has seen the locket. I will come presently."

But he lingered a long time after she left him, drinking against his will the sharp waters of bitter-sweet reflection. There came back to him an afternoon a year ago, when his sister Eva, out of childish love of mischief, had stolen up behind him, and cut off the lock of hair which fell over his brow.

"Mere masculine vanity," she had said, as the scissors snapped. He had sprung up instantly, and pursued her as she fled shrieking down the avenue. Helene, who was the only other occupant of the room had looked almost shocked at their conduct, and his pet lock of hair had mysteriously disappeared. Since then during how many days and nights had it been rising and falling upon the proud bosom, that he knew very well would be cold in death before it would give evidence of a quickened heart-beat in his presence. The knowledge he had gained by the discovery of the locket made Helene dangerously dear to him, and yet relieved him of not a particle of his duty towards Wanda. He saw neither of the girls again that day, but he carried home with him a stinging memory of both. Late that night he was pacing his room with sick heart and aching head, while in the next apartment Rose was assuring herself that the picnic had been a great success. "Really," she meditated, "nothing could possibly be worse--or better--than the way in which Wanda behaved."

CHAPTER XVIII.
THE COMMODORE SURRENDERS.

A few weeks later there was another excursion to the emerald glooms of the forest, but this was limited in number to the Macleods and DeBerczys, with a few of their intimate friends. Wanda was absent on one of her indefinite expeditions--indefinite in length as well as in object, though the wigwam of her foster-feather was one of the points of interest visited by the party. Conspicuous among the numerous Indians in the settlement in the neighbourhood of Orillia was the last of the Algonquins, partly because of the pathos which attaches to the sole survivor in any region of a nearly extinct race, partly because of the mantle of traditional glory that had fallen upon him from the shoulders of valorous ancestors. He declined to join the revellers at their midday feasting under the trees, but his unexpected appearance afterwards suggested a pleasant substitute for the noon-day siesta. "Talk about the storied memories of the past, in the old world," said Edward, leaning back on the mossy sward, and gazing up through green branches to the blue heaven, "this country has had its share of them, and here is the man," clapping a friendly hand on the Indian's shoulder, "who can tell us about them."

"Ah, do!" implored Herbert and Eva.

"Ah, don't!" entreated their father. "If there's anything that spoils the sylvan shades for me, it is to learn that they were once the scene of battle axes and blood spilling, and such like gruesomeness."

"But we *ought* to know about it," said Helene. "It's history."

"That makes it all the worse. If it were fiction I wouldn't care."

"Now, Papa," said Rose, "that evinces a depraved taste. People will blame your home-training. Consider my feelings."

"That is what I supposed I was doing, my dear, in praying to be delivered from a tale that would make your blood run cold."

"What a delightful way for one's blood to run in this weather," lazily remarked one of the Boulton girls, and the other said she was pining for a story of particular horror.

"Oh, a story, by all means," said the Commodore, "but let it be a tradition or something of that sort." Then turning to the Chief: "Does not our brother know the legend of the unfortunate wretch of a man who was set upon and abused by a lot of unmerciful women, because he barbarously forbade them to learn all the history they wanted? Something of that sort would be appropriate."

"Our brother" shook his head. "That is beyond my skill, but I can relate a story of the times before ever women were brought into the world."

"Rather dull times for the men, weren't they?" inquired one of the party.

"It is the belief of some of our race that they were very good times," replied the Chief, tranquilly. "The men of that period, free from the influence of the other sex, have been spoken of as a much better race of beings than they are to-day. At that time you never heard of such a thing as a man being cross to his wife, or too attentive to his neighbour's wife, and when the husband came back from the chase without meat there was no one to scold him. Every man had his own way, and dwelt in peace in his own wigwam. As fast as they died out the Manito created more, and as they had no families they had nothing to fight for, nothing to defend, and, consequently, there were few wars among them. There were, I am sorry to say, some disadvantages. The men were obliged to weed corn, dry fish, mend nets, fell trees, carry logs, and do other women's work, which, as we know, is a great degradation. Also, when they were sick or in trouble, some of the weaker ones were heard to declare that they wished women were invented, but as a rule they were blithe and gay as warriors in the dance that follows a great victory. There were many ennobling influences in this world before women entered it. Vanity did not exist. Simplicity was the rule, especially in attire, which ordinarily consisted of hunting coats and leggings, deerskin moccasins and coloured blankets, enriched with beads. It was only once in a while that they appeared in black eagle plumes, and gorgeous feathers, garters gay with beads, moccasins worked with stained porcupine quills, leggings of scarlet cloth, embroidered and decorated with tufts of moosehair, dyed blue and red, robes curiously plaited of the bark of the mulberry, and adorned with bear claws, hawks' bills and turtle shells. Besides being plain and quiet in their dress they were very upright in their lives. No man ever was known to lie to his neighbour; but now when you see a man and woman too frequently together you may be sure he is telling her things that come true about as often as larks fall from the skies. Neither were men in those days ever deceived; but now they are tangled in women's wiles as easily as a partridge is caught in a net. There were no cowards, for men at all times are staunch and bold, whereas a woman has nothing but the heart of a little bird in her breast. All nature shared in man's prosperity. The corn grew to the height of a young forest tree, and in the hunting-grounds the deer and bears were as thick as stars.

"But the chief glory of man in those days was his long, superb and glossy tail; for at that time it could not be said that the horses were more highly gifted than he. You must often have noticed the pride with which horses switch their tails about, apparently to drive off flies, but really to show their superiority to the race they serve. The reproach of having no tail is one that is hard to bear; but at the time of which I speak all men were endowed with luxuriant tails, some of them black as the shell of a butternut when it is fully ripe, others the colour of the setting sun, but all trimmed with shells, gay coloured beads and flowers, and strings of alligators' teeth. Those who say that there is nothing on earth so beautiful as a woman did not live in the time when tails were invented. Nothing could surpass the pride their owners took in them, nor the scorn that was heaped upon the hapless creature whose tail was short or scanty.

"But, as often happens to people who have all and more than they need, so it was with our ancestors. From being simply proud of their tails they began to grow vain and useless, caring for nothing but their own ease and adornment, neglecting to harvest the maize, feeble in the chase, sleeping sometimes for the space of nearly a moon, and unable to take more than a woman's journey of six suns at a time. Then the Manito reflected and said to himself: 'This will never do. Man was not made to be a mere groundling. His greatest luxury must be taken from him, and in its place there must be given him something to tax his patience and strengthen his powers.' So one fine morning every man in the world woke up to find his tail missing. Great was the surprise and lamentation, and this was not lessened by the sudden appearance of the women, who came in number like that of the flight of pigeons in the moon before the snow moon. No prayers could avail to stay their coming, and from that time all the troubles in the world began. No man was allowed to have his own way thenceforward, nor was he permitted to plod along in his old, slow, comfortable fashion, but each one in terror went to work as swift as a loon flying before a high wind."

The laugh that arose at the end of this not strictly authentic narrative was prolonged by a strange voice, and Allan Dunlop, who, unobserved, had made his appearance among them, now came forward to exchange greetings with his friends. Herbert and Eva Macleod hung enraptured about him, while he went to congratulate the old Indian upon his gifts as a story-teller. Then Edward's warm hand clasped his. "Come over and see my father," he said. "Oh, no, he is asleep. He generally sleeps in the afternoon of the day."

"A very good plan when one comes to the afternoon of one's days," observed Allan, and then he went over to speak to Rose.

Her little soft hand fluttered up to his as a bird flutters to its nest. They had not met since that stormy March night. Since then he had confessed, in correspondence between them, that life was a perpetual struggle between him and love, and she had asked--though not in so many words--if it would make it any easier for him to know that she was engaged in the same struggle with the same great enemy. Ah, with what a fine pen had she written that, and with what pale ink, and nervous, nearly illegible strokes, and how she had crowded it down to the very edge of the paper. But he had read it, and it was fixed on his mind as clearly as though it had been written in lightning on the dark horizon of his future. And now, though his brown eyes were warming into black, and her cheeks were the colour of the flower after which she was named, they talked of conventional things in an indifferent way, as is the customary and proper thing to do. They saw little of each other through the remainder of the afternoon, but when they were making ready for the sail home, Eva, at Allan's invitation, sprang into his little light boat.

"Come with me, Rose," she cried, "Mr. Dunlop is going to row me home, and it will be better worth while if there are two of us."

The excuses which Rose instantly invented were not so strong as the vehement tones in which her sister uttered her invitation, and to avoid attracting attention or remark she gently seated herself in the boat, which Allan exultantly pushed away from the shore. The delight of being for a little while almost alone with his love was intoxicating. The younger girl, who had counted so ardently upon the pleasure of Allan's society, found herself in a short time too sleepy to enjoy it. Her pale, pretty head nodded drowsily, and at last found a resting-place in the lap of her sister. The other two did not exchange many words. It would have been a shame to disturb the play-worn little maid. The night was very beautiful; the stars seemed softly remote. Beneath their light the woods gleamed mysteriously, and the waves were hushed into a dream of peace. The bay that at sunset had seemed a sea of melted gold, now held the young moon trembling in its liquid embrace. About them played the ineffable caresses of the light evening breeze.

"Rose," said Allan, softly.

She looked up with conscious resistance, but it was too late for that now. The imperious passion of his mood met the sad grace of her attitude. His speech flowed fast and warm as if it had been blood from his veins. She felt herself weakening into helpless tears. "Ah, spare me!" she cried. "It is all so hopeless. My father--"

"I am coming to see your father to-morrow," he said. "It will be a hard battle, but it must be decided at once."

He helped them to land, and they walked in silence to the house. At the doorway, in which Eva had disappeared, Rose took Allan's outstretched hand in both of hers, and drawing it close, laid her weary, wet little face down upon it. The sound of voices and laughter came up from the beach, and she hastily released herself and fled to her room.

The next afternoon Eva Macleod, with an air of considerable importance, tapped at the door of her father's apartment. "Papa," she said, with that fondness for a choice diction observable in carefully reared young ladies at the beginning of their teens, "may I have a private conversation with you?"

"Why, certainly, my dear! A little talk, I suppose, you mean."

Without heeding this undignified interruption, Miss Eva gave her parent a very accurate report of the dramatic scene in the boat the evening before, of which she had been an interested auditor.

"Of course," she added, in conscientious defence, "I didn't want them to suppose I was sleeping, but if I had opened my eyes it would have been very embarrassing for us all."

"Humph!" said her father. "Does Rose know that you were awake?"

"No, I have not broached the topic to her," replied Eva, with an affectation of maturer speech.

"Humph!" said the gentleman again; a quizzical glance at his younger daughter breaking for a moment through the gloom with which he was meditating the fate of the elder one. "Well, I am glad you 'broached' it to me; I shall--"

"Papa," interrupted Eva, with bated breath, glancing down from the window at which she stood, "there is Allan now."

"*Allan*! You are mightily well acquainted. I see I must prepare to make an unconditional surrender."

He walked in a nervous and disquieted manner out of the room. At the head of the stairs he encountered Mademoiselle DeBerczy, on her way up.

"Helene," he said, with the desperation of one who in the fifty-ninth minute after the eleventh hour does not entirely despair of a gleam of hope, "I wish you would tell me in two words if Rose loves Allan Dunlop. Does she?"

"*Don't* she!" exclaimed Helene, with explosive earnestness, and the two words were sufficient. Their effect was not lessened by subsequent occurrences. On opening the drawing-room door Rose hastened to his side, turning her back, as she did so, upon a young man of ardent but entirely self-respectful aspect, standing not far distant.

"Oh, Papa!" she cried in her extremity, "save me from him. He loves me!"

"Is that the only reason?" asked her father.

"No; there is a greater one. *I love him*!"

"Ah!" murmured Allan softly, "it is to *me* you should say that."

"She shall have unlimited opportunities for saying it to you," observed the elder gentleman, with kindly promptness, but with a sore heart. "After a while," he added, turning to Allan, with his hand on the door knob, "I will be glad to see you."

In this sentence, which is an interesting illustration of the power of manners over mind, the word "will" was purposely substituted for the customary "shall." It was only by an active effort of will that the good Commodore could be glad to see his daughter's suitor. But their interview, if it did not prove a death-blow to his prejudices, at least inflicted serious injuries upon them, from which they never afterwards recovered. He was won over by the young fellow's manliness, which, when contrasted with mere gentlemanliness, apart from it, puts the latter at a striking disadvantage, even in the mind of the confirmed aristocrat. There was also a tinge of absurdity in the idea of being ashamed of a son-in-law of whom his country was beginning to be proud. Perhaps it was as well that he should arrive unaided at this opinion, for Allan had won the rest of the household to his side, and a belief in which one is entirely alone must contain something more than mere pride of birth in order to support its possessor in comfort. Even the loyal Tredway would have failed to respond to his imagined need, for this faithful servitor had long since discovered that the happiness of his young mistress was more to be desired than the preservation of any fancied superiority on the part of the family to which he was devotedly attached.

CHAPTER XIX.
AT STAMFORD COTTAGE.

Not more than three miles from the Falls of Niagara, between them and Queenston, lies the pretty village of Stamford, in which, over sixty years ago, Upper Canada's Lieutenant-Governor built the summer home which became his favourite place of abode. Set in the midst of a vast natural park, its appearance corresponded perfectly to Mrs. Jameson's description of an elegant villa, framed in the interminable forests. Here, within sound of the great cataract and, on clear, typically Canadian days, within sight of York, thirty miles distant across the lake, Sir Peregrine and Lady Sarah Maitland found a grateful retreat from the cares of public life. Not that they loved society less, but solitude more; especially, to use a Hibernicism, when that solitude was shared. In the early summer of 1827 Stamford Cottage was filled with people after its pretty mistress's own heart. If she suspected one of her guests of being also after the heart of another, it did not endear him the less to her. Why should she not remove from the paths of her *proteges* the scarcely perceptible obstacles which prevented them from being as happily married as herself? But one day she discovered that the role of match-maker is as arduous as it is alluring, and with this she went at once to her husband's study.

"Dear," she began, "I have become greatly interested in a young man, and I thought it only right that you should know about it before it goes any further."

"Ah, yes, certainly." The gentleman looked rather abstracted. "And the young fellow--is he interested too?"

"Oh, interested is a feeble word. He is desperately in love."

"Then you haven't taken me into your confidence a moment too soon. Has he declared his passion?"

"No; that's just the trouble. He goes mooning round and mooning round, and never saying a word. And I'm sure," added the lady in an aggrieved tone, "I've given him every opportunity. Yesterday after infinite pains I brought him and Helene together in the arbour, and made some pretext for escaping into the house. What did that--infant--do but follow me out?"

"Quite natural, if his feelings towards you are such as you have described."

"Towards *me*! You don't imagine I am talking of myself."

"That is what your words would lead one to believe."

"Oh, dear husband, you know perfectly well what I mean. I do think that when a man sets out to be stupid he succeeds a thousand times better than a woman. Surely you have noticed how badly Edward Macleod and Helene DeBerczy are behaving."

"Really, my dear, I have not. I supposed they were behaving remarkably well."

"In one sense--yes. They are as 'polite as peas.' But why *should* they be polite?"

"Well, it is a custom of the country, I suppose. It's hard to account for all the strange things one sees in a foreign land."

"My object is not so much to account for it as to put an end to it. It's ridiculous for two people, who have known each other from babyhood, to be standing aloof, and looking as if the honour of each other's acquaintance was the last thing to be desired. And now Mademoiselle Helene wants to go home. She does not complain or repine or importune, but every day, and several times a day, she presents the idea to her mother, with varying degrees of emphasis, and in the tone of one who believes that continual dropping will wear away the stone. Madame DeBerczy as yet remains sweetly obdurate. She is enjoying her visit, and there seems to be no special good reason why it should be terminated. I particularly wish them to stay, as I want if possible to bring about a better understanding between Helene and Edward. We must not let them escape."

In pursuance of the policy suggested by his wife, Sir Peregrine took occasion to have a special kindly little chat with Helene, with a view to overcome her re-luctance to remain. Naturally of a reserved disposition his cordial hospitality found expression in looks and actions rather than words, and these took a greater value from the infrequency with which they were uttered.

"What is this I hear about your wanting to leave us?" he said, addressing He-lene, who, with her mother, was seated on his left at dinner that evening. "Have you really grown very tired of us all?"

The young lady laid down her knife and fork, and the unconscious movement, combined with her unusual pallor, gave one the impression that she was indeed very tired.

"No, Sir Peregrine, only of myself. I seem to be suffering from a prolonged at-tack of spring fever. Don't you think home is the best place for those who have the bad taste to be in poor health?"

"No doubt of it," replied the gentleman, at which she gave him a grateful glance, thinking she had won an unexpected ally; "but," he continued, "I hoped you would feel at home here."

Helene assured him that it was impossible for her to enjoy her visit more than she was doing. As she made this perfectly sincere statement her melancholy eyes by chance encountered the deep blue ones of her unacknowledged lover. In their depths lurked an expression of absolute relief. Could he then be glad to hear of their projected departure? She hoped so. It would be very much better for both. "Has it never occurred to you," she asked of Sir Peregrine, "that the pleasantest things in this world are very seldom the best for us?"

"I am sorry to hear you say that," he rejoined pleasantly, "as I was about to ask you to go out driving with me to-morrow morning. There is a view near the Falls that I believe you have never yet seen, and the gratification of showing it to you would be to me one of the pleasantest things in the world."

The young lady very willingly admitted that this was an exception to the rule she had just laid down. Lady Sarah, who thus far had approved her husband's tac-tics, now gave him a slightly questioning glance, but he returned her such a look of self-confident good cheer, that she knew at once he must be involved in a deep-laid plot of his own. As a rule she had small respect for masculine plots, and before another day had elapsed her sentiment on the subject was abundantly shared by at least two of her guests. Mademoiselle DeBerczy had always entertained a genuine admiration and liking for the Lieutenant-Governor. His chivalrous courtesy, picturesque appearance, and the exquisite refinement of his tone and manner pleased her fastidious taste. So it was with almost a light heart that she made her preparations next morning for the drive. But when seated in the carriage, and waiting with a bright face the appearing of her delinquent attendant, it was not pleasant to be told by the gentleman himself that important dispatches had just arrived by the morning's mail, which demanded his personal and immediate attention. "Besides that fact," said His Excellency, "I had forgotten an appointment I have with the Hon. Mr. Hamilton Merritt to talk over his great project of the Welland Canal between the two Lakes, and I cannot disappoint him." He couldn't think of asking her to wait until the sun was hot, and the pleasure of the drive spoiled, added the Lieutenant-Governor. But here was Edward Macleod, who would no doubt be glad to take his place. At this announcement Helene longed to fly to her room, but she could think of no valid excuse. The young man, sitting with the last *Gazette* in hand in a rustic chair on the veranda, listened to the summons with silent horror. He actually turned pale, but like Helene, he could think of no possible excuse for evading the turn affairs had taken. He rose mechanically, gave inarticulate utterance to the pleasure he did not feel, and took his seat beside the unhappy girl, who shrank visibly into her corner.

"Admirable!" exclaimed Lady Sarah, softly stepping out to witness the unusual phenomenon of Edward and Helene driving away together. "I never supposed a man *could* have so much sagacity and foresight. Here have I been cudgelling my brains to keep those two from playing hide and seek--no, hide and *avoid*--ever since they came, and now you accomplish it in the easiest and most natural way in the world. See what it is to have a clever husband! How did you happen to think of those important dispatches?"

Emphasis would indicate too coarsely the delicate stress laid upon the last two words. The gentleman looked extremely puzzled.

"*Happen* to think? I am *obliged* to think of them."

"Really? What a lucky accident! So you are not the sly designing schemer I supposed. Ah, well, you are the soul of honour, and that is infinitely better."

Certainly to her mind in the present case that was what appearances would seem to indicate; but the poor wretches who were tending slowly toward the brink of some indefinable horror, more awful to their imaginations than the great cataract itself, thought not so much upon the means by which they were brought into their present painful position, as upon the impossibility of escape from it. To the eye of a casual wayfarer these handsome young people, driving abroad through the dewy freshness of the morning, with the long lovely day before them, could not be considered objects of pity.

For a while they took refuge in commonplaces, relieved by lapses of eloquent silence; then as the winding road conducted them by easy gradations into greener depths of leafy solitude they looked involuntarily into each other's eyes, and realized that, beneath all the bitterness and pride and cruel estrangement, their love was the truest, most unalterable, part of their life.

"Perhaps," said Edward, speaking as though the words were wrung from him, "it is better that we should meet once more alone, though it be for the last time."

The girl gave a low murmur of assent. Her eyes were looking straight forward. The solitude was permeated by the deep thunder of the Falls, and it voiced the depth of her despair. "For the last time," she said within herself, "for the last time."

"I have a favour to ask," he continued, "a favour that I verily believe a man never yet asked of the woman he loved; and I do love you, my darling--there, let me say it once, since I can never say it again--I love you with all my heart and soul." He bowed his head, and she could see the blue vein in his temple growing bluer and swelling as he spoke. He had not laid a finger upon her, he could not so much as lift his eyes up to her face, but a mocking breeze suddenly blew a fold of her raiment against his cheek, and he kissed it passionately. Helene held her hands tightly together; they were trembling violently.

"I want to beg of you," he said, still without looking up, "to look upon me with suspicion, aversion, and distrust; to disbelieve any good you may hear of me; to hate me if you can; to treat me as long as you live with uniform coldness and indifference."

"I understand," she replied with icy brevity, "you think there is danger of my treating you otherwise."

Now, since the discovery of the locket, and its tell-tale contents, this was precisely the danger that Edward had feared, but he was a diplomatist.

"Have you ever given me the slightest reason to think so?" he demanded. "At my least approach your natural pride changes to haughtiness, arrogance, and scorn. But the one thing greater than your pride is my love. Ah, you know nothing about it--you cannot imagine its power. Madmen have warned those who were dearest to them to fly from their sight, lest in spite of themselves an irreparable injury be inflicted. And so I urge you to continue avoiding me, to cast behind not even a single glance of pity, lest in spite of your pride, in spite of my reason, I should bend all my power to the one object of winning you."

This calamity, it may be supposed, was not quite so great and horrible to the mind of the young lady as it was in the excited imagination of her lover. "I do not understand you," she said quietly. "What is it you wish to ask of me?"

"Only this: that you will never think of me with the slightest degree of kindness; that you will drop me from your acquaintance; that you will forget that I ever existed."

"Very well;" her tones were even quieter than before, and a great deal colder! "I promise never to think any more of you than I do at this moment." And all the time she was crying with inward tears, "O, darling, darling, as though I could think any more of you than I do now! As though I could, as though I could!"

"Thank you," said Edward, "you are removing a terrible temptation from my way, and helping to make me stronger and less ignoble than I am. Let me tell you all about it, Helene. Do you remember that night in the conservatory last winter, when you treated me so cruelly? Yes, I own I was a wild animal; but you might have tamed me, and instead you infuriated me. I went from you to Wanda, the Indian girl with whom I flirted last summer. She was in civilized garb, in my mother's home, quiet as a bird that has been driven by the storms of winter into a place of shelter. I too had been tempest-driven, and her warm welcome, her beauty and tenderness, stole away my senses. She soothed my injured vanity, satisfied my desperate hunger for love, and I lived for weeks in the belief that we were made for each other. But with the return of summer the untamed spirit of her race took possession of her, and when I saw her with you,--ah, dearest, is there need for me to say more? I cannot marry her; every fibre of my being, every sentiment of my soul, revolts from it; but neither am I such a monster of iniquity as to try to win any one else, and found my lifelong happiness upon that poor girl's broken-hearted despair. No, Helene, you have no right to look at me in that way. I never wronged her in the base brutish sense of the word--never in a way that the spirit of my dead mother might not have witnessed--but I have robbed her of her heart, and find too late that I do not want it. I cannot free her from her suffering, but at least I shall always share it."

And I too, was Helene's internal response. Aloud she suggested that it was time for them to return. Her indifference was precisely what Edward had begged for, but now in return for his confidence it chilled him. She noticed his disappointment, and with a sudden impulse of sympathy, she laid a tiny gloved hand upon his arm. "Oh, you are right," she breathed, "perfectly right. It is infinitely better to suffer with her than to be happy and contemptible and forget her. Believe me I shall not be a hindrance to you."

He took in his own the little fluttering hand, and held it in what he believed to be a quiet friendly clasp. It was an immense relief to unburden his mind to any one, and her approval was very sweet to a heart that had been torn for weary days and nights by self-accusation and self-contempt. Unconsciously he leaned nearer to her, still holding the little hand, which its owner did not withdraw, because it was for "the last time." In the reaction from the severe strain of the days and weeks gone past they were almost light-hearted. Before re-entering the village Edward stopped the horse in a leafy covert, where for a few minutes they might be secure from observation.

"It is only to say good-bye, my heart's idol," he explained. "Since I have proved myself unworthy even of your liking I must go away from you forever. But our parting must be here in private." He held both her hands now in a tight, strong grasp, and looked into her face with unutterable love. "Ah, heaven," he groaned, "I cannot give you up! I cannot, I cannot!" He bowed his face upon the lilies in her lap, but the languid bloodless things could not cool the fever in his cheeks. For her life she could not help laying her hand tenderly upon his head--the young golden head that lay so wearily close to her empty arms; but she said nothing. A woman's heart is dumb, not because it is created so, but because society has decreed that that is the only proper thing for it to be. "Helene," he murmured, lifting his head with a strange dazed look, "I believe I have been delirious all the morning. What possible good could my suffering be to Wanda? I don't know what I have said, but I wish you would forget it all. I wish you would remember nothing except that I love you-

-love you--*love you*!"

The girl laughed aloud and bitterly. "So that is the length of a man's remorse! No! You have begged me to despise you, and now I shall beg you not to make it dangerously easy for me to do so."

Her contempt was a tonic. It reminded the young man that he deserved, not only that but his own contempt as well. They drove home without exchanging another word.

CHAPTER XX.
THE COMING OF WANDA.

The spectacle of a pair of lovers equally pale and proud alighting at her door was rather dispiriting to Lady Sarah Maitland, but she did not lose heart. This she rightly considered to be the proper thing for *them*, not for her to do. At least they should not escape "the solitude of the crowd," and opportunities for bringing them into this sort of solitude were not lacking. The same afternoon an English lord, who had recently been making a tour of the States, with some officers of His Majesty's 70th Regiment, then stationed at York, arrived at Stamford Cottage, and in their honour a large number of guests were assembled that evening. The soft radiance of mingled moonlight and candle light, the artistic luxury of the place and its surroundings, the exquisite robes of soft-voiced women, the cultivated tone and manner of the men, with a sort of subtle and distinguished aroma of British nobility shed over the whole--all of these things held for Edward Macleod a potent witchery. This evening he was in unusually good spirits, and was entertaining a group of gentlemen, who had gathered about him in the centre of the large drawing-room, by an amusing account of his hunting experiences in the backwoods. The sounds of subdued mirth that followed his recital induced a passing bevy of ladies to join them. Lady Sarah took the arm of Helene, and gave him her flattering attention along with the rest. A young man never talks poorly from the knowledge that he has gained the ear of his audience.

"Really, a remarkably bright young fellow," confided Lord E---- to Sir Peregrine, at the close of another story, which was accentuated by little bursts of gentle laughter.

A slight breeze blew from a suddenly opened door upon the wax tapers, and the next moment a strange figure made its way through that brilliantly dressed assemblage, and laid its hand upon the arm of Edward. With his face flushed and eyes brightened by the sweetly breathed flattery that, like wine, was apt to go to his brain, he turned and beheld Wanda. She had evidently walked all the way from her home for the express purpose of finding him. Her dress, made up of various coloured garments, the cast-off raiment of those whose charity had fed and lodged her on the way, was covered with dust; her magnificent hair lay in a great straggling heap upon her shoulders. "My father has gone to the spirit-land," she said, "and now I come to you." Lady Sarah and Rose advanced immediately, with protestations of pity and sympathy, and entreaties that she would go at once with them to find food and rest. But she was immovable as granite. "I have come to *you*," she said, her beautiful eyes fixed upon Edward, and she uttered a few words of endearment in the Huron tongue. Nobody understood them but the young man, his sister, and hostess. The latter lady felt herself growing very cold, but she accompanied the pair to a private parlour, and returned to her guests with an amused smile upon her lips.

"Poor thing!" she said in a clear voice, distinctly audible to all. "Her foster-father died last week, and left no end of messages and requests to Mr. Macleod, his friend and constant companion in his hunting expeditions. The girl has that exaggerated idea of filial duty common to the Indian races. She could not rest until she had fulfilled his dying wishes."

No; Lady Sarah certainly did not merit the compliment she had given her husband--she was not the soul of honour--but what would you? With her cheery voice and confident laugh she had dispelled at a breath the vile suspicion of scandal. The company experienced a wonderful relief, and the conversation naturally turned to the peculiarities of savages. Rose had vanished, and it was generally supposed that she was with her brother and that queer Indian girl. In reality she was locked in her room, saturating her pillow with her tears.

Edward was alone with Wanda. For a moment the blood ran hot in his veins, and he longed to act the part of a man. He longed to take the hand of this beautiful travel-stained savage, and lead her back into the midst of those fashionably dressed, superficially smiling, ladies and gentlemen. He longed to declare, nay, rather to thunder forth, the words: "This is my promised wife! Through weary days and nights, with sore feet and sorer heart she has been coming to me. Burned by the sun and blinded with the dust, hungry and thirsty, and aching in every fibre, her trust never faltered, her love never failed. And her love is matched by mine. The loyalty and devotion of my life I lay at her poor bleeding feet."

That would have satisfied his imagination, but in real life imagination must always go a-hungering. He sat down beside her with a face far more weary than her own.

"Wanda," he burst forth, "my poor fatherless, friendless child, what can I say to you? I am a villain, a coward, a reptile! I thought I loved you, and I do not. No, though my heart aches for you, I do not love you. Oh, you look as though I were murdering you, and it is better for me to murder you now by a few sharp terrible words, than by a life-time of neglect and loathing."

The colour had all ebbed from her face. She fell on her knees beside him, and her liquid childish eyes and sweet lips were upraised to his.

"No, no, my little fawn, I must not kiss you. It is wicked to kiss what we do not love. And I do *not* love you." He was sheltering himself behind that assertion, but of a sudden he broke into crying, and his tears fell upon her face. "Child," he said, rising and pacing the room, "do you know what it is to many a man, who cares a great deal for your lips and eyes, and nothing for your mind and soul? It is to marry a beast! You would be wretched with me. We should grow inexpressibly tired of each other. Tell me," he cried, stopping short in his swift walk to and fro, and confronting her with parched lips and wet eyes, "could you endure to have me say cruel things to you every day? Could you bear to have me think bitter things of you in my heart, though I left them unsaid? How could you live under my coldness and neglect? You must learn to hate me--to scorn me,--to think as harshly of me as I shall always think of myself."

She was faint and dizzy, but she rose to her feet, and groped feebly to the door, cowering from him as she went, with her hands over her eyes. Then she turned back with a low wail of irrepressible anguish.

"I cannot leave you," she said, "I cannot give you up!"

Again he was bound in her chains. Her feverish hands held his, her burning eyes drank up the dew in his own, her pathetic presence thrilled him with a sense of love stronger than any he had dreamed of or imagined. Neglect, cruelty, bitterness, scorn! What did the words mean? Like poisonous weeds they had grown fast and rank before his eyes, but in the burning face of this all-conquering love they had shrunk, withered and dead to the earth. Yes, it was the vile earth from which they had sprung, and it was in the radiant heavens that this great love was shining. Wanda's victory was nearly complete. The only thing lacking to make it so was that she should renounce it altogether. And this she did--not with conscious art but by that sure instinct of womanliness which teaches that a man won by other than indirect methods is not won at all. Then she said, pushing him gently aside, "I will go away now, and never see you again, because I am a burden to you. No," for he had put his hand upon her wrist, "you must not touch me, because--" the words choked her for a moment, and then they fell from her lips with a sound of fathomless despair--"it is as though you were my little child that I was forced to leave forever." Again she had reached the door, but this time it was his arm around her that brought her back, his protestations of undying affection that revived her drooping frame.

There was a light tap at the door, which opened to admit Lady Sarah Maitland. "My maids will attend to this poor child," she said, addressing Edward. "She will have a bath, and food, and a bed. Meantime, I want you to help to entertain my guests."

"Really?" The young man frowned at the idea of rejoining that gay throng. He was in a state of mental exaltation--so far up in the clouds that the idea of attending a reception given by his brilliant hostess seemed by contrast spiritless and earthy.

"It would be a great kindness to let me off," he pleaded.

"It would be the greatest kindness to compel you to come," she insisted. There was a significance in the eye and tone of this thorough-bred woman of the world that were not without effect upon Edward, who at once accompanied her. His bright face, collected manner, and ready speech, lessened the impression made upon the company by the episode which had drawn general attention to him early in the evening. Not till after the guests had begun to retire did he again see Wanda. Running upstairs to get a wrap for the fair shoulders of a young lady, who preferred a moonlit seat on the lawn to the rather oppressive warmth within doors, he chanced into a little sitting-room in which Wanda, left alone for a moment, was resting with closed eyes in a great easy chair. Fresh from her bath, with her damp heavy hair lying along the folds of a loose white *neglige*, she looked almost too tired to smile. Edward advanced with beating heart, but stopped half-way, suddenly smitten by the sight of a pair of little bruised feet, carefully bandaged, resting upon a stool--the little feet that had travelled such a long hard road, that had been torn and wounded for his sake. A great wave of shame swept over him.

"I am not worthy to stand in your presence," he said penitently, kneeling at her side.

A low murmur of joy escaped the Indian Maiden's lips.

She drew his head down for a moment under the dusky curtain of her over-hanging hair, and then her eyes closed again.

Edward rose and beheld in the open doorway Helene DeBerczy; her large gaze, darker than a thunder cloud, was illumined by a long lightning flash of merciless irony.

CHAPTER XXI.
THE PASSING OF WANDA.

After night comes morning in the material world, but in that inner sphere of thought and feeling, which is the only reality, it frequently happens that after night comes a greater depth of darkness. The early light of successive summer mornings falling into the sleeping-room of Edward Macleod seemed to mock the heavy gloom which perpetually enshrouded his heart. He was back in his old home, for the pleasant circle at Stamford Cottage had broken up shortly after the unexpected advent of Wanda. A few days of enforced civilization had affected her more severely than the hard journey preceding it, and she had returned to her native wilds with the feeling of a bird regaining its freedom. Where in all the limitless forest she could be found at any particular time her lover could not tell. He was her lover still--he must always remain her lover. He had attempted to limit and define the strange irresistible attraction she exerted over him, he had voluntarily resolved upon life-long celibacy rather than subject her to the bitterness of seeing him belong to another; and if in thought he ever yielded to this great, untamed unrepressed love of hers, it was with something of the exaltation and ardour of one who makes a supreme sacrifice.

Edward Macleod was no sentimentalist, and yet he was conscious of a very delicate, infinitely sad satisfaction in the belief that he would expiate with his life the folly he had committed in permitting her to love him. In the loftiest sense he would be true to her. He could not be selfish and shameless enough to set forever aside the desolation that his hands had callously wrought. As her sorrow could never be mitigated it should always be shared. He would do everything for her. She should be educated, and inducted by gentle degrees into the refinement of civilization--he fervently hoped that it might not prove the refinement of cruelty. She should not be left desolate, forsaken, uncared-for; she should share everything he had except his heart. That was to be kept empty for her sake--for the sake of the sweet dusky maiden who had once possessed it.

Who had *once* possessed it! Ah, was it true then that she no longer held a claim? He had closed the door hesitatingly and with sharp pain in her face, but now the bare recollection of the little brown hands fumbling upon it thrilled him with a blissful sense that perhaps, after all, his life was not to be the utter sacrifice that he had supposed. Perhaps this peerless creature by some magical process of development might yet meet and satisfy his intellectual demands. She had already the soul of an angel--yes, and the beauty of an angel. And yet he was not satisfied.

It was this haunting dissatisfaction that kept him a prisoner in his room, one brilliant afternoon, when the fresh world without seemed too insupportable a mockery of his jaded and cynical state of mind. He stepped out upon the little balcony that ran under the windows of his own and his sister's apartments, and looked with a sore heart upon the eternal miracle of earth and sky. He sank heavily down upon a low seat, feeling very old and worn. If the back is fitted to the burden, it occurred to him that the painful process of adjustment would have to be continued through an interminable period of years. Perhaps it is only the stiff, bent shoulders of age that are really fitted to bear the burdens that impetuous youth find unendurably irksome.

While he sat in utter silence, thrilled occasionally with shrill sweet bursts of irrepressible bird song, and inwardly tortured by the hateful whisperings of doubt, remorse and despair, the door of his sister's apartment was opened, and a murmur of voices told him that Rose and Helene had returned together from an afternoon drive. Through the lightly draped open window their conversation, distinctly heard, forced him into the position of an unintentional eaves-dropper. There seemed at first no reason why he should withdraw, and when the reason became apparent he found it impossible to make his presence known.

"Is your brother in the house?" asked Helene, waiting for the answer before laying aside hat and gloves, and dropping languidly into an easy chair.

"Oh, no," returned Rose, "he is never at home at this hour of the day. Why? Did you wish to see him?"

"I? No! I wish never to see him!" The words were uttered in a passionate undertone.

Rose came directly and beseechingly over to her friend. "Dear Helene," she said, "what is this terrible trouble that is preying upon your life? Every day you grow thinner and whiter and colder--more like a moonbeam than a mortal woman. Soon I fear you will fade from my grasp altogether, and I shall have nothing left but the recollection that you did not care enough for me to confide in me. I am sure there is something dreadful between you and Edward."

"Something, yes, but not enough; there should be an ocean--a whole world between us."

"I wish I could help you a little."

"Help me, dearest? It is like your goodness to think of such a thing; but it is impossible. No, there is nothing tragic, or terrible, or awe compelling, in my fate. It is nothing, I suppose, beyond the common lot of a great portion of humanity. It is simply--" she hesitated a moment, while a choking sob rose in her throat; she clasped her white hands above her head in a stern effort at self control, and then flung them down with an irrepressible moan--"it is simply that I am hungry, and thirsty, and cold, and tired and I want to go back to my old home, to my only home in the heart of the man I love. My poor child, do I startle you by talking in this passionate lawless, way? You invited my confidence, and it is such a relief to give it to you. To every one else in the world I must keep up the desolate show of appearing heartless and lifeless, incapable of compassion, of suffering and yearning. But with you, for a little while, I want to be myself. I am not a mere drawing-room ornament, prized by its owner, and gazed at by curious beholders. I am a wretched woman. Oh, Rose, Rose, I am an inexpressibly wretched woman!"

She caught the little warm hands, sympathizingly outstretched towards her, and pressed them to her neck, where the veins throbbed fast.

"No, don't pity me yet--only listen to me. I am so tired of living on husks, I seem to be nothing but a husk myself, brainless, soulless, and empty. I am so tired of sham and pretence, of keeping up appearances. I hate appearances. They are all false, unreal, loathsome. Yes, I am a well-trained puppet; I smile and chatter, dance and sing, am haughtily self-satisfied; but at night--at night my sick heart cries like a starving child, and I pace the floor with it until I fear that its wailings will drive me mad. I heap insults on my darling, and profess to scorn his tenderness, and all the time I could fly to him, and rain caresses upon him, and hold him closely folded in the arms of my love perpetually. No, he is not to blame, and Wanda is not to blame, for all this wretchedness. I don't understand how a woman can hate her rival. The fact of their loving the same object gives them a closer kinship than that between twin sisters. Wanda's sufferings are too much like my own to permit me even to dislike her. She has rich beauty, a rarely luxuriant vitality, and the immense advantage of being free to show her love in a natural way. I have nothing but my love for her lover! If I could only trample on it, despise it, spurn it, but I can't, I can't! My love is stronger than my pride, stronger than my life. It is not a mere fancy of yesterday, it has grown and strengthened with my years."

"I remember one evening in York, last spring," Helene continued, "when it was warm enough to leave doors and windows open to admit the free breeze from the lake; I happened to pass a wretched little shanty in the lower part of the town. A commonplace woman within was cooking supper in plain sight of the street, and I thought what a miserable lot must be hers. Then her husband, a grimy-looking workman came home, and she put her toil-worn hands about his neck, and gave him a welcome that left me dazed and desolate, filled with unbearable pain and envy, because I knew then, as I know now, that for my darling and me there can be no sweet home-coming, no interposition of my love between him and the sordid cares of the day. The measure of my need will never be filled. Ah, **mon Dieu**, it is very hard--it is bitterly hard!"

The low passionate tones died away into absolute silence. Rose's tender arms were closely clasped about her friend, and her wet cheek was pressed against the pale face on her shoulder; but she could find no words to match the heart-sickness that had at last found free vent in speech. Perhaps the deepest sympathy can be expressed only by silence. In a few moments Helene looked up gratefully and with a quivering smile. "Dear little, pet," she said, "it is a sin for me to burden you with the shameless story of my griefs. I hardly know what I have been saying, so you must not attach too much importance to it. After all, it is only a mood." The inevitable reaction after deep feeling had come.

"I wish with all my heart that I could help you," said Rose, soothingly but despairingly.

"So you can. Give me those two blue eyes of yours to kiss. They are blue as wood-violets, and look grieved and sad--so exactly like Edward's." She leaned over and kissed them fervently. "Oh, I must not yield to such thoughts. I must control myself. I must be strong. I must conquer everything. Heaven help me!" The last words sounded like a piteous prayer, as indeed they were. "Come and sing to me, Rose. Sing my soul out of this perdition if you can."

The two girls departed to the music-room, and, shortly after, Edward, with the soundless step of a murderer, crept down stairs and far out into the forest. Like one driven by an indwelling demon into the wilderness he walked swiftly with great strides away from his trouble. No, not away from it, for it surrounded him like the atmosphere. Sometimes he stopped from sheer exhaustion, and leaned heavily against a tree, while the perspiration stood on his brow in large drops. At one of these times there was a rustling among the thick leaves behind him, and Wanda stole timidly, yet with the fearless innocence of a child, to his side. He groaned aloud as she hid her face upon his breast. "Ah, you are sad as a night in the moon of dying leaves," she said, pulling his arms about her.

"It is because I do not love you," he returned, and the cruel sentence was softened by the measureless sadness of his tone.

"Oh, but you shall love me!" Each passionate word seemed a link in a strong chain that bound him inexorably to her. "What does it matter," she pleaded, "that you care little for me now? My love is great enough for both. I can give my life up, but I can never give you up. You are dearer to me than life!"

She leaned over him, and he felt as in a dream the old potential charm of her flower-sweet breath and glowing beauty. Still, though he submitted to her caresses, he did not return them. Within his ears the impassioned words of Helene were sounding perpetually, deafening him to every other appeal. His visible presence was with Wanda, his breast was deeply stirred with pity and affection and remorse for her, but his soul was left behind with that stricken girl, to whose broken-hearted confessions he had been a forced listener.

The day had lost its brightness, as though twilight had suddenly laid her dusky hand across the burning gaze of noon; the shadows deepened perceptibly about them; the sky threatened, the darkened trees seemed full of dread, the last gleam of light faded swiftly into the black approaching clouds, and they were speedily engulfed in one of those impatient summer showers, whose sharp fury quickly spends itself. Edward was reminded of that time a year ago when they were alone in the storm. Again the Indian girl bent reverently to the ground, exclaiming in awed accents, "The Great Spirit is angry." "He has need to be angry," muttered the young man, hurrying his companion to a denser part of the forest, where the thickly intermingled boughs might form a roof above them. But before they reached it a terrific burst of thunder broke upon their ears, and a tree beside them was suddenly snapped by the wind, and flung to the ground. The girl, with the quick instinct of a savage, stepped aside, pulling hard as she did so upon the arm of Edward. But he, walking as one in a dream, was scarcely less unconscious of what was going on around him than when, a moment later, he lay, felled to the earth by the fallen tree.

Wanda uttered an ejaculation of horror and alarm, and exerting all her strength she dragged the inanimate figure away from its enshrouding coverlet of leaves. The rain beat heavily upon the bloodless, upturned face. "What can I do for you?" she cried in despair, taking his handkerchief and binding tightly the deep wound on his head. He opened his eyes languidly, and murmured scarcely above his breath, "Bring Helene!" She did not pause even to kiss the pale lips, but flew swift as Love itself upon Love's errand. And yet, in her consuming desire to obey the least wish of her idol, it seemed to her that every fibre of her eager frame was clogged and weighted with lead. The rain blinded her eyes, the tangled underbrush tripped her feet, and more than once she fell panting and trembling on the dead leaves. Only for a moment; then she sprang up again, leaping, running, pushing away the branches that stretched across her path, spurning at every step the solid earth that interposed so much of its dull bulk between her and her heart's desire. Reaching the lake she jumped quickly into a boat Edward had given her, which lay near, and she made haste for Kempenfeldt Bay.

The rain ceased before she reached Pine Towers, and with the first radiant glance of the sun Helene had come to the wood's edge for the sake of the forest odours, which are never so pungent and delicious as immediately after a thunderstorm. In the thinnest, most transparent of summer white gowns, with her lily-pale face and drooping figure, she looked like some rare flower which the storm in pity had spared. So thought Wanda, who, now that the object of her search was in sight, approached very slowly and wearily, her breast rent by fierce pangs of jealousy. Why had Edward wished at such a critical time for this useless weakling? What possible good could she be to him in what might be his dying moments? And all the time, Helene, fixing her sad eyes upon this wild girl of the woods, noting her drenched, ragged and earth-stained raiment, and the dark sullen expression that jealousy had painted upon her face, saw more than all and above all the overwhelming beauty, which belittled all externals, and made them scarcely worth notice. "What wonder," thought Helene, "that Edward is given up heart and soul to this peerless creature, when the mere sight of her quickens my slow pulses?"

The two loves of Edward Macleod stood face to face. Wanda explained her presence in a few cold words. "Some of the family can take a carriage and everything necessary and go to him by the road," she said. "You will reach him much sooner by letting me row you across the bay in my boat."

Helene trembled visibly, and a great longing possessed her to go instantly to Edward. Then a strong fear seized her. She felt a profound distrust of this beautiful savage with the coarse garments, rough speech, and strangely marred visage. Perhaps to revenge herself for Edward's suspected unfaithfulness she had killed him in the forest, and wished now to satiate her appetite for vengeance by taking the woman who loved him to view her ghastly work. Perhaps the whole story was a fabrication to lure her to some lonely spot in the boundless woods, where she would be horribly murdered. Perhaps--

"Come!" urged Wanda, with passionate entreaty. "He is dying."

"Is it you who have killed him?" demanded Helene, sternly voicing all her fears in that black suspicion.

The girl turned away with a quick writhing motion. "No," she groaned, "it is he who has killed me--with two words--***bring Helene***." She darted to the house with the news of Edward's accident, and then to the beach, where Helene was already before her. The tiny skiff was pushed off, and the two girls were alone together.

As long as she lived Helene DeBerczy remembered that swift boat ride across the bay. Great masses of black clouds still hung heavily in the western sky, occasionally pierced by a brilliant flash of sunshine, that emphasized by contrast the dreariness succeeding it. Below, the waters were dark and troubled, while from the flat shores rose the majestic monotony of the forest, chill, shadowy, inscrutable. But these were as the frame of a picture, that printed itself indelibly upon the heart of this high-born woman of the world--the picture of a tropically beautiful face, now for the first time deathly pale, and seamed with lines of unutterable anguish; of bare rounded arms, showing in their raised muscles, and in the tense grasp of the oars, a power of self-repression awful in its strength; of deeply-heaving bosom, beneath which was raging that old, old conflict between true and false love--the true love that gives everything, the false love that grasps everything; of the passionate, eloquent, suffering eyes, full of jealousy and yearning, fierce hate and fiercer desire, and behind all, yes, dominating all, the struggle for martyr-like self-effacement whose cry forever is, not for my sake, but for the sake of one that I love. Great waves of pity overwhelmed every other emotion in Helene's breast, as she leaned forward. "My poor child," she said, "how intensely you love him! Do not let my coming hurt you so, I have long ago yielded him to you."

"But he has not yielded himself to me," moaned the girl, her ashen lips framing the cry that came from her soul. The boat grated in the sand, and she sprang out, and pulled it upon the beach. Then, taking in a feverish clasp the delicately-draped arm of the other, she hurried her to the spot where Edward still lay, deadly pale but conscious. He did not look at Wanda--he had no eyes save for Helene. With a little cry of passionate love and sorrow she flung herself beside him, and drew the white wounded face close to her aching heart. His broken syllables of love were in her ears, his head was nestled, like that of a weary child, within her arms, his blood was staining the white laces on her breast. For a moment Wanda paused and looked upon them; then noiselessly as a dream she vanished away.

But where in the wide, pitiless world is there a place of refuge for a woman's broken heart? Instinctively Wanda went back to the boat, and rowed far out upon the troubled waters. The afternoon's storm had been but the warning of a wilder one yet to come; the heavy skies shut down on all sides, adamantine and inexorable as the fate enshrouding her; from the mute mysterious woods came the sighing of the wind, sinking now into deep moaning, then rising into a shrill anguish, that was answered by the sobbing of the waves upon the beach. All nature seemed stirred to the heart at the hopeless misery of this her cherished child. But Wanda's eyes were blank, and her ears deafened to the sights and sounds around her. With the desperation of despair she rowed fast and strenuously out into the heaving lake, while hours passed, and the black night, like a pall, enveloped all things earthly. At last, with her strength utterly gone, she dropped the oars and drifted wherever the wild tide might choose to take her. Low mutterings of thunder shook the air, and with them she mingled the notes of an Indian death-chant. Before the weird, heart-breaking tones had ceased, the black heavens opened, and tears of pity were rained upon this desolate human soul. She lay outstretched, her glorious face upturned to the starless skies, her tired hands far apart over the sides of the boat. Towards them with wolf-ish haste rushed the white-capped breakers, rising in fury as they reached the little craft, and flinging themselves wildly across it. Wanda paid no heed. Her voice rose once again, thrilling the air with its wild sweet melody, and then she sank, without even a convulsive clutch at the frail bark which overturned upon her.

So perished the life that was naught but a mere empty husk, since love, its strong sweet occupant, had departed. Alas, poor Wanda! alas, poor little one, whose sore feet and sorer heart could find no resting-place in all this wide hard world. The anguished winds moaned on far into the night; the sad waves, now racked and scourged by the tempest, sobbed ceaselessly upon the beach; the pitiful heavens outpoured their flood of tears, but the tortured soul that had committed the god-like sin of loving too much had found rest at last.

CHAPTER XXII.
LOVE'S REWARDS.

A few days afterwards the body of the Algonquin maiden, recovered from the waves, was lying in an upper chamber at Pine Towers. Whatever may have been the supreme agony in which this suffering soul parted from its human habitation, no trace of it remained upon the inanimate form. Free from scar or stain it lay, the languid limbs forever motionless, the cold hands crossed upon a pulseless breast, the beautiful figure, heavily shadowed in enshrouding tresses, stretched in painless repose, and on the wonderful face the expression of one who has gained, not rest and peace--when had she ever hungered for these?--but the look, almost startling in its intensity, of one who has found love. Somewhere, sometime, we who struggle through life--nay, rather, struggle *after* life--in this world that God so loved, shall find our longings satisfied; the one yearning cry of our heart shall be stilled. The poet shall touch the stars, whose pale light now shines so uncertainly upon his brow; the painter shall put upon canvas a beauty too deep for words; the worshipper of nature shall thrill with the knowledge of unspoken secrets; the seeker after truth shall learn the mysteries of heaven. The infinite Father cannot deny his children; He will not cheat them. But the lessons of patience are harder to learn than those of labour.

Upon this poor child of the wilderness had fallen a happiness so bewildering and so complete that it seemed as though the perfect lips must open to give utterance to a joy too full to be contained. But to the man self-accused of robbing her of love and life, this sweet reflected glory from the other side of the dark gateway brought no consolation. In that silent room, flooded with cold moonlight, Edward Macleod stood alone in the dead girl's presence, and felt the bitter waves of remorse sweep over his soul. Her beauty, touched by the light of absolute happiness, thrilled him now as never before. From mere wantonness, he had crushed out the heart of this faultlessly lovely and innocent creature, and his head fell upon his breast in shame and self-contempt. God might forgive him, but how could he ever forgive himself?

The door blew open, and, silently as a vision, Helene came in and stood beside him. It was a strange place for a lover's tryst--that bare room with its lifeless occupant, flooded with white unearthly moonlight "Let me stay with you, Edward," she pleaded, with quivering lips. "No," she added, in answer to the unspoken fear in his eyes, "I shall not try to comfort you." She knew intuitively that no consolation could avail in this hour of silent self-torture. "Only," she whispered, "you must let me share your grief, for I also have wronged her."

And so, with clasped hands, they bent together and kissed the beautiful still lips that could never utter an accusing word against them. Their love founded upon death had suddenly become as mysterious and sacred as the life of a child whose mother perished when she gave it birth.

Some months elapsed after the burial of Wanda before Edward ventured to bring his dearest hopes under the notice of Madame DeBerczy. This august personage, in whose memory yet lingered frequent rumours of the young man's flirtations with the nut-brown forest maid, cherished no particular partiality for him. If Helene's lover had ever entertained the unfounded illusion that her lily-white hand had been too lightly won, he might willingly have submitted to the just punishment of his presumption; but in view of his long struggle to win her favour, it was dispiriting to learn that there was still a greater height to conquer,--the lofty indifference of one whom he wished, in spite of her weaknesses, to make his mother-in-law. Ice, however, will melt when exposed to a certain degree of heat, and this was where Edward's naturally sunny disposition and the warmth of his love did him good service. Before the good lady fairly realized the change that was passing over her feelings with regard to her daughter's suitor, she had ceased to speak of him as that frivolous young Macleod, and had begun to see for herself in his handsome face the sincerity and sadness that follow in the wake of every deep and painful experience.

From approval it is but a step to appreciation, and this merges by natural degrees into affection. Helene, who, though she did not consider Edward faultless, was apt to find his faults more alluring than the virtues of some others, had at last the satisfaction of knowing that her mother inclined to take a like view of them; and her now impatient lover was made glad by a formal acceptance from Madame DeBerczy of his request for her daughter's hand.

Meantime, Rose and Allan, whose course of love, if it had not suffered so tempestuous a passage, had still flowed for the most part under gloomy skies, were at last in the enjoyment of undisputed sunshine. In this unaccustomed atmosphere the fairest flower of the Macleod family bloomed anew, and her lover at last beheld his prospects *couleur de rose*. Allan had accepted an invitation from the old Commodore to visit Pine Towers, and the impression he made upon his prospective father-in-law grew daily deeper and pleasanter, till, to the elder gentleman's sorrow at the thought of parting from his fondly-loved daughter, was added real regret that he had never before appreciated the sterling qualities of her chosen husband.

Politically, their views, which had once been wide asunder as the poles, had now almost unconsciously met and kissed each other. Nor was this the result of abandoned convictions. Both men continued to cherish their old notions of things, and to hold to the traditions of the party to which each was attached. But Allan Dunlop and the Commodore had come to know and to respect each other, and, as the result, each took a more dispassionate view of the questions which disturbed the country and which had ranged them politically on opposite sides. This change was specially noticeable in the elder of the two. Though allied to the party who prided themselves in being regarded as stiff, unbending Tories, Commodore Macleod had an acute sense of what was just and fair; and under a somewhat rough exterior he had a kindly, sympathetic heart. This latter virtue in the old gentleman made him keenly alive to the grievances of the people, and particularly sensitive to appeals from settlers, the hardships of whose lot, though he had himself little experience of them, were nevertheless often present to his mind. His manly character, moreover, though it was occasionally hid under a sailor's brusque testiness, disposed him to appreciate manliness in others, and to be sympathetic towards those whose aims were high and whose motives were good. Thus, despite his inherent conservatism and pride of birth, he was gradually won over to regard Dunlop, first with tolerance, then with awakened interest and respect, and finally with admiration and love.

Dunlop, on the other hand, though he abated nothing in his enthusiasm for the cause of the people, and never faltered in his loyalty to duty, came to regard the political situation, if not from the point of view of his opponents, at least from a point of view which was eminently statesmanlike and discreet. Influenced by a broader comprehension of affairs, and by a more complaisant regard for the country's rulers, who had done and were doing much for the young commonwealth, however sorely the political system pressed upon the people, Dunlop placed a check upon his gift of parliamentary raillery, and refrained from pressing many reforms which time, he knew, would quietly and with less acrimony bring about.

To these ameliorating influences both men unresistingly submitted themselves, and, as a consequence, each came nearer to the other; while the bond of love between Rose and Allan cemented the alliance political, and threw down all barriers that had once frowned on the alliance matrimonial. It was a consciousness of this change of feeling which led Allan Dunlop, on his return for a time to his political duties at York, to write to Rose in the following strain, and to assure her of the complete cordiality that now existed, and was sure to continue to exist, between her father and himself:

"YORK, November 30th, 1827.

"MY DEAR ROSE: From the paradise of the garden of Pine Towers, with you as its ineffably sweet, pervading presence, to the inferno of these Legislative Halls, with their scenes of discord and turbulence, duty and fate have ruthlessly and unfeelingly banished me. Coming from your restful presence, how little disposed am I to enter upon the strifes of these stormy times, and to take up the gage of battle thrown recklessly down by some knight of the Upper House, whose idea, either of manly dignity or of Parliamentary warfare, is not that of the "*preux chevalier, sans peur et sans reproche*."

Yet I would be unworthy of the little queen I serve, whose smiles and favour are a continuous inspiration to me, were I weakly to forego my duty, and desire to seek the solace of her presence without having first acquitted myself with honour on this mimic field of battle. What is to be the outcome of this strife of tongues, and what the future of our country, riven asunder as it is by those, on the one side, who are jealous merely for their own rights and privileges, and, on the other, by those who care only for the distraction and clamour of fruitless contention, it were hard to say. With the ever-increasing complications, the fires of discontent must some day burst into flame. Even now it wants but the breath of a bold, daring spirit to set the whole Province in a blaze; and I shudder at the prospect unless a spirit of conciliation speedily shows itself, and the Executive makes some surrender of its autocratic powers.

In the discussion of political affairs I had recently with your father, I am glad to say that we agree very closely as to the inciting causes of the public discontent, and have a common opinion as to the best,--indeed, the only satisfactory,--means of applying a remedy. This unity of feeling must rivet and perpetuate our friendship, and aid in bringing about, what I ardently desire, some necessary and immediate reforms in our mode of government. I need hardly say to you, who are so dear to me, how fervently I hail this mutual understanding on political matters, and how much I auger from it of weal to the country and of pleasure and happiness to ourselves. Heaven grant that all I expect from it may be realized!

I have no news to give you of social matters in York, save of Lady Mary Willis's Fancy Ball, which is to come off at the close of the year. Mr. Galt, of the Canada Company, the Robinsons, Hewards, Hagermans, Widmers, Spragges, and Baldwins--everybody but a few of the Government House people--are taking a great interest in the coming affair. There is to be a sleighing-party soon also, from the Macaulays to the Crookshank's farm, and on to the Denisons. I have been asked to join it, and wish you were to be here in time, to make one--the dearest to me!--of the party.

With my respects to your father, kind regards to Edward and Mad'lle Helene, and abiding love to your sweet self and the little people of your household,

    I remain, ever and devotedly yours,

    ALLAN DUNLOP."

But there was little need now of formal--or indeed of any--correspondence between Allan and Rose, for they were soon to be forever together, in the bonds not only of a common sympathy and a common interest in their country's welfare, but in that closer union of hearts which both had secretly longed for and both had feared would never come about. It was arranged that in the spring of the following year there would be a double marriage, and that the day that saw Edward united to Helene would also see the union of Allan and Rose. Even now, preparations for the interesting event had been set on foot, and society in "Muddy Little York" was on the tip-toe of excitement over the coming weddings.

As the winter passed, and the month drew near which was to witness the two-fold alliance, the young people of the Capital took a delirious interest in every circumstance, however trivial, connected with the affair. Of course, the double ceremony was to take place at the Church of St. James, and it was known that the Lieutenant-Governor and Lady Sarah Maitland, before finally quitting the Province, were to be present, and that the redoubtable politico-ecclesiastic, the Archdeacon of York, was to tie the knots, and, in his richest doric, pronounce both couples severally "mon and wife." The wedding breakfast, it was also a matter of current talk, was to be at the homestead of a distinguished member of the local judiciary; and it had also leaked out that, thereafter, the united couples were to embark on His Majesty's sloop-of-war, "*The Princess Charlotte*," and be conveyed as far as Kingston, on the wedding journey to Quebec, where Edward, with his bride, was to proceed to England to rejoin his regiment, and Allan and Rose were to spend the honeymoon in some delightful retreat on the St. Lawrence.

What need is there to continue the chronicle?--save to assure the modern reader of this old-time story that everything happily came about as foreshadowed in the gossip we have just related, and that the after-fortunes of the four happy people who took that early wedding journey on the St. Lawrence were as bright as those of the happiest Canadian bride and bridegroom that have ever taken the same journey since.

THE END.

The Codes Of Hammurabi And Moses
W. W. Davies

QTY

The discovery of the Hammurabi Code is one of the greatest achievements of archaeology, and is of paramount interest, not only to the student of the Bible, but also to all those interested in ancient history...

Religion   **ISBN:** *1-59462-338-4*   **Pages:132**

MSRP $12.95

The Theory of Moral Sentiments
Adam Smith

QTY

This work from 1749. contains original theories of conscience amd moral judgment and it is the foundation for systemof morals.

Philosophy **ISBN:** *1-59462-777-0*   **Pages:536**

MSRP $19.95

Jessica's First Prayer
Hesba Stretton

QTY

In a screened and secluded corner of one of the many railway-bridges which span the streets of London there could be seen a few years ago, from five o'clock every morning until half past eight, a tidily set-out coffee-stall, consisting of a trestle and board, upon which stood two large tin cans, with a small fire of charcoal burning under each so as to keep the coffee boiling during the early hours of the morning when the work-people were thronging into the city on their way to their daily toil...

Pages:84

Childrens   **ISBN:** *1-59462-373-2*   *MSRP $9.95*

My Life and Work
Henry Ford

QTY

Henry Ford revolutionized the world with his implementation of mass production for the Model T automobile. Gain valuable business insight into his life and work with his own auto-biography... "We have only started on our development of our country we have not as yet, with all our talk of wonderful progress, done more than scratch the surface. The progress has been wonderful enough but..."

Pages:300

Biographies/   **ISBN:** *1-59462-198-5*   *MSRP $21.95*

The Art of Cross-Examination
Francis Wellman

QTY

I presume it is the experience of every author, after his first book is published upon an important subject, to be almost overwhelmed with a wealth of ideas and illustrations which could readily have been included in his book, and which to his own mind, at least, seem to make a second edition inevitable. Such certainly was the case with me; and when the first edition had reached its sixth impression in five months, I rejoiced to learn that it seemed to my publishers that the book had met with a sufficiently favorable reception to justify a second and considerably enlarged edition. ..

Pages:412

Reference   ISBN: *1-59462-647-2*   *MSRP $19.95*

On the Duty of Civil Disobedience
Henry David Thoreau

QTY

Thoreau wrote his famous essay, On the Duty of Civil Disobedience, as a protest against an unjust but popular war and the immoral but popular institution of slave-owning. He did more than write—he declined to pay his taxes, and was hauled off to gaol in consequence. Who can say how much this refusal of his hastened the end of the war and of slavery ?

Law   ISBN: *1-59462-747-9*   **Pages:48**

MSRP $7.45

Dream Psychology Psychoanalysis for Beginners
Sigmund Freud

QTY

Sigmund Freud, born Sigismund Schlomo Freud (May 6, 1856 - September 23, 1939), was a Jewish-Austrian neurologist and psychiatrist who co-founded the psychoanalytic school of psychology. Freud is best known for his theories of the unconscious mind, especially involving the mechanism of repression; his redefinition of sexual desire as mobile and directed towards a wide variety of objects; and his therapeutic techniques, especially his understanding of transference in the therapeutic relationship and the presumed value of dreams as sources of insight into unconscious desires.

Pages:196

Psychology   ISBN: *1-59462-905-6*   *MSRP $15.45*

The Miracle of Right Thought
Orison Swett Marden

QTY

Believe with all of your heart that you will do what you were made to do. When the mind has once formed the habit of holding cheerful, happy, prosperous pictures, it will not be easy to form the opposite habit. It does not matter how improbable or how far away this realization may see, or how dark the prospects may be, if we visualize them as best we can, as vividly as possible, hold tenaciously to them and vigorously struggle to attain them, they will gradually become actualized, realized in the life. But a desire, a longing without endeavor, a yearning abandoned or held indifferently will vanish without realization.

Pages:360

Self Help   ISBN: *1-59462-644-8*   *MSRP $25.45*

www.bookjungle.com *email: sales@bookjungle.com fax: 630-214-0564 mail: Book Jungle PO Box 2226 Champaign, IL 61825*

QTY

The Rosicrucian Cosmo-Conception Mystic Christianity *by Max Heindel* ISBN: *1-59462-188-8* **$38.95**
The Rosicrucian Cosmo-conception is not dogmatic, neither does it appeal to any other authority than the reason of the student. It is: not controversial, but is: sent forth in the, hope that it may help to clear... *New Age/Religion Pages 646*

Abandonment To Divine Providence *by Jean-Pierre de Caussade* ISBN: *1-59462-228-0* **$25.95**
"The Rev. Jean Pierre de Caussade was one of the most remarkable spiritual writers of the Society of Jesus in France in the 18th Century. His death took place at Toulouse in 1751. His works have gone through many editions and have been republished... *Inspirational/Religion Pages 400*

Mental Chemistry *by Charles Haanel* ISBN: *1-59462-192-6* **$23.95**
Mental Chemistry allows the change of material conditions by combining and appropriately utilizing the power of the mind. Much like applied chemistry creates something new and unique out of careful combinations of chemicals the mastery of mental chemistry... *New Age Pages 354*

The Letters of Robert Browning and Elizabeth Barret Barrett 1845-1846 vol II ISBN: *1-59462-193-4* **$35.95**
by Robert Browning and Elizabeth Barrett *Biographies Pages 596*

Gleanings In Genesis (volume I) *by Arthur W. Pink* ISBN: *1-59462-130-6* **$27.45**
Appropriately has Genesis been termed "the seed plot of the Bible" for in it we have, in germ form, almost all of the great doctrines which are afterwards fully developed in the books of Scripture which follow... *Religion/Inspirational Pages 420*

The Master Key *by L. W. de Laurence* ISBN: *1-59462-001-6* **$30.95**
In no branch of human knowledge has there been a more lively increase of the spirit of research during the past few years than in the study of Psychology, Concentration and Mental Discipline. The requests for authentic lessons in Thought Control, Mental Discipline and... *New Age/Business Pages 422*

The Lesser Key Of Solomon Goetia *by L. W. de Laurence* ISBN: *1-59462-092-X* **$9.95**
This translation of the first book of the "Lemegton" which is now for the first time made accessible to students of Talismanic Magic was done, after careful collation and edition, from numerous Ancient Manuscripts in Hebrew, Latin, and French... *New Age/Occult Pages 92*

Rubaiyat Of Omar Khayyam *by Edward Fitzgerald* ISBN: *1-59462-332-5* **$13.95**
Edward Fitzgerald, whom the world has already learned, in spite of his own efforts to remain within the shadow of anonymity, to look upon as one of the rarest poets of the century, was born at Bredfield, in Suffolk, on the 31st of March, 1809. He was the third son of John Purcell... *Music Pages 172*

Ancient Law *by Henry Maine* ISBN: *1-59462-128-4* **$29.95**
The chief object of the following pages is to indicate some of the earliest ideas of mankind, as they are reflected in Ancient Law, and to point out the relation of those ideas to modern thought. *Religion/History Pages 452*

Far-Away Stories *by William J. Locke* ISBN: *1-59462-129-2* **$19.45**
"Good wine needs no bush, but a collection of mixed vintages does. And this book is just such a collection. Some of the stories I do not want to remain buried for ever in the museum files of dead magazine-numbers an author's not unpardonable vanity..." *Fiction Pages 272*

Life of David Crockett *by David Crockett* ISBN: *1-59462-250-7* **$27.45**
"Colonel David Crockett was one of the most remarkable men of the times in which he lived. Born in humble life, but gifted with a strong will, an indomitable courage, and unremitting perseverance... *Biographies/New Age Pages 424*

Lip-Reading *by Edward Nitchie* ISBN: *1-59462-206-X* **$25.95**
Edward B. Nitchie, founder of the New York School for the Hard of Hearing, now the Nitchie School of Lip-Reading, Inc, wrote "LIP-READING Principles and Practice". The development and perfecting of this meritorious work on lip-reading was an undertaking... *How-to Pages 400*

A Handbook of Suggestive Therapeutics, Applied Hypnotism, Psychic Science ISBN: *1-59462-214-0* **$24.95**
by Henry Munro *Health/New Age/Health/Self-help Pages 376*

A Doll's House: and Two Other Plays *by Henrik Ibsen* ISBN: *1-59462-112-8* **$19.95**
Henrik Ibsen created this classic when in revolutionary 1848 Rome. Introducing some striking concepts in playwriting for the realist genre, this play has been studied the world over. *Fiction/Classics/Plays 308*

The Light of Asia *by sir Edwin Arnold* ISBN: *1-59462-204-3* **$13.95**
In this poetic masterpiece, Edwin Arnold describes the life and teachings of Buddha. The man who was to become known as Buddha to the world was born as Prince Gautama of India but he rejected the worldly riches and abandoned the reigns of power when... *Religion/History/Biographies Pages 170*

The Complete Works of Guy de Maupassant *by Guy de Maupassant* ISBN: *1-59462-157-8* **$16.95**
"For days and days, nights and nights, I had dreamed of that first kiss which was to consecrate our engagement, and I knew not on what spot I should put my lips..." *Fiction/Classics Pages 240*

The Art of Cross-Examination *by Francis L. Wellman* ISBN: *1-59462-309-0* **$26.95**
Written by a renowned trial lawyer, Wellman imparts his experience and uses case studies to explain how to use psychology to extract desired information through questioning. *How-to/Science/Reference Pages 408*

Answered or Unanswered? *by Louisa Vaughan* ISBN: *1-59462-248-5* **$10.95**
Miracles of Faith in China *Religion Pages 112*

The Edinburgh Lectures on Mental Science (1909) *by Thomas* ISBN: *1-59462-008-3* **$11.95**
This book contains the substance of a course of lectures recently given by the writer in the Queen Street Hall, Edinburgh. Its purpose is to indicate the Natural Principles governing the relation between Mental Action and Material Conditions... *New Age/Psychology Pages 148*

Ayesha *by H. Rider Haggard* ISBN: *1-59462-301-5* **$24.95**
Verily and indeed it is the unexpected that happens! Probably if there was one person upon the earth from whom the Editor of this, and of a certain previous history, did not expect to hear again... *Classics Pages 380*

Ayala's Angel *by Anthony Trollope* ISBN: *1-59462-352-X* **$29.95**
The two girls were both pretty, but Lucy who was twenty-one who supposed to be simple and comparatively unattractive, whereas Ayala was credited, as her Bombwhat romantic name might show, with poetic charm and a taste for romance. Ayala when her father died was nineteen... *Fiction Pages 484*

The American Commonwealth *by James Bryce* ISBN: *1-59462-286-8* **$34.45**
An interpretation of American democratic political theory. It examines political mechanics and society from the perspective of Scotsman James Bryce *Politics Pages 572*

Stories of the Pilgrims *by Margaret P. Pumphrey* ISBN: *1-59462-116-0* **$17.95**
This book explores pilgrims religious oppression in England as well as their escape to Holland and eventual crossing to America on the Mayflower, and their early days in New England... *History Pages 268*

www.bookjungle.com *email: sales@bookjungle.com fax: 630-214-0564 mail: Book Jungle PO Box 2226 Champaign, IL 61825*

QTY

The Fasting Cure *by Sinclair Upton*   ISBN: *1-59462-222-1*   **$13.95**
*In the Cosmopolitan Magazine for May, 1910, and in the Contemporary Review (London) for April, 1910, I published an article dealing with my experi-
ences in fasting. I have written a great many magazine articles, but never one which attracted so much attention... New Age/Self Help/Health Pages 164*

Hebrew Astrology *by Sepharial*   ISBN: *1-59462-308-2*   **$13.45**
*In these days of advanced thinking it is a matter of common observation that we have left many of the old landmarks behind and that we are now pressing
forward to greater heights and to a wider horizon than that which represented the mind-content of our progenitors...   Astrology Pages 144*

Thought Vibration or The Law of Attraction in the Thought World   ISBN: *1-59462-127-6*   **$12.95**
by William Walker Atkinson   *Psychology/Religion Pages 144*

Optimism *by Helen Keller*   ISBN: *1-59462-108-X*   **$15.95**
*Helen Keller was blind, deaf, and mute since 19 months old, yet famously learned how to overcome these handicaps, communicate with the world, and
spread her lectures promoting optimism. An inspiring read for everyone...   Biographies/Inspirational Pages 84*

Sara Crewe *by Frances Burnett*   ISBN: *1-59462-360-0*   **$9.45**
*In the first place, Miss Minchin lived in London. Her home was a large, dull, tall one, in a large, dull square, where all the houses were alike, and all the
sparrows were alike, and where all the door-knockers made the same heavy sound...   Childrens/Classic Pages 88*

The Autobiography of Benjamin Franklin *by Benjamin Franklin*   ISBN: *1-59462-135-7*   **$24.95**
*The Autobiography of Benjamin Franklin has probably been more extensively read than any other American historical work, and no other book of its kind
has had such ups and downs of fortune. Franklin lived for many years in England, where he was agent...   Biographies/History Pages 332*

Name	
Email	
Telephone	
Address	
City, State ZIP	

☐ **Credit Card**   ☐ **Check / Money Order**

Credit Card Number	
Expiration Date	
Signature	

Please Mail to: Book Jungle
                    PO Box 2226
                    Champaign, IL 61825
or Fax to: 630-214-0564

ORDERING INFORMATION
web: *www.bookjungle.com*
email: *sales@bookjungle.com*
fax: *630-214-0564*
mail: *Book Jungle PO Box 2226 Champaign, IL 61825*
or PayPal *to sales@bookjungle.com*

Please contact us for bulk discounts

DIRECT-ORDER TERMS

**20% Discount if You Order
Two or More Books**
Free Domestic Shipping!
Accepted: Master Card, Visa,
Discover, American Express

www.ingramcontent.com/pod-product-compliance
Lightning Source LLC
Chambersburg PA
CBHW080730020726
47503CB00010B/2859